# *hers*

## BLOOD TIES SERIES

### A.K. ROSE
### ATLAS ROSE

*To all the girls who don't hover...they goddamn sit.*

# *warnings*

THE BLOODTIES SERIES is part of the Cosa Nostra world which contains several interconnected series. The tone is **dark**, involves a number of romantic interests for our female main characters and reader discretion is advised.

More information on the content warnings can be found here.

Please be aware of your own triggers and limitations. This is a Mafia/Gang related world and are not heroes or heroines, they are hungry, ruthless and they do bad things to themselves and to others.

If you're okay with this, please read on. I hope you enjoy this darkly rich, forbidden series. I can't wait to bring you *so much more....*

*Love Atlas, xx*

*Grab the playlist here on Spotify*

NICK

"YOU SURE YOU'RE ready for this?" I glanced at the darkening bruise below her eye. "You can take the day off, you know...after what happened."

There was more than the bruises, too. Ryth's hair was up in a loose ponytail. There was blood between the strands. Blood from what those bastards did to her.

*He had me by the hair.* Her words surfaced.

I clenched my fist around the steering wheel and the ache around my knuckles flared. Whatever we did to them last night, it wasn't enough. Goddamn cheating, jealous cunt. She and the piece of shit fuckboys she had to do her dirty work. I wanted to hurt them again. Real bad.

"Yeah. I'm good." She turned to me, forcing a smile. "This is my last year, Nick. It's important."

I swallowed and nodded. It was important. But in my mind, I demanded, *leave it, I'll get you a goddamn tutor if you want, you can take your exams somewhere else. Just not...here.*

She yanked the handle of the door and shoved it open before I said the words. Only, she didn't climb out. Not yet. Instead, she pulled back, leaned across the seat quickly and gave me a soft peck on the cheek. "Thanks for caring. I'll meet you here later?"

"I'll be waiting." I forced out the words.

She was gone then, climbing out and shoving the car door closed behind her with a *bang*, leaving me sitting here with my heart in my goddamn hands. *Go after her...*I stared at her back as she walked away. *Go after her, you pathetic fucking excuse...*

The sharp blare of a horn behind me pissed me off. Movement came from the corner of my eye. A group of girls stared as they made their way to the front doors, glancing from me to Ryth as she walked, oblivious to their attention. Fuck. I winced, shoved the car into gear, and pulled out of the drop-off point, not even bothering to look at the line of cars waiting.

I searched the drivers. But there was no Freddy this time. Looked like the Stidda, Mafia Prince Lazarus Rossi was true to his word and left her alone...for now.

How long that would be, I didn't know.

I punched the accelerator, forcing myself to not turn the fuck around. My heart was pounding. I pressed my hand against the ache. Christ, I had it bad. I wanted to go home, back to the savage glare from Tobias as he paced the floor, talking about hunting Gio down. We would...only not yet.

Not until all this shit died down and we figured out what was really going on. Her mom and our dad were on their honeymoon, but her real dad was still missing. That shit didn't sit right with me. One minute he was in prison...and the next, he wasn't.

He'd turn up...most likely in a damn body bag.

You don't steal from the Rossis and walk away, no matter what Lazarus said.

I pushed the car toward the city, finding familiar streets. Once everything settled, we'd hunt Gio down...and make the bastard pay for what he'd done to her. What kind of lowlife scum lured a woman out to a goddamn house in the middle of nowhere for her to be fucking ambushed? Jesus.

*Nick, I'm scared.*

I still heard those words. They haunted me, keeping sleep at bay. I'd stayed awake all night watching over her, replaying every goddamn second of the attack over and over again. Still, our little stepsister held her own, fighting them off long enough for us to get to her.

But that would not happen again. We would not let her out of our sight...except for school. I winced at the thought and pushed the pedal harder, headed to the converted warehouse on the upper east side, and pulled into the gated parking lot.

A yank and I shoved my hand inside the glove compartment, rifling around for the security card before yanking it out to press it against the scanner.

The boom gate lifted, leaving me to drive in and pull into the parking space assigned for my apartment. It felt weird when I climbed out. I hadn't been home in a week, barely even thought of the place. Not since Ryth and her mom had moved in, at least. I stepped inside the elevator, yanked the grate down, and pressed the button for the top floor.

The rickety thing shuddered and rose, taking me to the penthouse apartment. I shoved the grate up and stepped out, moved to the electronic keypad beside the door, and punched in my eight-digit security code.

The lock released, leaving me to push inside. The place was a converted warehouse, expansive, with an open floor plan. The only walls were for the bedrooms and bathrooms. Floor-to-ceiling windows gave a view of the city that was spectacular at night.

I loved the place and had spent a damn fortune on it. The building alone cost me almost three million and adding in the renovations, it cleared a cool eight. But when I walked inside, I

5

didn't feel that excitement anymore. The place felt...*empty* and no longer like a home.

My mind returned to Ryth. I didn't like leaving her.

Christ, I didn't like it. I glanced over my shoulder, tension making me antsy. Caged. Like something was wrong. I massaged the back of my neck as I made my way into the bedroom to the closet. I hit the light, pulled my duffel bag from the corner, and filled it with clothes.

I'd already made up my mind I wasn't leaving the house, not while Ryth was there. If dad wanted me out, then I'd buy the house next door...I'd buy all the goddamn houses, however many it took. I grabbed the bag and switched off the light. As I walked past my boxing bag hanging from the steel beam overhead, I lifted my gaze to the picture of mom hanging on the wall.

I'd come back someday soon to get the photo and the rest of my stuff. I might even put the place up for lease. But I didn't want to wait a second longer now. That gnawing ache grew in the pit of my stomach. It was her...my stepsister, drawing me in, making me desperate to be with her twenty-four-seven.

Fuck if this didn't feel like falling in love. But I sure as hell had no right to...there was more than my heart at stake here. I hauled my bag over my shoulder and walked out, yanked the door closed behind me, and set the code to lock it before making my way to the elevator once more.

I dropped my bag to the floor, pulled the grate down, and headed to the ground floor, then grabbed my phone and punched out a message to Tobias:

*We need to talk.*

Barely a second later.

*T: About?'*

About...

I shuddered as the elevator came to a stop. But I didn't step out, only stared at his reply. My damn hands shook as I typed:

*I think I'm in love with her.*

I swallowed hard, staring at the message...my thumb hovered over send...but I couldn't do it, not like this. Not over a damn message. I backspaced and instead typed out:

*Nothing. On my way home.*

I didn't wait for an answer, not that I expected one. Instead, I grabbed my bag and left, making my way to the car once more. By the time I tossed my bag into the back and slid behind the wheel I'd made up my mind, I was going to get her. Last year or no last year, I didn't give a shit. Not when assholes like Gio Romano were around.

I pulled the car out, desperate to get across the city. By the time the towering buildings were in my rear view, that clenched fist feeling had eased a little inside me. I relaxed my jaw and forced myself to concentrate on heading back to Duke's school. I grabbed my cell, ready to text her, as I turned into the street and made for the pickup point.

But as I lifted my gaze and saw the familiar car parked against the curb, thoughts of texting Ryth drifted away. "What the fuck?"

I checked the license plate...and turned back to the school. What the hell was dad doing here? Panic filled me as I pulled up hard, switched off the engine, and climbed out. I vaguely registered a white van parked across the street as I headed for the Mercedes and bent low, staring into the rear seat.

He was supposed to be on his honeymoon, so what the fuck was he doing here?

"Excuse me?" A man's voice came from behind me. "Can you tell me, is this the main entrance?"

I straightened, my mind already racing as I turned. "Yeah, you head—"

*Buzzz....*

Fuck, something bit me hard against the neck. Agony roared as my knees buckled, sending me crashing to the ground. Shadows descended...too many of them. I tried to fight, tried to yell.

"Grab him," one of them snarled as I unleashed a roar, lifting my head to find three massive guys surrounding me.

But these weren't punks...these were men, their steely stares dangerous.

*Fight!*

I shoved against the ground and drove upwards. My body trembled as that *thing* came for me again. A goddamn taser... they'd hit me with a fucking taser.

Electricity crackled, sparking at the end as I drove my shoulder into the closest guy. I cocked my fist, driving it up to catch him in the sternum. I was weak, my blows nowhere near my normal strength, still it made him gasp, clutch his chest, and stumble backwards.

"*You!*" I barked. "Picked the wrong guy, *motherfucker.*"

"Get him before the girl comes," another barked, stabbing a finger my way. "*Now!*"

The words froze me...my pulse raced, booming in my head. *Before the girl comes...he means Ryth.* "What the fuck?"

A shadow descended, moving fast, too damn fast. A blow came to the back of my head, leaving me stunned. *Buzz... buzz*...my insides turned weak as agony punched into my chest. Darkness moved in, stealing the light until I fell.

"Someone grab his keys. His car needs to be gone."

"No..." I slurred, my heart skipping. The sound was all I heard as they lifted me from the hot asphalt. I tried to surface, tried to open my eyes. Tried to do *anything*. But that darkness held me under as the crunch of boots came and hands gripped me.

I punched out, but my blows were slow and pathetic as the slow grind of a steel door came before the *thud* of it closing.

"*The car!*" One barked.

"Take it..." I whispered, and forced my eyes open. "Take everything...*just not her.*"

But they didn't listen, just heaved me in and piled into the back of the van as the engine started. The *snap* of something tight cut into my wrists, binding them together behind me.

"You're not gonna be any trouble for now, are you?" The growl was close as the van swayed, turning.

The growl of the Mustang's engine drifted to me. Desperation swelled at the sound. My car...*my fucking car*. But all I saw was Ryth in the damn thing. Her back against the door, legs splayed for me to see. I pushed the hurt away, focusing on what mattered...*where they were taking me.* My phone. My damn phone.

My thoughts were slow, too damn slow. A sledgehammer started somewhere in my head, trading blow for blow with my heart. The sound of the Mustang faded as we sped up. I blinked, focused on the assholes around me. Two in the back and one driving. The asshole in my goddamn car made four of them. "What do you want with her?"

One of them looked my way, and in the murky gloom, I caught the stitching on his shirt, an H inside an O. I scowled. I knew that symbol...

He watched me staring, then his lips curled as he lifted the taser. "Look away."

"Fuck you," I croaked, my throat on fire. "Do what you want with me...but you leave her alone."

"Is that right?" the bastard sneered, and leaned closer. "Don't tell me you're falling for the little bitch? I watched the recording...saw what you've done. You think she's special?

Believe me...we're doing you a favor. Get the fuck over her, Banks...and forget she ever existed."

*Forget she existed?*

*What the fuck?*

The van swayed, the engine growling louder.

I tried to stay calm, testing the plastic cuffs around my wrists. But inside, I was panicking, trying to put it all together. Dad. The wedding. I glanced back at the stitching. The fucking wedding. The Priest.

*HO...Hale Order.*

That name...that goddamn name. A chill coursed along my spine.

I clenched my jaw, my mind reeling, timing each goddamn turn as I tried to map out where we were headed. My muscles tensed, the tension on the plastic cuffs strained until heat filled my hand and I couldn't stand the pain. I made my move as we turned once more.

I shoved forward.

Head down, I rammed the bastard, slamming him into the side of the van.

The taser was all I saw. That and his fists. I took the blow to the side of my head, then dropped backwards when he shoved that thing at me, crushing my hands underneath as I fell.

Ryth's face filled my mind as I hit the floor hard. Tires squealed, and the force of the sway snapped the bindings. My hands were free, screaming in agony, but free. I shoved upwards, catching a fist in the face. My head snapped backwards and the tang of blood rushed into my mouth.

But she was all I cared about. I unleashed a roar, driving myself sideways, then kicked out, driving my boot into the asshole's shin. An anguish-filled scream followed.

I didn't have time to smile as I shoved forward, ramming into the bastard with the taser. My training kicked in. The heel of my palm met the bastard's nose. The blow was not as powerful as I wanted with the swaying, but still, it made him grab his nose and howl.

They were all fucking yelling.

*"Get him under control!"* the driver shouted, jerking his gaze to me as he veered into the other lane.

I shoved out my hand, bracing as I flew across the space. The blow was fucking brutal. Something crunched as my shoulder hit the side. *Snick.* My blood ran cold with the sound.

"Fucking come for me again and see what happens." The asshole with the taser pressed a knife against my neck. Blood streamed from his nose. "One fucking move."

If it was only me, I might've stayed down...might've swallowed that burning in my gut.

But it wasn't about me. *I was just in their goddamn way.*

I lunged, giving it all I had, aiming for the knife as we turned. Grunts followed my fists. I traded blow for blow. These bastards were dangerous...and trained. *Too fucking trained.*

My blows grew weak. The knife slashed, barely missing me as I ducked and slammed my shoulder into him. Agony stabbed into my stomach. I looked down, catching the glint of steel buried deep.

"*Fuck!*" the asshole roared.

I looked up, my movements far too slow. His fists came at me, catching me on the cheekbone. My head snapped sideways, once...*twice,* and darkness swallowed me whole.

# ONE

## *nick*

"NICK!"

I surfaced with the sound of a scream. Darkness stole the edges of my vision. I blinked and tried to understand what had happened as agony roared through my side.

*"What did you do to him?"*

"Ryth?" I stared into the murky warehouse, finding her. She was bucking and kicking, her arms gripped by two assholes as they dragged her inside.

In an instant, it all came rushing back to me. Dad's car outside her school. The attack...*the knife*. I let out a moan and looked down. *Fuck*. My pulse sped at the sight. Blood...so much blood. My shirt stuck to my side, wet and crimson. The metallic scent filled me like a rag shoved down the back of my throat. I forced myself to look away, to the only thing that mattered to me in this moment.

*Ryth*.

Voices murmured as I shoved up from the ground.

"No, you don't." The asshole from the van stood over me and pushed me back down, the taser in his hand. I winced at the sight. Cold, savage anger roared through me as I met his gaze.

"Can't have you messing up our plans." Elle Castlemaine's voice drew my focus as she stared at her daughter.

*No...not Castlemaine, not anymore.* Banks, right? A goddamn Banks. I shoved up from the ground again as those words echoed.

"Take her..." The bitch motioned to the two other guys who'd abducted me. "Take her to the Order...keep her away from the truth."

*"No!"* I roared as the warehouse swayed.

Ryth's eyes widened as her mother's words hit her. She stumbled backwards as those bastards closed in, grabbing her arms again.

*"Nick!"* she screamed my name, thrashing and fighting their holds. *"NICK!"*

I braced my hand to my side and surged. *"Get your fucking hands off her!"*

But the asshole with the taser grabbed me, shoving that thing at my face, sending bright sparks dancing across the probes. Adrenaline drove me forward as they dragged her back. She wrestled and shoved, fighting like a damn wildcat, giving it all she had.

I spun, gripped my fist with my other hand against my chest, and drove my elbow outward and up, slamming the piece of shit in the face. He stumbled sideways, dropping the weapon. It landed against the concrete with a *thud*. It was all I needed. Pain cut through me as I turned and lunged, radiating through my stomach like something stabbed me all over again.

Still, Ryth's screams cut deeper than the pain ever could. I leaped, but they moved too fast, lifting her feet from the ground as they carried her out. Her skirt rode high, exposing her bare thighs. Those assholes looked...

*They fucking looked.*

Creamy thighs, black lace panties.

Panties she wore for me.

*For...me...*

I lunged again as my father yelled out. *"Nick, NO!"*

I made it halfway across the warehouse, driving myself toward the sunlight, screaming out her name until I didn't just smell the blood...*I tasted it.*

*"The fuck you do!"* The bark came behind me. An arm wrapped around my throat as someone yanked me backward.

Heavy steps invaded. *"Stop fighting, Nick!"* dad roared. "You're making this worse than it is. Jesus Christ, you're fucking hurt. *Get him to a goddamn hospital, for Christ's sake!"*

Get me to a hospital? While they hauled Ryth away...*his own stepdaughter...HER OWN FUCKING BLOOD!*

I twisted, ignoring the roaring agony that ripped through my side and caught dad striding toward me. "Stop this...*you can stop this!"* Arms restrained behind my back, I slammed into him. "Stop this now!"

He grabbed me, pulling me away. Blood smeared all over his shirt, so much fucking blood. I stared at the mess on his hands, then the haunted look in his eyes.

*"Stop fucking fighting, and we'll get you taken care of!"* The bastard who wielded the taser came for me.

The warehouse blurred, jerking and jolting with my hard breaths. I moved, trying my best to dodge the blows when they came. But he moved fast, grabbing me around my arms and yanking me backwards. I hit the floor hard, knocking the air from my lungs. His hand ground my head against the floor. Car doors slammed in the distance. The sound pierced the gaps of his fingers and the sound of a car roared to life.

Footsteps rushed close, heavy, frantic, before they stopped.

"Nick...Nick, I'm sorry—" dad started.

"Get the *fuck off me!*" I bucked, twisting to stare up at him. "Stop this...you can stop this now. Give her back to me...*Dad, give her back!*"

A glimmer of sadness rose in his eyes before that bitch said one word. "No."

He lifted his gaze to her, and that sadness disappeared, leaving coldness behind. Then he left, his long strides leaving me behind with my head held hard against the filthy concrete floor and the ratcheting snap of handcuffs around my wrists.

*No...*

I bucked hard, yanking my wrists until the steel gnawed against bone and a radiating wave of nausea hit me. "No..." I turned, the edges of my world graying. *"No."*

"Get...the van," the bastard commanded above me, sucking in hard breaths as he lifted his gaze. "And let's get this bastard out of here."

Footsteps thudded as the other asshole left.

"Ryth," I moaned. *"Ryth..."*

The hand against my head shoved, grinding my ear against the floor as he rose. "She's fucking gone and she's not coming back. Not anytime soon."

Her screams still rang in my head, the terrified sound like a nail in my coffin, hammered home with the brutal thunder of my heart. Car doors closed. My father's Mercedes roared to life, then the sound drifted away.

"Gonna play nice now, asshole?" The bastard sucked in hard, savage breaths.

*Gonna play nice?*

How about...*no.* I jerked my body around, crushing the steel cuffs against my wrist and swung my legs out, catching him around the ankles. He buckled, crashing to the ground beside me with an unmerciful *thud.* I wasted no time shoving forward, even as a sickening wave of agony radiated through my stomach. I lifted my knees to my chest and fed my feet between my arms before lunging upward.

The sound of the van's engine started as I wrapped my cuffed hands around his throat and my legs around his body. He hit me, throwing his arm behind my head as I yanked. I dodged his blows, wincing as his fist caught me on the cheek. Pain followed, drowned out by her screams in my head.

I squeezed, muscles straining, jaw clenched.

*NICK!* Ryth's scream filled me. Not the sickening wheeze of the man against me, or the whine of the van's engine as it came closer. The bastard stilled against me. His hands hit the ground and there they stayed. I relaxed my hold, listening to the slow hiss of air.

My heart thundered, still I didn't slow long enough to realize what I'd just done. It was nothing compared to what I would do...*to them*. My father's face burned in my mind. But Elle's voice filled my head. Her icy fucking tone.

Hate seethed inside me as I unwound my hands from around his neck. His mouth gaped open and his eyes were life-less. I didn't waste a second, shoving my hands into his pockets, searching for the handcuff key, and felt the bite. I yanked them free. But they weren't the keys I was expecting.

My pulse thundered as I stared at my own keys. I jerked my gaze to the road...*my Mustang*. A moan tore free as I shoved upwards, jammed my keys into my pocket, then grabbed my attacker and yanked, pulling him out of sight. Brake lights flared as the rear of the van came into view.

I hid behind towering pallets, searching the guy's other pockets and yanked his phone free. *Tobias*...I jerked my gaze up as the van stopped and the other guy climbed out. "Okay, let's get this asshole to the hosp—"

He never made it to the end of the sentence, or the back of the van.

I lunged, grabbing him by the throat with one hand and pummeling him with my elbow, pulling away to drive the heel of my hand against his nose. The *crunch* was sickening as he slumped. Still, I kept him upright, shoving him against the van as I searched his pockets.

The small key was wedged in tight. My pulse boomed. Every second was pure fucking torture. I let him go, leaving him to drop hard as I twisted my hands, then unleashed a roar when I couldn't reach. My hands shook as I pushed the key between my lips and bent, guiding it into the lock before I gripped it with my teeth and turned.

I ran, leaving the cuffs to drop from my wrists, and grabbed my keys from my pocket as I stumbled into the glaring sun, catching sight of the Mustang in the distance. A surge of adrenaline hit me. I grabbed the bastard's phone and pressed the button, praying like hell it wasn't locked...

It wasn't...

But it wasn't exactly a phone, more like a tracker. A map filled the screen, a blinking red light moving. I didn't need an explanation to know what it was...it was Ryth.

I pressed the button, then punched in Tobias's number, listening to the damn thing ring...and ring...*and ring. "Fuck!"* I raced for the Mustang, yanked the door open, and slid behind the wheel, then punched the key into the ignition and started the car with a roar.

I checked the map, that blinking red light teasing me. *You won't catch her...you won't* — "Like hell I won't." I shoved the car into gear, wincing as agony ripped through me. Still, I yanked the wheel and punched the accelerator.

The V8 engine roared and the tires screamed as I spun the wheel and the beast surged forward. I divided my focus between the road and that blinking red light. They drove south...I tried to think of what was there. Nothing but emptiness. That I knew of, at least.

I risked losing them, grabbed the phone and stabbed the numbers for Caleb, listening to the goddamn thing as it rang.

"Yeah?" My brother sounded breathless.

"It's me."

*"Nick? Where the fuck are you?"* The squeal of tires echoed in the background and the high-pitched whine of his Lamborghini nearly flatlining told me only one thing...*he knew.*

"Doesn't matter. Tobias..." I grunted. "He with you?"

"They have her, Nick! *They fucking have her.*"

"I know." The road blurred in front of me as I gripped the steering wheel. "I'm putting you on speaker." I pressed the button and looked down at the mess on my shirt, and my head spun.

The car swayed across the white lines. I yanked the wheel, pulling it back. "I need you to listen to me. They're taking her somewhere." The bitch's words came back to me...*take her to The Order.* "The Order. Some place called The Order."

"The Order?" Caleb muttered. "I think I know of that place."

"The goddamn Priest," Tobias snarled, his low tone savage.

I hung onto his rage, needing it to drive me. I glanced at the blinking marker. "Head south. Past Caverns Corner..." the tires squealed as the car swerved.

*"Nick?"* Tobias barked my name.

*"Caverns Corner...then keep..."*

*"NICK!"*

I snapped back to reality and yanked the car across the lane, pushing the accelerator harder. "I'm here...I'm fucking here." The red light flashed...but it didn't move.

I blinked and shook my head. "Shit."

"What?" Caleb roared. Gears shifted, the Lambo scream-ing. *"WHAT THE FUCK IS IT?"*

"They stopped." I stared, squinted, and aimed the Mustang straight.

What the fuck happened? Was it Ryth? Did she make them pull over? Christ, I hoped so. I prayed she fought them, giving it all she had. "Come on, baby," I whispered. "Please come on."

But the road was hazy in front of me.

"Don't...think I can make it..." I slumped forward, gripping the wheel.

"What the fuck do you mean?" Tobias barked.

"Nick..." Caleb's cold, careful tone came through the speaker. "Talk to me, brother. Are you hurt?"

*Am I hurt?* I looked down at the sodden shirt stuck to my stomach, and a chuckle spilled free. Even though nothing was funny. My lips were dry, my thoughts weirdly hazy. But I held onto Caleb's voice. My brother...*no, my big brother.* "Yeah, you could say that."

"Where the fuck are you?" Concern etched his voice.

*On my way to save her...*

"Nick...*Nick*..." Tobias roared, his voice booming through the speaker.

"I'm here." I forced the words through clenched teeth, glancing at that map and the blinking light that moved.

"We're right behind you," Caleb called. "Look in the rear-view mirror."

I lifted my gaze, finding nothing more than the empty road behind me, until I caught the sight of a dot in the distance. A dot that grew bolder by the second. My sluggish pulse kicked hard.

"You see us?"

"Yeah." I pressed my boot harder against the accelerator and looked at the map. They were up ahead...on the other side of the trees in the distance. We were out of the city now. A long way out. Green overtook concrete buildings, stretching as far as I could see.

The Lamborghini gained on me. I pushed the Mustang harder, but I couldn't feel my foot on the accelerator, or my leg. Just an aching numbness.

"We've got you," Caleb urged. "Nick...buddy, we got you."

But I didn't care about myself. I cared about her...*Ryth*. "They took her." Agony roared through my chest with the words. "They fucking took her."

"I know, buddy." Caleb's voice was stony.

Blue filled my rear-view mirror. I didn't focus on them, only on the sweeping bend of the road up ahead...and the towering black wrought-iron gate on my right and the massive *Private Property - Trespassers will be Prosecuted* signs everywhere.

I jerked the wheel, kicking up dust and dirt as the Mustang left the asphalt and headed straight for the gate. But there were men waiting, a Humvee parked across the entrance with four men standing in front, wearing black fatigue suits and armed with military weapons.

I left the Lamborghini behind, unleashed a battle cry, and aimed the Mustang for the gate.

*Crunch.*

Metal shrieked on metal.

I flew forward and slammed against the steering wheel.

*"NICK!"*

Faint screams pierced the void as the Mustang's engine gave a splutter and died. My brothers' screams invaded. But I was already slipping, fading away. The darkness that had threatened my vision swiftly moved in. But not before I lifted my head and stared through the buckled, but still padlocked, gates.

The pungent stench of heated brakes drifted into the car. I blinked and tried to focus on the distance, looking for that fucking van...*and her.* But my vision swam, narrowing in on one of the guards as he stepped forward, slid the end of the semi-automatic rifle through the bars and took aim...*at me.*

# TWO

## *caleb*

"*NICK*!" I shoved open the door, staring at the crumpled front of the Mustang as the armed guard took aim at my brother. *"NO!"*

I lunged, hands up, desperation roaring through me as Nick slumped against the steering wheel...*and didn't get up.* *"T!"* I screamed. *"DRIVE THE FUCKING CAR!"*

I stared at the asshole with his gun pointed at my brother, yanked open the driver's door, and froze. There was blood...*so much blood*. A moan ripped free before I moved, grabbed his arm, and lifted. The heavy metallic stench of blood filled my nose as his cold shirt stuck against my skin.

*Fuck, he was heavy.*

There was only a year between us, but a lot of fucking personality, and muscle, it seemed. I drove upwards, my body howling under the strain as I lifted him from a crouch, pulling him from behind the steering wheel to over my shoulder.

Car doors thudded behind me as I yanked the rear door open and dropped Nick against the seat. "Be alive, you crazy motherfucker." I reached for his neck and pressed my fingers against the warmth. There was a pulse...but it was faint, real fucking faint.

I stepped backwards, shoved his feet inside and slammed the door. I glared at that bastard with the gun as I slid behind the wheel of my brother's Mustang and prayed like I'd only ever prayed once before in my life. This time, my pleas had to be answered. "Come on."

I twisted the key in the ignition, and the engine spluttered to life with a roar. *Yes!* I shoved the car into reverse and drove my boot against the accelerator. The Mustang didn't move, just roared, until I punched the pedal harder, listening to the squeal of steel until finally the car tore free.

Tires spun, kicking up rocks to pepper the underbelly of the car as I reversed hard and yanked the wheel. I glanced behind me. "Hang on, buddy." I glanced at the bloody shirt, my heart thundering at the sight.

I shoved the car into gear, hating how we had to leave Ryth behind. But right now, keeping my brother alive was all I thought of. I drove as fast as I could, taking the corners hard as I raced toward the city hospital. The Lamborghini hugged my ass. Tobias was a dark outline behind the wheel.

"You still with me, buddy?" I risked a glance behind me. His lips were pale, his skin graying. *Shit,* that didn't look good. "Nick...*Nick!*"

There was no answer. I forced myself to focus on the road, aiming the busted-up car toward the Hope Emergency Department and pulled up hard outside the doors. I killed the engine and shoved out of the car, bellowing as the double doors opened automatically. *"We need a doctor here! Someone help me! WE NEED A GODDAMN DOCTOR!"*

*"What the fuck happened?"* Tobias shouted. The heavy thud of his footsteps was so fucking loud in my ears. But I couldn't answer him, because the truth was...*I didn't know.*

Time slowed, everything slowed. Two men came running out, one pushing a gurney my way as I yanked open the rear door and reached for him, lifting Nick out of the car. Immediately, they took him from my arms.

Voices barked at me, but I didn't hear a damn word. All I could do was watch as they wheeled my brother into the emergency department. Nick's arm fell limply to the side as they carried him away. It was all I could do not to fall apart

"Sir, we're going to need some information."

I just nodded.

"He fucking did this." Tobias raked his hand through his hair, pacing back and forth at the rear of the Mustang. "That *motherfucker* did this..."

"T," I muttered, staring at the emergency doors as they closed.

My mind was racing, unable to put the pieces together. All that time he was driving, he was bleeding out. I winced, a coldness claiming me until all I felt was distance.

Distance from this...

From Tobias.

From *everything*.

"We need to go in," Tobias muttered, glancing at the Mustang's open driver's door. "Caleb...*Caleb!*"

Tobias barked my name, snapping me out it. "I got it." I walked around my little brother, staring at the blood soaking the seat, and climbed back in. The Mustang gave a whine as I drove it away, pulled into the parking lot, and found a space.

T pulled the Lamborghini into the next space along and locked the car, handing the keys to me as we headed back to the emergency room. I gave my name and my brother's to the receptionist, taking a seat when she motioned, telling me we'd be notified when they knew more.

It was bad...I knew that.

But how bad was it?

I sat, lowered my head into my hands...and froze. Blood was drying in the creases of my fingers, staining the nailbeds under my fingernails.

"You the two who brought in the stabbing victim?"

I lifted my head to the two cops standing in front of me.

"Yeah," Tobias answered, taking a step forward, protecting me. "He's our brother."

"Want to tell us what happened?" one of the cops asked.

"I have no idea," I answered. "I didn't know he was stabbed until I opened the car door and saw the blood."

"So you have no idea who did this?"

Neither of us answered for a while, then I slowly shook my head. But we knew...we'd both seen the blood on our father's shirt.

"We're going to need a full statement at some stage," the cop said, handing me his card. I took it, nodding, knowing full well they'd wait.

Because they weren't the ones who needed answers. We were. I watched them walk away, going over and over the conversation in my mind.

*I need you to listen to me...they're taking her somewhere. The Order. Some place called the Order.*

The Order.

I'd heard that name before, but right now I couldn't think. Instead, I sat, staring at the blood on my hands while it dried and my brother paced. Hours felt like a lifetime. I rose, paced the waiting area, and turned when a young doctor neared.

"You're Mr. Banks' family?" he asked.

"Yeah," Tobias answered. "How is he?"

God, the doctor looked like a damn kid. "We have him in surgery. That's all they told me. But we have moved him to floor four, surgical, if you want to wait up there."

I just nodded. "Sure."

The kid lowered his gaze to my hands. "There's a bathroom up there, if you want to clean up."

I just stared at him until he nervously turned and walked away. After a few minutes, we made our way up to floor four, stopping at the vending machine to grab coffee before we found some vacant seats in the waiting room.

I strode to the bathroom, scrubbed my hands three times to get most of my brother's blood from my skin, and stared at my reflection in the mirror. "What the fuck happened, Nick?"

Were they attacked?

They had to have been. He'd never let her go, not knowing my brother. No, he'd fight...and he'd keep on fighting. *Christ, don't let him die.* I lowered my head until the howl of the door hinge invaded and some guy walked in.

"Sorry," he muttered, taking one look at me.

I didn't respond, just yanked the door open and walked out, finding Tobias pacing in the hallway, running his fingers through his hair once more. If he kept doing that, he'd end up bald if he wasn't careful.

He jerked that savage glare my way. "I'm gonna fucking kill him. Gonna kill that motherfucker."

I couldn't stop it. I just cracked, grabbed him by the shirt and yanked him closer. I kept my voice low. "Hey. That's our fucking dad you're talking about."

T looked me straight in the eyes. "He's not my father, hasn't been for a long goddamn time, Caleb. It's about time you woke up to that."

I stared at my baby brother and tried to figure out where this all had gone wrong. Him. Dad. *Everything.* Tobias had been quick to throw Ryth under the bus for all his problems, but the truth was, shit had gone south a long time before she and her mom had moved in.

But this...

This was a whole new level of fucked up.

"What the fuck is that place, C?" Tobias looked at me. "What the fuck is going on?"

I released my hold on his shirt and pulled him close. We may not have seen eye to eye a lot of the time, but underneath all of that, he was still my brother, and right now, he needed me. More than ever.

"I don't know," I answered. "But you can bet your fucking life I'm gonna find out. I'm going to get Ryth out of there, and we're going to figure out what the fuck is going on...just as soon as Nick pulls through.

"If he pulls through."

I pushed Tobias back, seizing his gaze. *He's going to pull through...he has to*—I opened my mouth to say the words, but there was nothing, just movement in the corner of my eye.

We both turned at the same time, watching a doctor as he pushed through a set of double doors, swiped the covering from his head and the mask from his face, and headed toward us. But he didn't smile or look relieved.

He gave a frown, one that made my pulse thud hard in my chest. "Oh, fuck."

# THREE

*ryth*

*NO...THE* word rose as I surfaced. *Snap.* Something closed around my ankle, making me flinch. I tried to force open my eyes, but exhaustion weighed them down, keeping me under.

*No! No! NICK!*

I snapped awake with the words, driving myself to the surface. Nick...*Nick*...the image of him rose slowly in my mind. Lying on the concrete, bleeding, desperation and rage burning in his eyes. The sight was a shot of adrenaline. I forced open my eyes.

"Easy," someone snapped at my right.

A sting came at my arm, making me wince. I turned my head, squinting at the glaring light, finding a man dressed in black pulling a needle free. Panic moved through me, making my heart thunder. "What the fuck are you doing?" I tried to push up, but the room swayed.

"Easy." The man pushed me back down, the bed hard and cold underneath me. The spotlight pulsed. *Throb. Throb. Throb.*

"Let me up," I growled. "Nick. Nick. I have to save—" The room tilted with any movement.

*Buzz buzz buzz.* I tried to blink with the sound, but that

29

darkness reached for me, dragging me back under. "Gotta stayeee awwakkeee...*Niiiccckkk...*"

I tried to fight that cruel grip as it clutched my ankle and tugged me back down and as I succumbed to the emptiness, that grating sound echoed once more. *Buzz buzz buzz...*

*Ryth!* Nick's screams surfaced. Faint, so very faint. *RYTH!*

Only darkness waited for me now, pressing down like a weight.

Until a sound drew me higher. The heaviness that weighed me down lifted a little.

A hand pressed against my mouth. "Shh," a female whisper came against my ear. "If they find me in here, they'll take me."

Air trickled in when I sucked in a breath, but warmth pressed over my mouth, making me jerk open my eyes. I blinked into the murky gloom, seeing movement over me. In an instant, the room came rushing back. The sting in my arm. The panic I felt. The man...*the man.*

"Easy," she urged, her voice soft and careful. "I'm gonna take my hand away, okay? Just don't...scream."

The hand slipped away, leaving me to gasp and stare.

"I'm Viv...Vivienne," she whispered. "I saw them...when they came for you. You can get out of here, can't you? I mean, not right now...but soon. Soon they'll come.

My slow thoughts crept closer until they slipped away again. "Who?"

She stared at me. "The ones who rammed the gate."

The gate? What gate? I dropped my hand to the cold steel beside me and shoved, wincing as agony pummeled my head. I blinked and tried to think. "Where am I?"

"Don't you know by now?" she murmured. "You've come to Hell, a brand new version." Her head snapped up, her eyes moving across the room before she moved back. "You gotta survive this place, gotta get free. They'll come for you now that you're awake, but I'll find you. I'll find you and help you get out of here. Only when you leave, you gotta promise to take me with you." She stepped away, moving toward the door.

"Wait." I shoved upwards, hearing something clatter near my foot as I moved. A burn came at my abdomen, sharp, stinging as she cracked open the door. "Don't go."

She stilled, and in the faint light from the hallway, I saw her. Her auburn hair was more red than brown. But her sad, despairing eyes held me. God, she looked desperate. "You have to take me with you," she murmured, her voice barely reaching me. "Or I'm not going to survive."

She slipped out of the room, closing the door soundlessly behind her, leaving me alone.

Fear slipped through me, making me try to push up from the stainless-steel table I lay on. Something clattered against the steel from my foot, the same sound from before. I leaned forward, wincing at that sting as it came to my abdomen once more, and reached out.

Something was clasped around my ankle. I yanked the thing as the sound of heavy steps came from outside. The door opened once more. I yanked the webbing harder. Panic plunged deep as two men stepped in the room and closed the door.

Darkness slipped from my mind now, leaving chilling clarity behind. "No." I yanked the thing and when I couldn't tear it free, I lifted my head as they came for me.

"Easy," one of them murmured. His predatory movement triggered the memory of what had happened.

The abduction. The warehouse. "Nick." I stiffened, as I whispered.

They leaped across the room, coming for me. I screamed, lashing out, kicking when they grabbed me. I didn't care about the pain anymore. Didn't care about anything but getting out of here.

*They'll come for you.* Vivienne's words surfaced as my abductors lifted my feet from the floor. I kicked and screamed until my throat burned. Still, they didn't care, hauling me toward the door.

"Get the fuck off me!" I swung my fist.

One of them caught it as they dragged me by my arms toward the doorway. The sight of that glaring hallway triggered something in me. *FIGHT!* Tobias roared in my head. His savage roar giving me energy. I lifted my foot and drove it against the doorframe, pushing myself backwards.

"Stop fucking fighting!" one of my attackers barked, and thrust me forward.

I fought harder, twisting and thrashing, until I caught a blur in the corner of my eye. The blow hit me on the side of the head and exploded in my ear. I stopped fighting, dazed and stunned, giving them the precious seconds they needed to drive me through the doorway and out into the hall.

"Fucking pain in the goddamn ass!" one barked, the sound hollow and thudding in my ear.

I pulled away from them, still fighting. Pathetic movements were all I had left. I braced my bare feet against the slick tiled floor as my head thumped and boomed.

Still, they dragged me along the hallway, stopping for one of them to press an access card against a sensor before shoving me through a set of double doors. Their boots echoed in the empty hallway. I tried to look behind me as they pushed. But all I saw was the stark white walls.

They stopped at a room, pressed the card against the scanner outside the door, and pushed the handle down. Bright lights blinked on with the flick of a switch before they shoved me inside. I stumbled, throwing my arms out wide to find my balance.

"There," the asshole who'd hit me snarled. "Make yourself comfortable. You'll be here a while."

I spun, rage burning inside me. *"Fuck you!"*

But they left, yanking the door closed behind them with a *bang,* leaving me alone. I rushed the door, throwing my fists against it as I stared through the glass panel at them. "Let me out! *Let me out NOW!"*

The asshole stared through me before he turned, giving me his back, and walked away. I slammed myself against the door, pummeling it with my fists. "Let me *out of here!"*

Rage came. Tears blurred them as my abductors left. *"Let me out!"* I punched the door. "Let me the fuck out of here!"

Warmth trailed down my cheeks as I drove my fists against the door time and time again. But my blows and pleas were futile. "Please," I whispered, and turned, sliding my back against the door as I sank to the floor. "Please let me out of here."

Mom's words rang in my head, cruel and unkind. *We can't have you messing up our plans...take her...take her to the Order.*

"The Order," I whispered, my voice thick and blubbering. "Why, mom? *Why?"*

She'd betrayed me...*again.*

I drew my knees to my chest and gripped them tight. She'd betrayed me, just like she'd betrayed dad. I wanted to kick and scream for the guys, but Nick was the one who gripped my heart tight. Nick and Tobias and Caleb. My shuddering breaths stilled as that desperate look from Nick filled me once more. Blood filled my mind as the memory came roaring back. Blood that spread as he'd kicked and fought in a desperate attempt to get to me.

"Nick." I squeezed my eyes closed. *"Oh, Nick..."*

FOUR

*caleb*

THE SURGEON SLIPPED the surgical cap from his head and walked toward us, a grave look of worry etched on his face. He glanced at Tobias, then settled that focus on me. "Are you the family of Nicholas Banks?"

"Nick," Tobias answered, rising from the hard plastic seat along the hospital corridor. "His name is Nick."

"Nick," the doctor repeated.

"He's our brother." I rose with Tobias, my pulse pounding, my voice sounding strange. "Is he..."

"Alive," the surgeon hurried to answer. "But barely. He's lost a lot of blood. The knife barely nicked one of the major arteries, any deeper and we'd be having a very different conversation right now. To say it's a miracle your brother's alive is a massive understatement." His bewildered expression said it all. "I honestly don't understand how he survived."

"I do," I murmured, remembering the desperation on Nick's face when he'd looked up at me, slumped over the steering wheel.

*Ryth,* he'd croaked. *Ryth.*

"We've given him four units of blood so far and we have

34

more on standby. Once he comes out of recovery, we'll assess his situation and give him more if he needs it. But for now, we're keeping him..."

"Sure," I nodded. "Whatever you need to do."

"He's one determined man," the surgeon added. "I don't know what happened, but he had an angel watching over him today."

Mom's face rose from the darkness of my mind. I knew I wasn't the only one thinking the same thing.

Tobias swallowed hard. "When can we see him?"

"Once he's conscious. But we're keeping him heavily sedated. You might not get much out of him. "

"That doesn't matter." I shook my head. "That doesn't matter at all."

A nod, and the surgeon glanced at Tobias. "I'll have a nurse come and get you when he's awake."

I just stood there, watching the guy turn and leave, before I sank to the hard seat once more.

"Jesus." Tobias' voice shook.

I didn't trust my own. I could only lower my head into my hands. Nick was alive...he was alive, and that's all that mattered. Relief flooded through me. I closed my eyes and tried to remember how to function.

"It was mom."

I opened my eyes slowly and turned my gaze to Tobias.

"Mom saved him today. That's exactly what she'd do," Tobias insisted, his stare pinned to me. "That was her all over."

I nodded slowly. It was...it was so her to protect her sons. She was selfless and driven, and I could just see her standing there, screaming and savage, when Nick fought for his life.

Pain bloomed in my chest with the image. I didn't know what I'd do if I'd lost Nick too, so soon after her. I'd fall apart...

even more than I was right now. I'd fall apart with no hope of putting myself back together.

"That was Nick's blood on dad."

I flinched and jerked my eyes to his. "You don't know that."

"Don't I?" That dangerous tone was back in my brother's voice. "Let's just see what our brother says when he's awake."

I wanted to argue, wanted to tell him to take the words back. But a shiver of apprehension tore through me. All I could see was the blood on dad's shirt, and hear the lie when he said *he's at the hospital.* If he didn't stab Nick himself, then he'd seen it. Either way, he was involved, and had still had the balls to come home. He couldn't even stay with him...

I leaned my head back against the wall as Tobias took a sip of his coffee. "It's cold."

"I'll go," I answered, pushing myself to stand. "Wait here in case the nurse comes."

My brother nodded, looking up at me, and in that moment, I couldn't get out of there fast enough. I lengthened my stride, fighting the urge to break into a run, and headed not for the vending machines but for the elevator.

I wanted to run, and keep on running. I pressed the button and stepped inside as the elevator doors opened, and closed my eyes as it carried me down to the foyer. My head was dull and throbbing when I opened my eyes and stepped out.

I heard nothing.

I felt...*nothing.*

Just the rush of adrenaline coursing through my veins and the burn at the back of my throat. I tried to slow my breaths as I strode out of the lobby of the hospital and plunged into bright, piercing sunlight.

My hands shook as I headed across the parking lot to where Tobias had parked my car. I couldn't look at the

Mustang, not yet. I kept my focus on the Lambo's midnight blue paintwork as I hit the button and slid behind the wheel

I should be up there, should be sitting beside my brother, waiting for Nick to wake. But I couldn't. Not yet. I yanked the door closed and sat behind the wheel, staring at the bushes planted at the edge of the lot. *He'd betrayed us...*

"You piece of fucking shit." The words slipped free as I punched the steering wheel. *"YOU PIECE OF FUCKING SHIT!... I trusted you!"*

Desperation howled inside me. I sucked in a hard breath and tried to keep from completely losing my shit. "I trusted you."

*Ryth...* Nick's whisper came back to me, stopping me cold.

*Ryth...*

*Ryth.*

Her name hummed in my veins. She was a storm brewing on the horizon, rumbling, igniting. I could almost taste her ozone. The rear-view mirror is where I lifted my gaze. I needed to get her out of that place. I needed to get her out of there *now*. *The Order...*

The Priest's image came back to me. The stitching on his crisp black suit. That same stony, detached look I'd seen before. Panic surged. The same panic I'd pushed away at the wedding when I'd thought I recognized him before. But the place that came back to me wasn't a compound behind razor-wire. No, it was in the depraved, secret clubs of the elite where powerful men didn't just fuck women...*they bought, traded, and owned them like property.*

"Fuck, let it not be the same." That panic thundered inside me. I rubbed the back of my neck, then pushed open the door and climbed out.

I needed to get back to Tobias, to be the big brother he needed. Then I needed to get our little sister out of that place, whatever it was. I made my way back through the parking lot and into the hospital, riding the elevator up to the fourth floor. The hiss of the vending machine was the background for my thoughts. I grabbed fresh coffee before finding Tobias pacing the floor like a caged animal.

"Where the fuck have you been?" he snapped.

I handed him the steaming cup, watching as he unthinkingly took it.

"We need to get in there," he snarled. "We need to find out what he knows."

My little brother didn't need any more stimulation, but not having anything in his hand was worse. "Drink your coffee, Tobias."

He flinched as rage sparked in those dark eyes. Still, he did as he was told, blowing on the coffee before taking a sip. Words of war hung heavy in the air. *I'll fucking kill him...I'LL FUCKING KILL HIM.* My chest ached knowing this was what our family had come to.

Our mother's cancer had almost broken us, but then when Lazarus reported about my father cheating, that had driven Tobias toward revenge. That was bad enough. But when he brought Elle and Ryth into our lives, we were ready for war... until Ryth...

Ryth changed it all.

I'd almost forgiven him, almost given into his selfish attempt at happiness—the surgery doors pushed open up ahead and a nurse strode out, scanning the hallway until she settled on us and headed our way—I'd almost forgiven him for one smile on our sister's face.

But now...now I wanted blood.

"Mr. Banks?"

I met her gaze. "Yes."

She glanced at Tobias. "Your brother's awake."

He strode to a nearby garbage can and dropped the coffee inside. I followed, taking a first and last sip, steadying myself for what we were about to find out. We followed her through the doors and along a hallway, making our way to a private room where our brother lay.

His eyes were closed, his lips pale as fuck. I froze in the doorway as Tobias moved to his side. "Hey. You awake?"

Nick's eyes fluttered, then opened, moving from Tobias to me. For a second, he didn't speak, then he licked his lips. "Ryth."

"We couldn't get her," Tobias answered. "But we will, even if I have to go in, guns blazing, all on my own."

Nick glanced at me. He knew...knew more blood would be spilled.

"No, no guns." I stepped closer. "But we'll get her. We'll get her back and we'll figure all this out."

Nick gripped the bedrail and pulled.

"Hey!" Tobias barked, and lunged, pushing against Nick's shoulders. "What the fuck do you think you're doing?"

"I'm going..." our brother slurred. "With you."

"The fuck you are." Tobias looked my way, his gaze demanding I say something.

But Nick wasn't backing down, baring his teeth. "Get the fuck off me, T."

Tobias leaned closer. "You were fucking stabbed!"

The words stopped Nick. He breathed hard, then glanced at me. Panic flared as he frowned.

"What happened?" I asked. "Tell us everything."

His scowl deepened. "I was at home, at the apartment, I mean. I remember grabbing my things. Something made me drive to the school, I can't quite remember. But when I got there, I saw dad's Mercedes..."

"Go on." Tobias urged, his tone dark and dangerous.

"I got out, thinking something was wrong, then I was fucking hit from behind. They had a damn taser, got me down and into that damn van. I fought as hard as I could...but there were three of them and they were trained." His eyes widened and fixed on mine. "They were fucking trained."

"Ryth." Tobias drove him closer to the truth.

"By the time they dragged me into the warehouse, I'd been tased and fucking stabbed. They brought her in, kicking and screaming. Her mom was there...and dad, as well. They said something about not messing up their plans, and they took her away." He closed his eyes and winced. "I tried to fight, but they had me handcuffed."

"Dad..." I murmured. "He saw you were hurt?"

Nick nodded, and the sight was a punch to my gut.

"I don't care about that," he added. "I only care about getting her out of there."

"Is it some jail?" Tobias asked, then looked my way. "Some fucking girls' school?"

I shook my head. "I don't know." But inside, that fear grew.

"He did this." Tobias turned and paced the floor. "Him and that goddamn bitch!"

I wanted to tell Tobias to drop it, wanted to keep him close, as close as I could. But if he was going after dad and Elle, then he wasn't going after the compound. Either way, I had to keep him safe. A shiver tore through me as I answered. "Then we find out the truth."

"Get her out." Nick held his side as he dropped back onto the bed. "Whatever it takes. Promise me."

It was me Nick stared at. Me Nick made promise. "I will. Just get better. We need you."

A soft knock came at the door and a nurse entered, moving to his side. But we were already done getting all the information we could.

I hated leaving him, but I hated leaving Ryth more. We left and headed for the elevator. We walked in silence, stepping inside when the doors opened. Neither of us stopped at the front desk, we just walked back out into the sunshine and headed for the Lamborghini. I pulled my phone out of my pocket, brought up the details for the towing company, and called them to take care of the Mustang as I climbed in behind the wheel.

Tobias slid into the passenger seat without a word. The silence was chilling as I backed out of the hospital parking lot and headed for home. It felt like we'd been here forever. But it'd only been hours since I'd pulled in, screaming for help. I focused on driving. The moment we got near the house, Tobias spoke.

"You stay out of my way, Caleb," he warned. "Got me? Just stay the fuck out of the way."

I'd almost lost a brother today...the fear of that was enough.

Now I was about to lose my dad, too...

Only there was no sign of the Mercedes when I pulled into the driveway. Only Tobias' black Jeep sat there. Tobias was out before I could kill the engine. His heavy steps echoed like thunder as he slammed through the front door and raced inside.

*"Where the fuck are you!"* Tobias screamed as he threw open the study door, then turned back.

"T," I called as he raced past me, taking the stairs two and three at a time. I was right behind him, driving myself hard to keep up.

Tobias was a savage as he slammed against their bedroom door and tore inside. I swallowed harsh breaths, staring at the mess of clothes discarded on the floor. "What the fuck?"

"They're gone." Tobias left dad's walk-in closet and went to mom's.

No. Not mom's, not anymore.

*"Fucking bitch!"* he screamed. His face was a mask of menace, teeth clenched and bared. The whites of his eyes were neon as he went to the bathroom.

The room was a goddamn mess. Bottles and makeup were scattered everywhere across the counter, some on the floor, crushed under hurried steps as they raced to leave. I could almost hear dad scream, *Leave it! Just fucking leave it!*

So, they'd abducted Ryth...

Had Nick stabbed...

Then they ran.

"His offices." Tobias jerked his gaze my way.

"Go," I urged. "Call me as soon as you find anything."

Tobias nodded and left, flinging himself through the doorway and back down the stairs. The snarl of the Jeep's engine came seconds later, almost smothered by the squeal of tires. God help my father when Tobias caught up to him, but there was no one else who would.

I looked at the destruction they'd left behind. Whatever was happening, they'd thought of themselves first, and fuck the rest of us. I strode out of the bedroom. The house was so goddamn empty without the sound of her laughter and moans.

I climbed the stairs, made my way to her bedroom, and pushed open her door.

Hours...

That's all it'd taken to tear her away from us.

*They said something about not messing up their plans, and they took her.* Nick's words resounded in my head as I stared at her bedroom. *Whatever it takes. Promise me.* I stole a breath. "Whatever it takes."

The memory of her assaulted me as I stepped into my bedroom and glanced at the bed. Her bare ass driving against my fingers, her pussy quivering as I'd made her mine. Hunger hit me like a blow, more dangerous than I'd ever felt before. If she was in that place controlled by the Order...then there was only one way to get her back. I reached for my phone and pressed the number for my contact.

"Banks," the male answered. I could almost hear the smile on his face. "Long time, no bullshit, brother."

"Evans," I said carefully, my voice stony and controlled. "You're still with Copeland?"

"Yeah. Why, you want in? You know Major has a thing for you. You'd have a damn fine office waiting for you tomorrow. Hell, it'd probably be bigger than mine."

"That's not why I called." I licked my lips. "You still have those connections? The ones with Davidson and Hale?"

There was silence from the other end before he answered carefully, his words muffled against the phone. "You know I don't take part in that scene, same as you."

Revulsion burned in my belly. "But you *still* have those connections, right? You can still...get me in?"

"Do you know what you're asking me to do?" His voice turned low and desperate. "You know what happens there. You really want in on that?"

I closed my eyes, remembering the young women they'd paraded in front of us, like lambs to the slaughter. Women that were trained to never say no. "I think I'm in trouble," I answered. "And I need your help."

"Trouble..." His voice turned stony. "What kind of trouble?"

A shudder ripped through me as I closed my eyes. "I think those bastards have my goddamn sister."

# FIVE

I SAT in the dark with my back pressed against the door, my thoughts frozen on that last image I had of Nick bleeding on the ground. I couldn't think of anything else. Not this place or mom's words, or the searing betrayal that burned its way through my chest.

I forced everything else away, closing my eyes, forcing all my concentration on one single prayer. "You keep him alive, and I'll do anything. Anything you want. I'll leave them, if that's what you want. I'll go away. So far away you won't hear from me again. I won't ask for another thing. Just him...okay? *Just him.*"

Footsteps thudded, and it took me a second to realize what that sound was. *Click.* The lock sounded. As the door swung open, I scurried backwards, shoving my heels against the floor. I expected them to come charging in. I expected cruel hands and roars as they made their demands.

But none of that came.

My heartbeat thundered. My breaths were hard fists in the back of my throat I had to swallow. I lifted my gaze to the shadowed figure standing in the doorway and met ice-blue eyes.

"Ms. Castlemaine," he murmured, staring down at me as though this was the position he'd expected to find me in. Fear coursed through me with the slow drag of his gaze along my body, stopping at my ankle. "I'm sure you have questions. If you'll follow me..."

*Follow me?* I opened my mouth to bite back, but he turned and strode away, leaving the door open. *Run.* That need drove me as I shoved against the floor and rose. His steps thudded, growing fainter as I moved to the open doorway.

I glanced along the hallway and stopped, my gaze fixed on the locked double doors and the card reader. Even if I tried to make a break for it, I wouldn't get far. I was betting they weren't the only locked doors in this prison either.

*You've come to Hell. Just a brand new version of it.* Vivienne's words echoed within me as I swallowed and shifted my focus to the fading footsteps. I had no choice but to follow. I needed answers...and I prayed I'd get them.

I moved to the corner, catching sight of the man as he walked along the hall and stopped at an open doorway with his back to me. My heart was pounding as I followed, my eyes searching the locked doors and darkened rooms behind the glass windows, then stopped, well out of his reach.

*My little lioness...*

Dad's nickname for me surfaced now as I watched the man turn and motion to the doorway. "Please." The word was careful and controlled. I gave a shake of my head. There was no way in hell I was going into a room with him, or anyone, for that matter.

One brow rose as the double doors behind him gave a *click* and opened. As though on cue, a guard stepped out. Tall, with striking white hair. His unflinching gaze moved to mine as he stopped at the man's side and leaned close, whispering something in his ear.

But the man didn't lean toward him, just stood still, his gaze fixed on me. My stomach trembled with the focus. He'd made no move to hurt me, hadn't even raised his voice, and yet in that moment, I was more afraid of him than the bastards who'd dragged me kicking and screaming into this place.

*I'm sure you have questions.*

I swallowed, staring at his hand that hovered in the air, knowing I couldn't stand here forever. The white-haired guard straightened and glanced my way. His eyes sparked and his lips curled in a silent snarl. He looked at me with the kind of malice that sent a chill along my spine. My stomach trembled at the sight of him. I didn't want to be alone with him...not if I could help it.

"The answers you seek start in this room, Ms. Castlemaine, or I can leave you to my associate here." He stilled for a second, his voice turning dangerous. "But his methods are decidedly less tasteful than mine."

My heartbeat stuttered as terror surged through me. Cold tiles kissed my bare feet as I stepped through the door, flinching as the automatic lights came on. It was a bathroom. Open. Stark and white. There were no doors for privacy, not for the toilets or the showers. My chest tightened at the sight. There was a set of clothes on the edge of the sparkling vanity, white lace panties and some kind of sheer covering. I froze at the sight.

"There's bodywash and shampoo." I spun, finding him and the guard standing behind me. He glanced at the clothes, then at me. "We expect our initiates to be meticulously clean at all times."

My eyes widened, rage racing to the surface. I gritted my teeth. "Go fuck yourself."

There was a twitch at the corner of his lips as he lifted the phone in his hand. One swipe of his thumb, and he pressed the screen.

*"NICK!"* My own screams rang out from his phone. He lifted it toward me and I saw the interior of that warehouse once more.

*"RYTH!"* Nick roared. *"RYTH!"*

My heart punched my ribs. The pounding in my ears was deafening as he pressed the screen, stopping the video. "I understand your...*stepbrother* was hurt in the intervention."

I jerked my gaze to his, and the white tiles of the bathroom faded to black. He was all I saw in that moment, every glimmer in his eyes and every rise of his chest.

"I'm sure you're concerned about him," he continued, that unflinching tone never once wavering. "I could make some calls to find out the extent of his injuries. But by the looks of this...it seems rather unlikely he survived."

*No...*

I stumbled backwards as my knees buckled, sending me crashing to the floor.

*Thud...thud...thud...*his polished shoes came into view. "If you do what I ask," he demanded. "Shower, scrub...and dress in the garments I provided."

I stared at the tops of his shoes, black against the stark tiles, and fought the tears when they came. "Please," I whispered. "Please tell me he's alive."

My captor said nothing, nor did he move. He just waited while the screams of agony howled inside me and eventually fell silent. On quivering legs, I rose, gripped my shirt, and dragged it over my head. I was still in the same underwear I'd put on that morning. The same underwear Nick had picked out for me at Victoria's Secret.

My captor lowered his gaze as I reached around and

unhooked my bra, leaving it to fall free. I swallowed hard, thumbed my panties, and pushed them down.

"You can call me The Principal," he murmured, staring between my legs. "Now shower...and don't forget to shave...*everything.*"

My tears came as I slowly turned to the shower and hit the taps. The sting on my abdomen was instant, drawing me back to the pain I'd felt before when I came to. I looked down, and moaned. Black against my pale flesh. Panic roared as I touched the marking. A *tattoo*...

"*No,*" I cried and rubbed the red, raised flesh, whimpering.

*H* inside the *O*. I'd seen that marking before...seen that *ugly fucking mark*—I stiffened as the image of the Priest came rushing back to me.

*Can't have you messing up our plans.* My mom's voice slipped through the cracks of my mind.

The Priest. The wedding. *The betrayal.* I touched the tattoo on my skin and felt the bathroom sway. They'd marked me...*they'd marked me.* Like I was nothing but property. One they owned...

I lowered my gaze to the strap around my ankle, feeling their gazes on my ass. *Don't panic...just don't panic.* I stepped under the hot spray and tilted my head back. I used their body-wash and shampoo, then swallowed, sneaking a glance over my shoulder as I picked up the razor.

My thoughts turned dark as the memory of Vivienne's desperation returned. How many girls had done this? How many had taken the razor to their wrists instead of their legs? I didn't need to meet my captor's gaze to know the truth.

So I set to work, taking the razor to my underarms, my legs, and finally between my legs. When I was done, I was smooth.

Whatever it takes.

I held onto that thought.

*Whatever it takes.*

I dried off and dressed in the soft white lace lingerie, fighting the wince as I slipped the sheer covering on and tied it. But I stiffened when the heavy footsteps of the guard sounded behind me.

"No." I shook my head, drawing on that strength my stepbrothers had given me. The one who called himself The Principal was behind the guard. "I won't go. I won't do a damn thing you ask. Not until I know..." *Nick.* "Not until I know he's alive."

The Principal's smile was slow and sadistic as he strode past the guard to stop in front of me. "I can make some calls, if you like." He brushed my hair so gently, curling the strands behind my ear. "If that would ease your mind."

Hope surged inside me, until he grabbed me by the throat and dragged me close. "But please don't mistake my kindness for weakness." His eyes searched mine. "Let me show you what happened the last time someone thought that."

He let me go. I coughed and touched the ache his fingers had left behind as he turned and strode from the bathroom.

A heavy hand from the guard gripped my arm as he demanded. "This way."

I followed without a fight, desperation burning inside me. My body twitched with the pounding in my ears. I had no choice but to follow The Principal as he led me to the double doors, then through. The lights dulled as I walked along the corridor. Shadows grew in the corners and spilled across my feet, which only increased the panic inside me.

The Principal stopped at a set of double doors and waited. When we neared, he pressed his card to the scanner and opened the doors. Darkness waited inside and with it came the low whimpers of someone in pain.

Not just someone. A woman.

*Whack!*

I flinched at the sound and jerked my gaze to him...to the devil with the ice-blue eyes as he stepped inside, leaving the guard to drive me forward. The guard shoved me into the barely lit room, leaving me to stumble.

But I didn't fall. Not with his bruising grip around my arm. No, he just manhandled me, driving me deeper into the darkness. I bucked, yanked, then froze as a *slap* came once more.

The moan that followed from the darkness chilled me to the bone. The Principal's footsteps stopped before the *whoosh* of something came. Those murky lights grew a little brighter behind what was a heavy black curtain. And in the sultry glow, I caught the panicked gazes staring back at me.

My heart punched into the back of my throat as I was shoved forward again. There were at least twenty of them. All dressed in the same hideous gown...only different colors, white, black...*and red.*

"Olivia," The Principal called as he strode toward a woman who stood naked in front of the others. Her arms were chained and pulled out wide, her legs secured the same way. Heat rushed to my cheeks at the sight of her, bare and exposed. "She decided she'd rather try to end her life than to stay with us."

A guard stood beside her, a long leather switch in his hand.

"The problem with that is...it's not her life to take." He turned that icy gaze to the naked woman. "Is it?"

A nod and the guard stepped closer, then cracked that whip through the air...and right between her legs.

*Crack.*

She bucked, her eyes wide, her skin glistening with sweat as she moaned.

"Her life belongs to me...as does her body," The Principal declared, staring into her eyes. "I'm hoping you learn that lesson quickly, Ryth."

My breath caught at the sound of my name.

I scanned the women watching the display. They all watched me. Familiar brown eyes met mine. *Vivienne.* They'd dressed her in white, in the same clothes as I wore.

"You are not your own person here. You've been sold." The Principal swiveled to meet my stare. "To me."

*"No."* I shook my head and stepped backwards. "No fucking way."

But I didn't get far. The white-haired guard held me in place, those arctic blue eyes fixed on mine.

Sold...

My mom had sold me. *Can't have you messing up our plans.* Her words came back to me. I bit down on my tongue, fighting the moan that pushed into the back of my throat. This was what it had come down to. They wanted to break me...they expected me to be meek and mild. They expected I'd do whatever they wanted. The chilling truth was, a few months ago they might've won.

But not now.

Nick, Tobias, and Caleb came roaring back. They'd rather die than see me fall at this bastard's feet. That same power I'd felt that night at mom's wedding came roaring back to me. The power *I wielded.* The power *I* controlled. I clenched my jaw as my power came back to me. "Fuck you," I snarled. "Fuck you all the way to Hell."

# caleb

"ANSWER YOUR GODDAMN PHONE, T." I forced the words through clenched teeth and paced the floor. "Just answer the fucking phone." For all I knew, the little punk could be stabbed or bleeding somewhere in a goddamn gutter. "Fuck, this is such a goddamn mess."

I lifted my phone, trying one last goddamn time.

*"Why the fuck are you calling me?"* Tobias snarled in his voice message.

I hung up, tossed the cell to the bed. It wasn't just Tobias that had me riled. It was this whole thing. I massaged the throbbing knot on the back of my neck and tried to figure out what the fuck had happened.

As always, my mind skimmed past mom's passing. I didn't want to think about that, not yet. But fuck, it had left a goddamn hole in all our lives. Dad went off the rails. We'd thought it was grief...but now.

Now, I was starting to know better.

Elle Castlemaine. It had to be. She was bad fucking news...*really bad.*

Ryth said the FBI had arrested her dad. But I knew they

didn't just act like that out of nowhere. No, something like that took planning. And that meant time. A pang tore across my chest when I thought of Ryth, now in that goddamn place all alone.

She was nothing like her mom. Nothing fucking like it...

*Get her back.* Nick's husky words surfaced. *Get her back.*

No matter what it took, right?

Only, my brother had no idea the kind of danger our little stepsister was in now, from the kind of men that revelled in the darkness. My pulse thundered as I glanced at the darkening sky once more. Christ, I didn't want to do this. I didn't want to go back to that part of my fucking life. And it wasn't because I was scared of *them*...

It was because I was scared of myself.

I shifted my focus to the bottom of my bed. *Good girl.* My own words rang in my head, muffled by Ryth's tortured moans of release. I'd escaped the clutches of depravity once, but I didn't come away unscathed. The kinds of things I'd witnessed had left a goddamn mark. One I hadn't been able to scrub away.

I liked what they did at those clubs, liked the rush owning someone like that gave me. I liked using them in the moment... but I didn't like the wave of sickness it left behind.

What I longed for was both.

Someone to love...someone to be cared for...*someone I could use to temper that debased need inside me.* I hated how my body hummed, knowing I was about to dive headlong back into that darkness once more. Only this time it was for a reason...*her.*

I left my room and made my way to the bathroom. The house sounded empty without them. Still, I forced myself to undress and shower. I took my time scrubbing and washing as that hunger slowly burned. I killed the water and stepped out, toweled my body dry, and strode naked along the landing to my bedroom.

Black. That's what I dressed myself in.

Black as the sins I was about to commit...*for her.*

I sprayed myself with scent, adjusted my belt, and slipped my shoes on, taking a glance at myself in the full-length oval mirror at the end of my room. They wanted cold...detached. The spark dulled in my eyes as I sank down into that emptiness. Then detached is what they'd get.

Only I clung to one tiny glimmer...

*Her.*

*Ryth.*

"I'm coming, princess," I murmured. "Hold the fuck on."

I left my room and went downstairs, then out the front door. My headlights carved through the night as I backed around and shot forward. But I didn't head straight for the elite members-only club, not yet...I had to confess first.

I made my way to the city, to a small bar notoriously known for the city lawyers who patronized it. A band of brothers I was once part of...and somehow that strange yearning rose inside me. It'd been months since I'd stepped foot inside my office, months since I'd thought about reviving my failing study of the Law.

But now it had been shoved into my face whether or not I liked it. I only hoped the loyalties were still there. I carved through the busy downtown streets, pulling the Lamborghini into a parking space near Fourth and First before I killed the engine and climbed out.

Sideway glances came from a group of women as they strode past. I adjusted my jacket and hit the button on the remote, ignoring the smiles and stares. They could look all they wanted. They weren't my type in the least.

But they were headed my way, following me into The

Associate. That's where I left them, headed to the back of the bar where the men leered, drank and talked about pussy like they had game. They didn't. Still, they thought it made for pleasant conversation. It was exactly the kind of thing that had turned me off coming back.

I nodded at Havers as he lifted his gaze to me. His brows rose. "Banks?"

"Hey," I answered, scanning familiar faces and stopped at Michael Evans, defense lawyer at Copeland Law, one of the oldest and most prestigious firms in the city. Getting a position with them depended on two things: clout and money, and Evans had both.

"C." Michael nodded my way.

I glanced toward the private booths at the back of the bar. "Want to grab a drink in private?"

"Sure," he muttered and slid from his stool, nodding at the other guys around us.

They all stared, mostly at me. Luckily, I was used to it. I moved to the back of the bar, sliding along the seat of a booth way in the back, and waved the waitress over. Evans ordered rum and coke. I motioned for two and waited for him to take a seat, acutely aware that every second Ryth was in that place, was a second too fucking long.

He took a seat, glancing over his shoulder at the others as they still looked our way. "Told them you were thinking about coming back," he muttered, then turned toward me. "But that's not why you're here, is it? Want to tell me what the fuck is going on, C?"

A shiver coursed through me. I'd known Evans since our first goddamn day at Harvard. Both of us straight-laced and full of dreams. A little pathetic, looking back on it now. Only he'd kept that idealism, letting it drive him, whereas I'd sunk slowly into that hunger.

The need for revenge and the tainted. Christ, I was like an addiction just waiting to happen.

"So, I heard your father got remarried," Evans started.

I winced and nodded, waiting as the waitress neared carrying our drinks. She smiled, glancing at Evans before turning to me, and stilled. "Anything else I can get for you?" She slid napkins on the table, one in particular pushed my way.

"Thank you, but no," I answered.

There was a flicker of annoyance before she turned and walked away. Evans reached over, grabbed the napkin, and turned it over to reveal her phone number.

"Good to see nothing changes with you." He smirked and shook his head, pushed back in his seat, and let the smile fade. "Now, you want to tell me what the fuck is going on?"

"Nick's in the hospital," I started.

He froze, his brows rising. "Oh shit. He okay?"

I gave a slow nod and played with my drink. "He will be, but he almost fucking died today...and that's not all."

"I'm listening," he urged.

"I don't have all the facts yet. But she double-crossed her own husband, set him up with the FBI and put him in prison. Now he's missing...and she just conveniently disposed of her daughter." My voice went low. "In a place called the Order."

His breath caught...and there was a flicker of fear. "You know what they do in that place?"

I swallowed hard. "I have a feeling I'm about to find out."

He leaned forward. "She really worth this? You know what they'll do to you."

"Worth it?" I repeated. "Yeah, she's worth it."

He went silent, staring at me, and I hated his fucking attention. "Jesus Christ, you like this girl?"

Ryth filled my mind, sending my pulse soaring. "She's not a girl...she's my goddamn stepsister."

"You fucking fell for her, didn't you?"

I didn't have to answer. It was written all over my face.

"Jesus," Evans muttered. "How the mighty have fallen. You fell for your kid sister."

"Stepsister," I snarled. "And she's not a kid."

He took a sip of his drink. "So you're really going to go through with his?"

"Know of another way inside?"

"Not if you want to stay alive. I heard the compound is guarded with ex-mercenaries."

All I thought about was that gun being leveled at Nick's head after he crashed into the gate. There was only one way in without getting ourselves killed...only it was going to be just as fucking brutal.

"So you're really prepared to do this?" Evans probed again.

"I don't have a choice." I met his gaze. "My heart won't let me. Besides, it's just an introduction, then I'm leaving you. An introduction is all my damn conscience will allow."

I knew what even that small thing was costing him, and it had nothing to do with money.

Evans stared at me for another moment, then he grabbed his drink and downed the rest of the contents. "Then I guess we're about to walk into the lion's den."

I flinched and shook my head as he slid out of the booth. "You don't have to—"

"You saved my ass back in college more times than I'll ever admit. You think I'm about to bail on you now?" He shook his head as I drained my own drink and rose from the seat. "Besides, I'm gonna like having one up on you, Banks." He threw an arm around my shoulders. "Don't think I've given up on us starting our own firm together. My money, your looks. We'd fucking kill it."

I cut him a glare. "Don't get ahead of yourself."

"Buddy." He tightened his hold around me. "With the shit I'm about to do for you, getting ahead of myself is the only thing that's going to get me through."

I let him make his jokes as I placed my empty glass down on the napkin with the waitress' number. He was on the phone as we walked out, calling in favors...a whole lot of them. When we stepped out of the bar, he lifted his hand, motioning for his driver.

Evans came from old money. The kind that was taken for granted, and it showed. The Mercedes pulled up, double-parking long enough for him to climb in the backseat, leaving the door open behind him for me to follow.

"Ninth street, Neil," Evans instructed. "Near the Water-house brewery."

Neil looked over his shoulder before slowly giving a nod. I caught a glance my way in the rear-view mirror, but he said nothing, just put the car into gear and pulled out.

Evans stared out the window in silence. It was a heavy silence. I knew what I was asking, which is why I'd never expected him to come. An introduction. A request. Hell, call in a favor or two. That's all I'd wanted.

Not this.

We drove until the bars and the nightclubs disappeared and the streets turned dark and quiet. Ninth street. Ninth street, that was owned by rich old men who paid a hefty price to keep the law away.

The driver pulled up outside a building and parked. None of us moved. The sound of the engine filled the silence until with a slow, hard exhale, Evans muttered. "Well, it's time to sell our souls."

Then he yanked the door handle and climbed out.

I followed, closing the door behind me as the car took off once more. With every step, that emptiness bloomed up from deep inside me. I drew on everything I had. Every ounce of pain and rage, fixing on the betrayal of my father, as I headed to the security manned front door with Evans.

We were stopped, IDs checked, and patted down before the heavy black door was unlocked and we were allowed entrance. Once inside, we handed over our phones and keys to a waitress waiting meekly at the door. We placed our things on the silver tray before the waitress left, taking them toward the back room.

They'd be locked away, leaving our minds to capture every perverted act that happened in this place. Deep, throbbing music filtered in through the back room, the sound drawing my gaze until Evans gave me a nudge in the side.

Seated on one of the plush leather sofas were three men. Men who watched us with careful eyes until one motioned us over with a wave to the seats opposite. I swallowed hard. My damn heart thundered as Evans took a step forward and I forced myself to follow.

Darkness and sin smothered this place. The waitress neared with the same damn tray, only on it this time were two tumblers of top-shelf Scotch. I knew by experience, only the best for the Hale Club. I took the drink, praying they didn't notice the shake of my hand when I drank.

"Evans." Killion Dare nodded, motioning to the seat opposite before he turned that piercing stare my way. "Banks. Long time no see." His voice softened. "We were all very sorry to hear about the passing."

I ground my teeth as a flinch came in the corner of my eye, hating that my mom had ever had a place in his sick goddamn mind. Still, I gave a nod and forced myself to answer. "Thank you."

"Please." Dare motioned to the seat opposite. "Sit, let's open up some dialogue. Evans tells me you wish to come back...our only question is, why?"

He crossed his legs, but I knew it was all an act. Just like everything was in this place. A cry tore free from the back area of the club. Short, painful, followed by a *slap*. This place...this *fucking* place.

# SEVEN

## *nick*

*BEEP...BEEP...BEEP...*THE grating sound pulled me closer to the surface. I cracked open my eyes to find only darkness...just like I'd found inside.

I closed my eyes again and tried to shift on the hard hospital mattress. But no matter which way I turned, I couldn't find relief.

*NICK!*

Her haunting screams filled my head, and I couldn't let them go. She kicked and screamed, howling for me.

*NICK, NO!*

I opened my eyes once more, and that *beep...beep...beep* in my ear sounded like gunshots. Movement came in the corner of my eye. I jumped as the curtain was drawn back and a nurse neared, her focus buried in the open file in front of her...until she stilled and lifted her gaze. "You're awake."

I just nodded.

She placed the file down at the foot of the bed. "Just here to check your vitals."

*NICK!*

I turned away as the nurse moved the blood pressure

machine close, peeled the cuff free before winding it around my upper arm, and hit the button. The sounds. The smells. It was like the side of a blade that was running along my skin. One tilt of the hand and it'd cut me...and I couldn't just fucking wait for that, not when Ryth was trapped in that place, behind the fences and the guns...

God knew what they were doing to her.

My pulse sped at the thought, but the panic wasn't just for her. I needed my brothers to get her out, or fucking die trying. Because I would.

"Perfect, Nicholas." The nurse was just too fucking cheery. And I was too savage. Especially for a place like this.

"My things," I muttered, desperation burning inside me.

"Your phone's in the cupboard beside you. I can grab it for you, if you like?"

I shook my head. "No...thank you."

She scribbled the details down in my folder before tucking it under her arm. "I'll be back in a few hours. Try to get some sleep."

I just nodded, knowing full well that wasn't happening.

Still, I waited for her to leave before I gripped the railing and pushed my feet to the side of the bed, wincing at the deep flare of pain as it carved through my side. Inch by inch. It felt like hell.

My breaths caught. I clenched my jaw, biting down on the groan that threatened to come, and slid my feet free, letting momentum take over. One shift of my hold to the handle that hung over my head, and I pulled myself upwards.

Agony roared through me, burning in my chest as I straightened. Christ, it felt like I'd been stabbed in the gut. I winced and looked down at the large bandage around my waist, savagery rising in me once more. That fucker...that fucker...*had it coming.*

I used that anger to drive me as I reached out to the cupboard, grasped the tiny key, and twisted it. My things were stacked in the drawer. I held my breath, steadied myself, and reached in, then grasped my phone and dragged it free.

No charger…

It had better have battery.

I pressed it on and almost moaned with relief. *10%* battery. "It'll fucking do."

I scrolled through my contacts and pressed Caleb's number, listening to it ring…*once…twice…three fucking times.* "Answer the goddamn phone, brother."

I hung up, my thoughts seething. What the fuck was he doing that was so fucking important he couldn't answer my goddamn calls? I pressed the button and tried again, that sense of unease growing inside me.

It rang unanswered…*again.*

My lips twitched in a snarl as I pressed Tobias' number, and surprise, the snarly punk answered. "Yeah?"

"Where the fuck are you?" I snapped.

A groan came from the background, low and tortured, and suddenly I didn't want to fucking know. *Good.* That's all I thought. *Let him hurt as many as he needed as long as it led us to Ryth. It was like letting a starving pitbull loose.*

I'd use him. Hell, I'd use us all.

*NICK!* Her screams howled as I swallowed and snapped. "Come and get me the fuck out of here."

"The hospital?" he snapped. "Fuck no."

"You'll come and get me, T, or I'll pull on these fucking clothes and get out of here myself. Then I'll beat your ass."

He went quiet. Was he thinking? Christ, I hoped not.

"Fine, give me twenty," he answered. "I just need to take care of a few things."

A scream was muffled in the background before a *thump!*

Then there was silence. The kind that, in that moment, made me smile. "Caleb with you?"

"No. Why?"

"Doesn't matter," I muttered. "Move your ass, brother. I need to fucking hunt."

I hung up the call, *8% battery.* I winced and cast the phone on the bed, turned my head and listened. She wouldn't come back—I glanced at the monitor—*beep...beep...beep.* Until I disconnected that.

I turned my focus back to the drawer, yanking my jeans and boots out. *What? No shirt?* I remembered the blood. Yeah, probably not. The damn room swayed as I pushed up, drove myself to stand, reached around me, yanked the ties and tugged the damn gown free to leave it hanging on the cord of the monitor. I didn't have time for boxers, so I yanked on my jeans and shoved bare feet into my boots and braced myself before bending over, pulling the laces tight.

*Beeeeeeeeeeeepppppppppp...*

"Fuck." The cord had slipped free. I rose too fast and the damn darkened room grew even darker, tilting to the side. "No, you fucking don't."

I clung to the pinprick of light in the middle of my vision and tried to breathe, and slowly...the gloom brightened. My pulse kicked. Adrenaline was my drug of choice. I used it, snatched my phone from the bed, and drove myself to my feet. I tugged the rest of the sensors free and slowly headed to the drawn curtains, then out of the room.

The hallway was blinding. I blinked, squinted into the glare, and moved further along the hallway. Movement came in the distance.

I focused straight ahead as someone called out. *"Hey! I don't think you're supposed to be out here!"*

I clenched my jaw and kept on walking, heading to a bank of elevators at the end of the hallway.

*"Mr. Banks!"* Came the shout as I punched the button for the elevator and glanced back along the hallway.

The nurse was hurrying toward me with a look of concern. But she never made it. The doors opened, and I was inside in an instant, pressing my hand to my side. I stabbed the button for the ground floor and prayed Tobias was on his way.

Wouldn't matter...I'd walk if I had to.

Ten-foot-high fences and armed mercenaries filled my mind as the elevator sank to the ground floor. But the moment I stepped out into the brightly lit, empty foyer of the hospital, I caught sight of the headlights of the Jeep as it swung under the drop-off canopy.

With my hand pressed to my side, I lengthened my stride and headed for my brother. Automatic doors opened as I neared, leaving the cool night air to hit me hard. Tobias glared as I grabbed the door handle and yanked.

"You crazy ass motherfucker." He shook his head as I climbed in.

"Nice to see you, too," I muttered, pulling the door closed as I sank into the seat. *"Now fucking drive."*

## EIGHT

*caleb*

WHY?

The sharp, short *slaps* that came from behind the curtain grew louder. I forced myself not to jump at the sounds and met Killion's stare. "Why come back?" I reached up, massaging the back of my neck. "That's an excellent question indeed."

I couldn't stop from glancing at where the moans came from. Moans that I knew from experience were torturous in the most degrading way. My pulse picked up pace at the thought. *Christ.* I couldn't catch my breath. Couldn't taper that need inside me. Couldn't hold that darkness at bay...*and right now it was all I had.* I glanced sideways at Evans and winced before answering. "Because no matter how much I try, I can't get this place out of my head."

Killion smirked at the words, his eyes glinting. The sight of that made me want to throw up.

Because I saw the same hunger in myself.

"We don't normally allow probationary members back in once they leave." Killion shook his head. "In this case, that's a pity."

He gripped the armrests on the seat and pushed to stand.

My heart punched all the way up into the back of my throat. Evans jerked a panicked gaze my way as the other two senior members rose with Killion.

"Wait..." I croaked, desperation driving me upward. "Tell me what you want, and I'll do it."

Killion stopped, giving me his back as he adjusted his jacket, then slowly turned. That sickening shimmer was shining brighter in his eyes now. "How do I know this isn't a setup? After all...you could be wearing a wire right now."

*A wire...*

*That's what he was afraid of...*

*That I was wearing a damn wire?*

My stomach clenched as that booming in my head turned heavier. I lifted my hand and moved it to the buttons on my shirt, holding his gaze as I worked them one by one. Killion's brows rose as I undressed in front of him. I had nothing to lose in that moment...*apart from Ryth.* One lick of his lips and I knew I had him.

He slowly faced me, taking a step to close the distance. His gaze roamed, and his hand followed as he shoved my shirt from my shoulders, then placed his hand flat against my chest. I shivered with the contact.

They liked women; I knew that. But the kind of hunger Killion had inside him was fucking ravenous.

He lowered his gaze to my cock. "As much as I'd like to see the entire show, Caleb, I think you're out of time."

He dropped his hand and stepped away. His gaze fixed on my bare chest. "But Christ, I'd like to watch you fuck."

My balls clenched. Ryth roared into my mind and my own desperate growls returned. *When I take you, Ryth...I'm going to take you all fucking night. You're going to be my favorite fucking toy...my wet, perfect plaything...*

Hard breaths deepened as I captured his stare, letting him

see exactly what he wanted to see. Me, raw and desperate, and Killion was entranced.

"You want back in?" he murmured, drawing the focus of the other two members. "Fine...but you're going to need to prove yourself."

Panic pushed to the surface. I strangled that fear, driving it back into the dark, and slowly nodded. A turn of his head and he nodded to someone in the gloom. Movement came, black on black as the heavy velvet curtain was pulled aside.

"After you." Killion motioned us forward.

I took a step, my hands moving to the buttons of my shirt.

"No." Killion stopped the movement. "Leave it open."

The cool air-conditioned air danced across my skin. But that wasn't the chill I felt. Killion looked at me like I was a woman he used. I gave a slow nod and lowered my hands.

"Evans." Killion motioned. "This way..."

"He's not—" I started.

"He is, if you want back in."

Evans jerked his wide gaze my way. There was a tiny shake of his head. His pupils were huge, swallowing the blue.

"Maybe you're not ready," Killion started.

"I'll do it." Evan's voice was nothing more than a husky whisper. "Okay...I'll fucking do it."

Killion smirked once more. "Then, by all means." He motioned toward the curtain. "Let the party begin."

This wasn't what I'd wanted. Not for me...or for him. If there was any other way to get Ryth out of that place, I'd take it, short of putting a bullet through my head. But as I followed Killion and the two other members toward the back room of the Hale Club, it felt like I was killing myself anyway...

Just slowly.

I glanced at Evans as we walked. With each step, he grew

paler. His eyes were wide and fixed straight ahead. A soft man shouldn't be in a place like this, and as disgusted as I was, I was just as fucking excited. We stepped around the curtain and were led to a hallway, then to a door in the back. The guard pressed his finger to the keypad, and the lock gave a *click*.

*Slap!* The sound came from another room. Another torture...another act of degradation.

"Caleb," Killion called my name.

I turned my attention back and followed him inside. Evans closed the door with a clunk. The locks engaged, making me swallow hard. The room in front of us brightened. A spotlight on the floor glowed where a young woman stood. She was scared, dressed in a black negligee and matching bra and crotchless panties.

Killion took a seat on one of the plush armchairs, then glanced my way and motioned with his head. No one spoke. They all watched her as they sat. The other two silent members took seats on either side of Killion, leaving those closer to the door vacant.

"Sit." Killion commanded, when we didn't move. "This is what you want, right?"

*No...*

*Yes...*

Torment consumed my mind. Still, I followed suit, taking a seat, Evans taking one at my right as we all turned our focus to the woman who stood shivering in front of us. The air was colder in here, so cold my nipples tightened, just like hers.

"Commence," Killion demanded, and from the corner of the room, a man stepped forward.

He'd been hidden in shadows. But as he stepped into the light, I saw exactly what this was. That gold stitched H inside an O. Hale Order. That's what this was...the same men who had Ryth captive. I flinched and jerked my gaze back to the woman.

"Strip," the guard commanded, staring at her.

She jerked a panicked gaze his way, those wide, terror-filled eyes fixed on him. "Please," she whispered.

"Going to make me ask again?" The implied threat made my gut clench.

One tiny shake of her head and her trembling hands rose, working the ties of her negligee. Out of nowhere, music started. Slowed. Reverbed. The beat was heavy and thick, competing with my pulse.

Under the stare of the guard, she moved, stepping forward on bare feet. That tremble of fear sparked in her eyes before it dulled. Right in front of us, I saw her fade away and leave the shell of a woman behind.

"Jesus." Evans glanced away.

"Touch her," one of the others commanded. It was the first time one of them had spoken.

The guard lashed out his arm, grasped a handful of her hair, and jerked her head backwards. She cried out, her hands flailing, but it wasn't in pain. The strands of her hair pulled taut, but that's where it stopped. With his other hand, the guard shoved the negligee aside and yanked her bra down to softly pinch her nipple, rolling it between his calloused fingers.

Her spine was bowed. She stared up at him like he was *everything*.

"She likes it," Killion murmured.

I didn't want to look his way...didn't want to see how much *he* liked it. But I did. I did because I was fucking sick. Only, when I looked at him, it wasn't Killion's cruel stony stare I saw...*it was Nick.*

Nick, who'd sat and watched Tobias touch Ryth, his fingers

working the puckering peaks of her tits...*Ryth, who'd stared up at him filled with torment and desperation.*

Part of me saw this woman as the guard unsnapped her bra and yanked it roughly free. I saw the panicked glance at all of us watching her. Her hands lifted, covering her breasts, until the guard snarled and shook his head. The other part of me sank into the fantasy of what we had in my brother's bedroom. *Ryth*...it was Ryth I wanted here and now, so it was Ryth I forced myself to see.

"Get them down," the guard growled, then with a shove, she stumbled forward.

Killion just watched her as she stood there, her tiny hands trying to cover her perky breasts. "You heard him, lower them. *Now.*"

She did, her eyes fixed on him.

That is what he wanted, that pained look in her eyes as her cheeks reddened.

"Panties." Killion glanced at them. "Off."

She swallowed, then her head gave a little shake. "Please, no. You don't have to do this..."

Killion glanced at the guard, who took a step closer to her. She stumbled a step sideways, casting a panicked gaze toward the brute. "Please, no."

"*Panties,*" Killion demanded, softer this time, although no less forceful.

In the corner of my eye, Evans cast a panicked glance my way, silently urging me to do something. But I didn't know if he wanted me to save her, or him. But I couldn't...because this was a test.

The guard feigned a step, and she jerked her hands to her hips, sliding her fingers under the elastic of her panties and slowly lowered them.

"Closer," Killion demanded.

She jumped and, trembling, stepped as close as she dared.

"Now turn around."

She stiffened and jerked her gaze along the others until she stopped at me. I don't know if she was surprised, or desperate to reach someone, but she whispered. *"Please..."*

Ryth. Ryth was all I saw. Ryth under Tobias when I walked into my brother's bedroom. "You want out of this?" I asked. She nodded. "Then do what we ask. It's that simple. Turn around."

Killion shot me a glance. Hope surged inside me.

Ten-foot-high fences and armed mercenaries. It didn't matter. If I had to stand here and watch a girl made to strip in front of us, it'd be worth it. Even if she now looked at me with betrayal.

She lowered her head and her shoulders curled as she slowly turned until her back was to Killion.

"Stop," he ordered. "Now bend over."

The guard stepped closer until he towered over her and, with one hand placed on her shoulder, made her bend at the waist.

"Spread," Killion demanded.

She unleashed a whimper and lifted her hands to either cheek of her ass. Humiliation tore across her face as she spread herself wide.

One of the other men shifted in his chair, moving forward. He reached out and stroked her pussy before sliding his fingers in.

"Jesus," Evans whispered, although this time it wasn't in disgust. He stared wide-eyed as one partner slowly finger-fucked her, then shifted in his seat. And suddenly, Evans wasn't so sickened by the events in front of us. No, he seemed...*enthralled.*

"You like that?" the other partner murmured as he moved to the edge of his seat.

Her eyes closed the moment he slid his hand along the curve of her ass, then pushed his finger into the tight ring of muscle. My cock grew hard, not at the sight of her, but at the memory of Ryth in my bed.

It had been *my* finger that pushed in, *my* touch that had made her moan.

Just like this woman moaned.

"That's it," Killion murmured. "Now she's getting somewhere."

She unleashed a tortured sound and pushed back against the slow thrusts, her body betraying her mind.

So wrong...

So fucking disgusting.

"Whore," Killion said, his voice stony. "Such a dirty fucking whore."

She squeezed her eyes shut harder, trying to block out his words, but it was too late for that. Fingers glistened as they sank deep into her pussy. Killion, who hadn't even lifted a finger to touch her, rose from his seat and took a step closer.

"On the floor," he commanded, looking down at her.

The others' fingers slipped free from her body as she lowered herself to the floor onto her hands and knees.

Killion stepped closer, still staring down at her. "Lower."

She sank down.

Killion lifted his foot and placed his boot on the back of her neck until she pressed her face to the floor. "Now crawl."

"Fuck me," Evans whispered.

But Killion didn't even glance at Evans. No, his focus was all for me. "Do you want one, Banks?"

I swallowed hard, my heart hammering.

"That's why you're here, isn't it? You want your own private fuck toy, someone you can control." He pressed his foot harder against her until she moaned. "Someone you can own."

"Yes," I answered, my voice nothing more than a croak as I met that stare. "I do."

*ryth*

SOLD...MY *mom* sold *me?* The words howled inside my head. But everything else was distant...faded, the sound of tortured cries from the naked woman in front of me reverberated like an empty drum.

"Now, get in line." The sadistic white-haired guard shoved me forward.

I stumbled toward the others, but caught my fall, moving closer to Viv. She said nothing, didn't look my way, didn't appear to even see me at all. But the moment I fixed my sight on the naked woman, I felt the slightest brush of a finger on the back of my hand.

She saw me...comforting me in the only way she dared. I swallowed hard, my heart thundering as I watched the terrifying display.

*Slap!*

The leather switch lashed the woman's belly, leaving bright red welts behind.

"Have you learned your lesson, Olivia?" The Principal walked behind the guard dealing out the punishment. "Or do you wish to take this further?"

She closed her eyes. Sweat ran in rivulets down the sides of her face. "No."

"Who do you belong to?"

My breath caught with the words. That fire in my belly grew, seething from the ember my stepbrothers had ignited. *No.* I wanted to say the words for her, *Fuck you!* That urgency was a roar inside me. I wanted to turn away, wanted to look at anything else but this most vulnerable moment.

This shouldn't be happening to her...

And especially not here in front of an audience.

I risked a glance at the others, who stood separated by the color of the skimpy underwear they were wearing, red, black, and white. I fixed my gaze on those who wore red. There was a hardness in their eyes. A coldness, the same coldness I saw in the hard eyes of the man torturing her. Not the man wielding the whip, but the man controlling the narrative. The man *really* torturing her.

"*Who do you belong to?*" The Principal demanded an answer.

*Slap!*

I flinched at the sound of the lash. But those dressed in red didn't even seem like they heard. There were no winces, no breaths caught. One of them even smiled, the corner of her lips curling as she watched. There was no spark of anger at the brutality of what we were forced to witness. This sick show of dominance was disgusting...but they...they seemed to enjoy it.

My stomach clenched as I forced myself to look away.

"Please." Olivia whimpered. "I'll do whatever you want."

"Whatever...*I...want.*" The Principal repeated as he stalked closer.

He reached out and grasped her chin in a cruel grip. She resisted, fighting against his hold for a second at least. But then she gave in, turning that tearstained gaze to his.

"You're beautiful when you cry," he said, staring into her eyes like they were the only ones in the room. "You think I enjoy this?"

"Yes," she croaked, meeting his piercing gaze with hate. "I do."

The smile on his lips grew wider. Viv stiffened, as did the other girls around me as the white-haired guard neared.

"Take her," The Principal muttered, never once looking away. "She eats in her room tonight. As for the rest of them, have Derek escort them to the hall."

"No," Olivia's eyes widened. She shook her head. "No...no."

Her panicked look toward the rest of us went unacknowledged as the brutal guard stepped forward and released her arms, while the other guard, who, I was guessing, was Derek, bent to her feet. Her knees buckled when the chains were removed. But the savage bastard was there, gripping her by the arm in a hold that would no doubt leave bruises.

"Move," he snapped, shoving her forward.

They left with the thud of boots and soft, wounded whimpers. Derek moved closer, glancing at each of us. "You want to eat?" he snapped, then gave a jerk of his head. "So fucking *move*."

Viv brushed her fingers against my hand. "Follow me," she whispered. "And don't make a sound."

The pounding in my chest didn't ease. Viv's grip wound through my fingers. She clung tight, pulling me after her as she slipped between the others. I suppressed a shiver, fear making my knees quiver as we walked through the parted curtain and toward another set of locked doors.

I tried to take note of where we were headed, but the hallways all looked the same and there were too many locked doors to count. We passed through three, making our way toward what felt like the rear of the building, then stopped at another set of double doors.

The only doors that weren't locked.

Still we waited, like a line of terrified soldiers on their first day of training. Only we weren't here to fight...*no, we were here to be sold.*

Derek pushed past us, then through the doors. Those who wore red followed, then those in black, leaving those of us wearing white to step inside last. The scent of food hit me, making my belly howl with hunger. I realized I hadn't eaten all day. I lined up with the others and moved toward the serving counter as plates were handed over one at a time.

But this wasn't any prison cafeteria. Seared steak, chicken, seasoned vegetables, and fruit were available. We each took a plate, depending on what we wanted. Viv took the steak, motioning for me to take the chicken. I did, and followed her to a table along the wall. The others moved without a sound, taking seats, eating in silence.

I stabbed my chicken and cut slowly, watching the guard from the corner of my eye as he neared our table. The moment he passed and moved on toward the others, Viv murmured, "They'll come for you. It's better if you don't fight back. Don't give them a reason to hurt you."

"Who?" I whispered, glancing up at her. "The Principal?"

She shook her head. "No. The men from the club."

A pang of fear cut across my chest.

She lifted her head, risking the connection. "They want someone to play with."

Warmth flew from my face. "Is that...is that what happened to you?"

"No," she whispered as the color drained from her face. "I'm already owned."

*Owned.*

My throat closed up tight.

"But hang on. We're going to get you out, okay?" she whispered, jabbing carrots on her plate. "Just be ready when I come."

"When?"

She glanced around at the others. "Tomorrow. I'll come tomorrow."

*nick*

THERE WAS A HAUNTED, detached look in my brother's gaze when he looked at me. One that made me look down, but that sight wasn't any better. Bright red splatters of blood shone on his shirt, brightening as we passed under the streetlights before they dulled once more. But the blood wasn't mine. I knew that. So who the fuck's was it?

"T," I spoke carefully, staring at the mess. "What were you doing when I called?"

He didn't answer, the muscles of his jaw flexing the only sign he'd heard me. I sucked in careful breaths and tugged the seatbelt away from my side as the Jeep rocked and jolted. The damn thing wasn't the smoothest ride, not like the Mustang. I winced when I thought of it, the brutal *crunch* as I'd hit the gate the goddamn soundtrack to my thoughts. My goddamn car...

I'd get it back. Fix it up...*after I found Ryth.*

I swallowed hard and glanced at Tobias as he turned the corner, heading deeper into the city instead of to our home. "Where's Caleb?"

Tobias shot me a glare, hate detonating in his dark eyes. Fuck, the dude looked scary. "How the fuck do I know?"

Something went down between the two of them while I was in the damn hospital. That was all we needed, for us to hate each other. I looked around at the familiar buildings, spotting the glinting windows of dad's office up ahead. My pulse sped as I glanced at the blood on my brother's shirt once more.

Was that dad's blood?

Tobias jerked the wheel and the Jeep swung hard, making me brace against the dash. We pulled into the underground parking garage, tires squealing as we pulled up next to the elevator. Tobias glanced my way, that menacing spark burning in his gaze as he reached behind him and grabbed the jacket that'd been tossed on the backseat.

He tugged it on, zipped it up to cover the bloodstains, and shoved out the door before stopping. "You coming?"

I stabbed the seatbelt release, desperation humming in my veins. "Want to tell me what the fuck's going on, T?" I asked, but deep down, I really didn't want to know.

I'd seen T like this only once before. Pushed to the limit... deadly as fuck. Both times had involved our father. I braced my hand against my side, yanked the handle, and slowly climbed out. The glaring underground lights blurred with the effort.

"T." I sucked in hard breaths as the Jeep's locks gave a *clunk*.

Part of me wanted to talk him down from what he was doing, but a bigger part of me didn't. I sucked in a deep breath as Tobias turned to the nearby locked doors and dragged an ID card from his pocket.

I caught the image printed on the card and it wasn't our dad.

It didn't relieve me.

I followed him through the doors, leaving them to slam and lock behind me as I followed T to the elevator. He pressed the card against the scanner and the elevator doors opened. An uncomfortable silence filled the air as we stepped inside.

I'd made a point to avoid this goddamn place at all costs. Dad and I might not have been at war after mom's death, like he was with Tobias. But we sure as fuck were far from okay. The elevator gave a jolt as it stopped at the twenty-third floor.

Tobias strode out and headed left, like he knew this place intimately. I followed as he pressed the unknown dude's card to the scanner and stepped inside. The reception area was sleek and expensive. Dad liked to maintain an office here. But that was as far as I knew.

I had no idea who his clients were, or what called him out of town so damn often. Now, I was regretting not being more involved. Maybe then I could've seen all this coming. Blame weighed heavily on me as I strode through the doors after my brother and followed him through the small reception area. It was clean. A phone, coffee cup, and pictures of two young kids gave me the impression someone still worked here.

A low moan cut through the air, coming from the rear offices. I gripped my wound, fighting a wave of pain, and followed my younger brother along a hallway.

Bright red smears shone on the glaring white tiled floor. A twitch came at the corner of my eye at the sight before I jerked my gaze high. Tobias stopped at a closed door, pressed the card to the scanner, and opened the door.

The sight inside assaulted me. The guy from the ID lifted his head, his eyes wide with terror. His hands were bound behind him as he sat in his office chair. Tobias never even flinched from the sight, just glanced my way, watching the door as it closed with a *click* before he moved toward the terrified guy.

"Now, Harvey. I've given you some time to think about this, from the goodness of my heart." My brother unzipped his jacket and peeled it from his body before clenching his fists. It was then I saw the blood between his knuckles.

"Jesus, T," I muttered, revulsion making my gut clench.

The guy wasn't a fucking threat. He was far from it. Young, fucking scared, beaten all to hell. His lips were split, one eye already swollen until it was nothing more than a slit. He even had crusted blood inside his nostrils.

He whimpered and tried to speak, but the words were muffled by the rag stuffed in his mouth. Tobias reached forward, snagged the edge, and yanked it from the poor bastard's mouth.

The guy coughed, sucked in harsh breaths, and narrowed his gaze at T. "You...*you're fucking crazy.*"

"Crazy?" Tobias repeated, and flexed his hands. "More like determined. Now, are you going to give me the truth? Hale Order, what is it and how the fuck can we get inside?"

The guy just shook his head. I glanced at the desk behind him. He was obviously some schmuck who worked for our dad, so how the fuck did T expect the guy to know?

"You know his clients," T continued. "You know who he sees. You know where he is right now, don't you?"

The guy flinched and paled. But he didn't say no.

*He didn't say no...*

"Where?" I croaked. "Where the fuck is he?"

The guy suddenly looked even more terrified. Yeah, he knew something...

I stepped closer, fighting the agony that pulsed in waves through my middle, making the rest of the room washed out and gray. "I'm not going to ask again, Harvey. Where the fuck is our father?"

The guy whimpered as I shuffled closer, staring down at him. "Please," he whispered. "I'll lose my job."

"Lose your job?" Ryth's torment howled inside my head as I leaned down to the idiot. "You're about to lose more than your fucking job."

His breath caught and his eyes widened. There was a glimmer of desperation before he stuttered. "H-he...he t-told me to not say a w-word to any of you. H-he s-said you were nothing more than thieves and b-bullies. Said you only c-came around for your mother's m-money."

I stiffened, unable to fight the burn in my gut. "He said *what?*"

The guy looked from me to Tobias. "B-but the jokes on y-you. Th-there's...n-nothing...l-left. It's all g-gone. Every cent."

"You think..." Tobias moved, grasping him by the shirt and jerking him forward. "You think we'd do this for *fucking money?*"

The guy didn't understand. He truly didn't fucking understand the hole he'd just dug for himself.

But he was about to find out.

Pain moved through me as I straightened. But this time it had nothing to do with the stab wound in my side and everything to do with the agony that welled in my heart. My sweet mom's face rose to the surface.

The indignant little prick jutted his chin upwards, his eyes burning with misplaced loyalty. But in that moment, I couldn't give a shit. I had no energy left to explain. I doubted it'd make a difference, anyway. "T," I murmured, and straightened. "Show this asshole what it means to cross us."

Tobias gave a nod, clenching his fist. "My goddamn pleasure," he muttered, right before he lashed out and punched the asshole in the jaw.

The blow launched him sideways so hard the chair toppled

and fell. He hit the floor with a crunch. I stepped backwards, letting Tobias be what he was born to be. Savage. Dangerous... wrath in its most primal form. He grasped the guy and hauled him from the floor, screaming.

"*I'll tell you!*" Harvey howled.

But it was too late. Tobias drove his fist into the guy's chest and was rewarded with a *crack*. A roar of agony followed, the asshole turning a sickening shade of gray.

*Whack!*

*Whack!*

*WHACK!*

Over and over, until there were no more screams left. By the time Tobias was done, he was breathless. Blood glistened on his knuckles as he straightened and looked down at the guy. He was breathing, barely. But we were done.

"I told you once before, Nick. So, I'm telling you again, just to be sure." Tobias' voice was devoid of emotion as he turned and met my gaze. "When we find our father, stay the fuck out of my way. Don't make me have to hurt you too."

I'd never seen my younger brother so cold.

So void of the life our mother had given him.

He didn't just want our father's blood.

*He wanted his goddamn life.*

# ELEVEN

## *caleb*

"WHAT THE FUCK?"

I surfaced with a savage snarl, cracked open my eyes, and instantly regretted it. Tobias stared down at me, his face chiseled in cold, hard rage as he bent and picked up the empty bottle of Scotch next to my bed. "You were fucking drinking?"

I winced at the words. My pulse was already in flight, racing, *aching*. I tried to blink through the sting of my eyes and closed them once more. "Go the fuck away, T."

"So, you're out there, drinking and what...*partying,* while Ryth is in that fucking Hell?"

I kept my eyes closed as my heart howled in agony. There hadn't been a second of rest for me, not even under the blur of the alcohol. I'd tried to drink to forget what I'd seen last night. Tried to muffle the moans and the whimpers that resounded over and over inside my head. Tried to drink to hide my own sick fucking need. Because when I looked at Killion, all I saw was myself. But never *once* did I *ever* drink to forget her.

She was all I thought about.

All I *wanted* to think about.

*Ryth.*

But she was in that place. That fetid, *foul,* disgusting place, and every second she was there was a second too fucking long.

"You fucking disgust me, brother," Tobias growled as he kicked another bottle.

*Thud!* The bottle landed on the floor beside my bed with a deafening sound, one that made my heart punch hard against my chest.

"You're drinking and just *living it up* while we're out there trying to *FUCKING GET TO HER!*"

I opened my eyes, hating how his words cut right to my core. "Get the fuck *out,* Tobias!"

*We're...*

What did he mean *'we're'?* I shoved upwards, still dressed in my shirt and trousers. The stench of cigars and pain clung to me, making the torment even worse. "Get the fuck out of my room." I rose from the bed, glaring down at T.

He hated me at this moment.

Fuck, he hated everyone.

I pushed him toward the door, catching the clench of his fist and the flare in his jaw. I waited for the swing, but it never came, and I was too fucking heartsore to care. If he beat me, it might even make me feel better. Maybe the pain I'd feel would be worth it. Maybe...

I drove him to the door and out of my bedroom.

"What the fuck is wrong with you?" Tobias stepped backwards, glaring at me.

From the doorway across the landing, I caught Nick stepping out. Panic flared as I took in the darkened circles under his pain-filled eyes, and the dressing strapped around his bare chest. *What the fuck?* Fear struck me at the sight of my bother.

He shouldn't be out of the hospital!

Fuck, he shouldn't even be alive, let alone walking around,

yet there he was, staring at me in...*disappointment.* I swallowed hard.

"You fuck—" T started, and I didn't wait for the rest, just closed the door in his face.

That constant ache bloomed in my chest as I walked back to the bed and slumped down. I didn't care that I was still dressed in the filth, didn't care that my brothers' hate still roared outside my bedroom. I turned over, grabbed my pillow, and clamped it around my head, trying my best to muffle the screams.

*You want your own private fuck toy. Someone you can control.* Killion's voice resounded, no matter how hard I pressed. Whimpers followed, feminine whimpers. But it wasn't Killion's sick words that made that *thing* twist in my chest. It was my own words, my cold, desperate tone...

*Yes.* The words echoed. *I do.*

# TWELVE

*ryth*

I WAITED all day for Viv to come. Sitting on the hard floor with my back pressed to the door as I listened to the heavy thud of boots approach before they faded again. Viv was coming. She *had* to be coming. I twisted my fingers and clenched my jaw, my heartbeat booming in my head.

So why wasn't she here?

I shoved up from the door and paced. The single bed, the basin, and the set of built-in drawers were the only things in this cold, hard room. There were no windows to see outside. No light apart from the illuminated panels overhead, controlled from somewhere outside. Gray polished concrete floors and gray painted walls. Viv said they passed this place off as a reform school for girls, but the only things they taught were obedience, and how to be fucked...*literally*.

As always, my mind turned to Nick, Tobias, and Caleb. I stilled midway across the floor. Nick...*Nick*. I clenched my fists and massaged my knuckles. I still hadn't been told anything. *He* told me he'd find out. The bastard who kept me here. The one who wanted us to call him The Principal.

He wasn't a goddamn principal.

He was a sadistic fucking piece of shit.

A man who ran his own private whorehouse.

A whorehouse my mother had sent me to. No, not sent me...*sold me*. I shook my head, casting the thought aside. That pain was too much to unpack. I needed to keep my wits about me here. I needed to stay alive and away from these sick motherfuckers.

The thud of boots heading my way drew my gaze to the door. I swallowed hard as the shadow spilled across the glass panel and the gray guard's uniform filled the pane. The click of the lock sounded, and the door swung wide.

"Out," the guard commanded. "Bathroom."

I swallowed the tremble of fear and stepped forward, glancing along the hall as other doors were unlocked by more guards and the girls stepped out, wearing the same flimsy goddamn nighties we were told to wear last night. I tried to find Viv amongst the others, but she wasn't there.

Images of what could've happened to her flashed through my mind.

Was she taken away...was she...*hurt?*

Did they find out what she was planning and put an end to it, and her?

"Move," the guard ordered, shoving me on the back of the shoulder. I stumbled forward with the others, keeping my head down, keeping quiet. But inside, that seething rage boiled. We made our way to the bathroom and stepped inside. The hiss of the showers already filled the space. I scanned the naked bodies of the others, searching for Viv, but she wasn't here either.

"In," the guard behind me snarled.

Revulsion made me hug my arms across my body. I could tell those who wore red and black from those of us who wore white. They never hid their bodies from the guards' gazes, just washed and scrubbed, breasts on full display.

Another jab at my back. "Clothes off and in...don't make me have to rip them off you."

I swallowed hard and thought about turning around and punching him square in the jaw, until from the corner of my eye, the white-haired guard stepped into the bathroom, scanning the others, until those ice-blue eyes settled on me. There was a spark of excitement as he took in my defiance.

"You going to haul off and hit officer Garland here, Castlemaine?" He leaned his big frame down, "'cause it sure looks like it to me."

I clenched my jaw so hard my teeth nearly cracked. Whimpers and the brutal sound of the lash hitting flesh still rang in my head from last night. I only needed to give this bastard an opportunity, and he'd make an example of me, like Olivia was last night.

"No," I murmured.

He leaned closer. "Sorry, what did you say?"

I forced my gaze to his. "I said, *no.*"

The smile was instant. "That's what I thought." He glanced at the showers. "So, what are you waiting for?"

My breaths raced as I gripped the thin satin and lifted the nightie over my head. Heat burned in my cheeks as my nipples puckered. I felt their gazes on my body as the nightie hit the floor, then I reached for my panties, shoved them low, and stepped into the warm spray.

Others hurried out, grabbing towels to dry and dress. I washed my hair, dropping my head back into the spray, holding the asshole guard's gaze. Taps squealed. Showers were abandoned, leaving me the only one behind. I tried not to let fear get the better of me, washing and rinsing before I turned to switch off the water.

But the white-haired asshole was in my way. I tried to step around him, but he moved, forcing me sideways until he pressed me against the cold tiled wall.

"I like you, Castlemaine bitch," he growled, his breath warm on my neck.

I kept my gaze down as water ran in rivulets down my back.

"I think you and I are going to become very good friends indeed. I'm coming for you." He brushed aside my wet hair. "Fuck, you're gonna scream when I do."

My stomach rolled with revulsion, but I forced my gaze to his, letting the savagery rise inside me. "One day I'm going to get out of here," I hissed. "I can't wait for you to meet my step-brothers."

"Oh, yeah?" He pushed me hard against the tiles. "Think your big brothers are going to save your pretty ass?"

He grabbed my face, smashing my lips against my teeth. With the other hand, he traced the mark on my cheek. "I bet they'll enjoy watching me ride their little sister."

The image of that roared inside my mind, making the bathroom gray at the edges.

I wanted to cry. I wanted to throw up.

I wanted to wrap my arms around my body and rock in a corner while my mind fractured and my will slipped away. I knew now why those dressed in red didn't cry, scream, or fight. It was because of men like him slowly breaking them down.

"I-I think you might be surprised." Even though my voice was trembling, I forced the words. "I'd watch your back if I were you...for the rest of your life."

He grinned then, and the sight of that was almost as foul as his words.

"Tig," the other guard called.

92

The sick bastard slowly turned his head, but his grip didn't ease around my jaw.

"The Teacher is waiting."

There was a heartbeat where he didn't move, long enough for my fear to move even deeper, before the grip eased around my jaw and he straightened. "Get dressed, Castlemaine bitch," he muttered, holding the other guard's stare.

I stepped around him and scurried to grab a towel. Self-preservation drove me as I roughly toweled my hair and yanked on a clean white nightie and panties.

I didn't even try to brush my hair, just raced out of the bathroom, to stop in the empty hall. The sound of voices called me forward, and there was no way I was giving the white-haired bastard another opportunity to corner me. I rushed toward the voices, my wet hair sticking the nightie against my back.

"Classes are important." A male spoke in front of the women. "I expect you to be clean, ready...and punctual." He glanced my way as I entered. "Attention matters. You, on the other hand, *do not.*"

I stepped around the others, wincing at a cold rivulet of water that slipped between my breasts. The Teacher moved closer, staring into the other girls' eyes. "You do not matter, not your wants or your needs. The *only* thing that matters is the needs of your master, your owner. Your entire being will be dedicated to them. *Their* wants. *Their* needs. You will find what they crave. You will *become* what they are searching for, even if they don't know themselves."

Disgust moved through me.

He moved closer until he stopped at one of the girls in white. She whimpered at the closeness, winced, and tried to pull away until he lashed out, grasped her around the back of the neck, and dragged her close. "Some of them will want a woman who's a whore, who greets them at the door on your knees with your mouth open, ready to take their cock. Others will want someone timid, afraid. They want that rush of power that comes when they take a woman who's begging...beg for me." He focused on her. "Show me how afraid you can be."

His stare never moved, burrowing into hers even as she tried to pull away.

My heart thundered as I took in his stance, his body, the way the rolled sleeves of his black shirt pull taut. He was exactly like The Principal. Hard, cold. Powerful. His light green eyes reflected the overhead lights, making him almost beautiful, in a vicious, terrifying way. His big, powerful hand tightened around her neck until the tips of his fingers pressed against her veins.

She whimpered.

Her legs shook, and it was his hold that kept her upright, kept her rooted to the spot as he leaned close, so close he could have kissed her. "Show...me..."

"P-please," she whispered.

"Please?" he whispered back, forcing her head to turn so he whispered the word against her cheek. "Please what?"

"P-please d-don't h-hurt m-me."

"Keep going," he urged.

"I-I..." she stuttered and closed her eyes. "I..."

*"KEEP GOING!"* he roared.

The entire class jolted at the sound. My heart hammered as he pulled his head away from hers and stared into her eyes. "Did they tell you about the recruits who fail their training?" His voice was so calm, so controlled, so *chilling*. "You think it's hard here?" He gave a small chuff. "There is always harder, crueler. Those who are shown to be...*unusable* will be used in other ways. You've been sold, traded...discarded. And if the Order cannot get its use out of you in this way...then there are less...*favorable* conditions you will be sent to. Either way, we get our use of you until the very end."

My stomach clenched with terror as my breaths raced. She dropped to her knees as they buckled, thick, heavy sobs tearing from her mouth. "Please don't hurt me. I'll do anything...*anything*."

He stood over her, looking down like she was nothing, as she dropped her head on his feet. Her body shuddered and shook, the bones of her ribs moving like shadows under her skin.

"Good," he murmured. "Good."

*Good?*

Good, that he broke her?

"You will be the key to their lock. You will hone yourself, carve yourself. Change your hair color, change your eyes. You will change everything about yourself and become the one thing they can count on, can love...can fix."

He said the last words softly.

So softly, I barely heard them.

So softly, the others didn't.

They just stared at the woman on the ground in horror... after all, she could've been them.

"Today you will sit in your cells and mourn the life you once had. You will cry, you will scream. You'll bang on the walls and howl until your throat burns and your voice is hoarse, then tomorrow...tomorrow you will become someone else. Someone who will either break, or someone who survives."

He lifted his head and scanned the room, taking in every pair of downcast eyes until he stopped at mine. I didn't look away, just held his stare until my gaze watered and my body shook.

"To your room," he commanded.

I stepped away from the others, my pulse racing as I headed for the door. I was first through, punching the handle and shoving the door wide, until I stopped.

Viv stood there, her back pressed against the wall. A man held her there. A man who wasn't a guard. He was older, gray hair splattered amongst the black at the sides of his.

"You think the contract will save you, Vivienne?" he murmured, tracing the line of her jaw with his finger.

Her head turned just enough that her eyes found mine. There was a flicker of panic, one that was quickly replaced by a dull, controlled stare.

"It's a fucking piece of paper," the man growled into her ear. "One I can tear up any time I wish. You are my ward, Vivienne. You belong to me."

The rush of footsteps from the women from the classroom swarmed around me, drawing the gaze of the man who pressed Viv against the wall. He didn't care about us, didn't flinch, didn't step away...until the slow, heavy thud of steps came behind me, and the man they called the Teacher stopped at my side.

The older man dropped his hands from Viv's face and stepped away. There were no words spoken between them. Even if there were, I wouldn't have heard them. Because screams came. Silent, tormenting screams that burned in Vivienne's gaze.

Ones which resounded in my soul.

# THIRTEEN

## *caleb*

CALEB...CALEB, *help me.*

I cracked open my eyes to darkness. But I didn't move, not yet. One tiny flinch and the fantasy would slip away, taking the image of Ryth along with it.

"*Not yet,*" I whispered, my voice a burning croak. "Please, not...yet."

The stench of cigars and pain clung to me, my shirt, my soul. I tried to force away the realization. Only it didn't matter how hard I held onto her. She faded anyway, slipping away into the nothingness.

An ache tore across my chest. I forced myself upwards to sit on the side of the bed, kicking the empty Scotch bottle on the floor, my senses sharpening. Silence waited for me. Numb, stony silence. The kind I didn't like.

I shoved up from the bed and swayed. My body ached, but my head felt worse. I rubbed the throbbing ache in the back of my head and slowly made my way to my bedroom door. In the split second when my hand landed on the door handle, I thought maybe this had all been a bad dream and none of this was real.

Nick hadn't almost died. He was playing Call of Duty in his bedroom while he made his next million. And Ryth was in her bedroom down from mine, working hard on the school assignment she had to submit next week. One I'd work hard to distract her from with a night spent in my bed.

But the moment the door cracked open and the emptiness rushed in, it hit me.

It wasn't a bad dream, every bit of it was real.

She was gone.

Nick was alive, barely.

And our father and her mom were to blame for it all.

I stepped out onto the landing and glanced to T's room. The bitter stench of his hate still lingered. My brother was a train wreck in slow motion. He'd already left the tracks, already hurtling toward whatever darkness waited. But I could no more help him than I could help myself.

My phone vibrated, still in my pocket. I flinched at the sensation, realizing I was still dressed in the clothes I'd worn last night...*last night.* Memories invaded, making me swallow the bile in the back of my throat and think about raiding my father's liquor cabinet once more...until I realized I'd already done that and there was no more alcohol left.

I reached and pulled my phone out as I headed barefoot toward the bathroom. It was late, *really late.* Dark outside. How long had I slept? I tried to blink away the sting in my eyes. Not long enough. That's how long. But there was no rest for me, not anymore.

*Crawl...*

Killion's snarl rose as I stepped close to Nick's door, pushed the handle and shoved the door open. The bedroom was empty. I moved to T's, finding the same. They were pissed at me, and doing who the fuck knows what.

I shook my head, hating how I shoved that desperation

aside. I couldn't care about them, not now. I had too many of my own demons to wrestle. But not battle, right? No, because to get her out, I needed to let my demons win.

I stepped into the bathroom, hit the light, and glanced down at my phone, finding six missed calls. Five of them were from Evans. But the sixth call was from a private number. I pressed the button to my voicemail and listened to Killion's deep baritone. *"There's a private party over at Crestwood tonight. Your name and Evans' are on the register. I expect to see a lot more of you tonight."*

Disgust moved through me. No doubt that's what the five missed calls from Evans were about. I'd wanted in...so this was in. I lifted my gaze to the haunted eyes in the mirror. He wanted to see more of me. That only meant one thing...

He wanted to watch me fuck.

My balls clenched at the thought.

I didn't care about an audience. But what I did care about was *her*.

Ryth.

There was no goddamn way I wanted to fuck anyone else.

Not now...not ever.

Only I wasn't sure I had a choice. I pressed Evans' number and listened to it ring, until it was answered with a moan. "C." Evans sounded panicked. "What the fuck do we do now?"

## FOURTEEN

*nick*

MY BROTHER WAS SILENT...TOO fucking silent. We sat parked in the dark, hidden by the towering trees of the forest. The Jeep's engine was idling, but the headlights were out, leaving us all but invisible from the compound on the other side of the road.

I scanned the fence line, watching for movement. The Order was well protected, too fucking well. The guards patrolled at intervals. One team checked the fences, while another patrolled the inner grounds. Even if we knew where they were keeping Ryth, we'd be found before we got anywhere near the damn buildings.

Tension clenched my gut, sending a stab of pain through my side. I winced and pressed my hand against the fresh dressing as T shoved the four-wheel drive into reverse and backed up.

Red brake lights flared in the dark as we slowed, turned, then surged forward. T waited until we were far enough away before he hit the headlights and lit up the dirt track. He said nothing, just drove while I pressed my hand against my side and held on.

There was no way in there, not without abducting a guard, torturing him for information, then taking him out. I thought of money, but a bribe would take too fucking long...and we didn't have time to waste. Every second she was in that place was a second too long.

The odds of getting one of the guards on their own were slim. Still, I thought about that as we headed back to the city. Only we didn't head home. Instead, we made for the seedy suburbs of the south. I glanced at T as he headed for the strip, slowing when the punks pulled up beside us in their Lamborghinis and revved their engines.

But Tobias didn't seem to notice or care. He stared straight ahead, jaw clenched, fists tight around the wheel. Headlights splashed against his face, making his dark eyes look even darker than they were. He looked haunted...*no; he looked fucking dangerous.*

He was slipping from us, falling into that dark place.

Still, we slowly made our way south, leaving the street-racing punks and the glittering lights of the city's heart behind. But with each turn, it felt like he was heading somewhere. Somewhere he didn't really want to go. So we took the back streets and roundabouts, dancing around the more dangerous and seedier suburbs, until I couldn't hold back anymore. "Want to tell me where we're headed, brother?"

"I might have a contact that can get us inside," T murmured. "But I haven't seen him in a while."

I jerked my gaze his way. "You do? Why the fuck didn't you say that before?"

T said nothing. But it wasn't a pissed off nothing...it was a concerned nothing. Like he wasn't sure about this at all. We turned toward the back streets of Penance, where the bikers occupied the backyard warehouses and shopping centers were overrun with street gangs. Four punks on ATVs pulled out behind us. I caught the movement in the side mirror, and that sinking feeling hit hard.

"When we get there, Nick, you say nothing. Got that?" T pulled into the shabby mall and headed for the underground graffiti ruined parking garage. "Don't ask questions, don't make small talk...especially small talk. You stay quiet, leave the talking to me."

T handled the Jeep, pulling in past the shattered boom gate and the trashed security booth. I scanned the area, spotting a brand new black Escape parked sideways at the rear of the lot. Three guys on sport motorbikes were parked, watching us as we neared.

These didn't look like just any punks, especially not in a place like this. A cold feeling swept through me at the sight. "Want to tell me who the hell those guys are?" I scanned them, finding three more guys standing further back.

"No one you want to know," T answered, pulling up hard. "Wait in the car. We're not staying long."

He climbed out, leaving the engine idling, and walked over to the guy leaning against the Escape. I glanced at the side mirror, catching movement further back. Three guys watched from behind the parked cars in the distance. Guys who sat astride Harleys, wearing MC patches. Who the fuck were those guys?

The asshole from the Escape gave T a patdown, then stepped away. They spoke, saying words I couldn't quite hear, until the guy turned his head and motioned to the bikers at the rear.

The bikes started with a throbbing roar. The others climbed onto their motorbikes as T just turned and headed my way once more. I said nothing when he slipped in behind the wheel, waiting until we were headed out again. "T, you want to fill me in here?"

"They can get us in."

That's all he said.

"Get us in," I repeated, watching an Audi swing in hard behind us. "At what cost?"

He didn't answer, which was an answer itself. That cold feeling burrowed deeper inside me as we followed the guys on the Harleys out of the mall and east on Penance.

East where no one went. No one who wanted to stay alive, anyway. I winced and jerked my gaze to T. There was no way he knew the kind of men who occupied these kinds of streets. No way he even moved anywhere near the kind of blood-drenched circles these men did. No fucking way...

Not my kid brother.

The Escape overtook us on the bend, engine gunning, dark tinted windows rolled down, the driver glaring at me as he passed. T followed to where the low-income housing spread out to the east. There were watchers on the corners. Guys straddling bikes, others in sleek, dark rides. The expensive kind. We drove to some kind of an empty lot with a towering fence and a heavy, locked gate and waited while the driver of the Escape climbed out and casually made his way to the lock, working the keys old school style. Then he got back into his ride and led us further.

The worn path led to a set of warehouses in the distance. Three steel mountains backed against nearby derelict houses. The dirt track kept going past the warehouse, giving those inside multiple exit points. Seemed strategic, smart. T shoved the Jeep into gear and followed the Ford, leaving the asphalt behind. I winced and held my breath as we jolted and rocked, making our way to the front of one warehouse.

The driver of the Escape parked and climbed out, waiting until T killed the engine. I followed my brother, holding my side as I stepped out and slammed the door behind me.

"Remember, let me do the talking," T muttered as I headed around the front of the Jeep and followed him to the door.

Sickening howls of agony came from inside. There were dogs, and a lot of them. Fighting, killing something, by the sounds of it, something small and terrified. I clenched my jaw with the pain and ducked under the roller door as it lifted. But the moment I stepped inside, I wanted out.

*Right the fuck...now.*

The stench of shit and piss and blood hit me like a fucking chainsaw. Two massive pitbulls were attacking a single dark puppy within a bloodstained pit. I caught flashes of tan streaked by blood. The closer we came, the more I realized what this was. *Sport. This was a fucking sport.* "What the fuck?"

T shot me a glare, one that said two words: *say nothing.*

A group of pathetic pieces of shit yelled and screamed, cheering the bloodbath on. I couldn't look...I didn't fucking want to, but there was something about those howls of agony that echoed somewhere deep inside.

The howls went silent. The disappointed screams from those gutless bastards made me want to tear them apart, piece by rotten piece. I had to force my gaze from the tiny bloody form in the middle of the pit as two of the men climbed inside and tethered the Pitbulls with chains and muzzles. Money changed hands. The sight of it made me want to throw up as one of the brutes neared that still, tiny form, gave it a kick, then bent, grabbed the puppy by the hind legs, and tossed it over the fence, where it landed on the concrete floor with a sickening *thud.*

I was wrong.

This wasn't sport. This was just fucking *bloodlust.*

"T," I growled, tearing my gaze from that tiny form lying so still on the floor.

"You want in?" T growled, casting me a glare. "Then shut your fucking mouth."

He lengthened his stride, heading for the brightly lit office in the back. I scanned the warehouse, making sure I saw every ugly motherfucker in there. I wanted to make sure I knew who to take out when I returned.

"Tobias," the asshole behind the desk murmured as he leaned back in his chair. His legs were crossed, boots in the middle of his desk. But there was nothing relaxed about him. The man was a snake, and he showed that with the flicker of annoyance, like the man was about to strike. "Last time I saw you, T, you told me you weren't interested in the game. What changed?"

"The right motivation," Tobias answered.

The guy didn't speak, just watched him while the dogs started growling and barking further back in the warehouse.

"Nice place," I muttered.

A slow, sly smile crept across the asshole's face as he slowly turned his head, giving me his focus for the first time since we'd walked in. "Interested in placing a bet?"

I swallowed my rage and tasted acid. "Not particularly."

The smile was cold, a fucking mask, as he shifted his gaze to my brother. "Why are you here, T?"

"The guards at the Order. They look like your men."

He gave a careful shrug.

"I want in."

"You want in?"

Tobias stayed silent. I watched the two, growing even more desperate to find out how the fuck T knew these assholes. It had to be Lazarus. There was no doubt about that, but I was surprised that even the Rossis stooped so low.

"Jackson," the dog killer called.

The heavy thud of boots came behind me. I didn't turn, didn't shift my gaze from the man in charge.

"Yeah, boss?"

"Tobias here wants in on the guard duty at Hale. You got a spot for him?"

"Can he hold his own?"

"I dunno." He stared at my brother. "Can you hold your own?"

"You tell me, Amo," Tobias answered, his tone hard.

I waited for the tension to break, for the asshole T called Amo to break out in laughter and give us exactly what we wanted, a way into the Order to get Ryth out.

"Guess there's only one way to find out." Amo gave a nod to Jackson, then leveled a look at T. "We're short a man for a job."

I stiffened and jerked my gaze to my brother. "A job?'

"What do you think, T?" he continued, not once looking my way. "Gotta prove yourself, brother."

I didn't like this two-bit gansta, didn't like him at all, and I sure as *fuck* didn't like him calling T his goddamn kin. T looked from Amo to me, then slowly nodded.

"You don't have to do this," I murmured.

"He does if he wants a spot on the team." Amo slid his feet from his desk and rose, walking around the desk.

"It's okay, Nick," Tobias growled as he turned away.

Fuck that. I started after him. "Then I'm coming too."

"Nick." Amo placed his hand on my arm as the two assholes from the fighting ring stepped in front of me, cutting me off from my brother.

I didn't give a fuck who this guy was, or if I pissed him off. All I cared about was watching T stride toward the rising rolled door, going where and doing what I didn't know.

I jerked my arm away. "Get the fuck off me." I stepped around the dog-killing piece of shit. "Tobias!"

T glanced my way as he disappeared under the door. The engine of the Escape roared to life. Headlights flared a second later, casting shadows across his face.

My brother looked like a stranger as he left. I shifted my gaze to that still, lifeless little body on the concrete floor as fear found me once more. What the hell had we done?

FIFTEEN

FEAR ROOTED me to the spot as the man pressed Viv against the wall outside the classroom. He grabbed her jaw, squeezing until her lips pouted and she winced. Still, the show of pain didn't stop him. Instead, he seemed to like it. He dragged his thumb across her lip, his gaze fixed on the slow slide. "This fucking mouth is mine, you got that?"

The other girls stayed in the classroom behind me, watching.

Still Vivienne didn't buckle. "Fuck you," she spat, her words coming out warped and strange.

"Fifteen days." He pushed his thumb inside her mouth, sliding over her teeth to tug the side of her mouth wide. There was something debased and erotic about the act. "I'm going to enjoy stretching you out, Vivienne. *Very much.*"

"London." The curt, bitter tone came from behind me.

The older man never looked our way, just bored his gaze into Viv's, then slowly straightened. There was a twitch at the corner of his mouth, like he wanted to do a great many things to her.

*Ward,* wasn't that what he'd called her? So, if she was his ward, that meant he was her...*master?*

No. God, no.

No wonder she was desperate to get away from this place.

A silver pin glinted against his black satin tie as he straightened. The man looked impeccable, even if he did look old enough to be her father. His tailored black vest molded to a hard body. Thick veins traced a map along his powerful forearms. But it was his steely blue eyes that seized me, detached, unfathomable, meeting the Teacher's stare.

"I want her home," London demanded.

"As soon as Vivienne has finished her training." The Teacher brushed by me, stepping out into the hall.

The muscles of his jaw flared as the older man turned to her. "I can teach her everything she needs."

"I'm afraid it's part of the contract." The Teacher held out his hand to Vivienne. "I can summon The Principal if you need to discuss the terms?"

A second was all it took. A second for him to realize what he was doing. "No...no need," he muttered. "I've waited this long. What's a few more days?" He turned to Viv. "Vivienne."

He waited. When she didn't answer, he lifted his hand and thumped it against the wall beside her head.

She just held his stare, forcing the word through clenched teeth. "Daddy."

He traced the line of her jaw. She jerked away. Still, that didn't ease the hunger in his stare. He just pushed off the wall, turned, and strode away. My chest burned until I exhaled. I wanted to go after him, to push *him* against the goddamn wall and terrify him with sickening threats.

"Vivienne," the Teacher murmured, watching the asshole stride away. "Take Ms. Castlemaine with you to the cafeteria for some refreshments. I'll come and find you in a moment."

Viv just nodded and lowered her gaze.

I grabbed her hand and pulled her away from there. She followed, but her skin was pale, her eyes fixed straight ahead, like she was in shock. Red marks from that man's hand lingered on her mouth, making me sick to my stomach. I tried to remember which way to go, but ended up needing Viv to point toward the correct hallway.

When we were inside the cafeteria, I pulled her into a hug. I didn't know what else to do, how to give her comfort. "It's okay." I pressed her agIainst me. "It's going to be okay."

"No," she whispered. "It isn't."

I pulled away to stare into her eyes. "Let me get us a drink and you can tell me who that man is and what the fuck is going on, okay?"

She didn't nod, but I didn't wait, just headed for the counter with a range of juices and drinks, pouring us each an OJ before returning. She sat at one of the tables hugging the wall, staring at her hands clasped in front of her. I pushed the glass toward her.

But she didn't drink, just sat there.

"That man, he called you his ward. What the fuck does that mean?"

"It means I'm one step away from being sold, that's what."

"Jesus," I shook my head, shoving aside my mom's face as it rose. "How can this happen? How can..."

"They treat us like property?" She lifted her gaze. "Because we don't matter, that's how."

*I need this, Ryth. Please, honey, can't you be happy for me?* Mom's words hit me hard. *Had I ever really mattered to her?*

"The why doesn't matter." She picked at her nails. "You start down *that* road and it's only going to take you one place... and that's down. You'll dig yourself into a hole so deep you won't ever escape. The only thing you can control is now.

You're nice, Ryth. Nice and innocent, and you should stay that way. You don't understand what they want from us, how they make us..." She looked away.

Innocent...I might've been before Tobias, Nick, and Caleb, but I sure wasn't anymore. Heat raced to my cheeks as that night after the wedding filled my mind. Still, I forced my focus back to Vivienne. "How they make us, what?"

"Nothing," she answered, picking up the juice and taking a sip. "You wouldn't understand."

"Then tell me. Help me understand. What is this contract?"

She gave a chuff. "The contract isn't shit. They all think it is. But it's nothing but a worthless piece of paper. It doesn't stop them from...doing things to me."

I leaned closer. "Who?"

Her voice was as emotionless as her eyes. "The man I'm supposed to call Daddy...and his goddamn sons."

My insides clenched and my stomach dropped. "They... hurt you?"

"Yes," she whispered. "And I like it. I fucking like it, okay?" She drank, then placed her empty glass down. "That's why I want out. I want away from this place and all the fucking assholes inside it. And I especially want away from *him*, London St. James. He's going to destroy me, Ryth...him and his sons."

My pulse boomed, making me stand. "Then we get out of here."

She lifted her head, and for a second, the emptiness in her eyes sparked with hope. She glanced over her shoulder. "They'll come for us soon. The Teacher and probably The Principal."

My heart was racing with the memory of that cruel bastard. I wanted to be as far away from him as possible, him and that white-haired asshole guard. "We need to find a phone."

She glanced over her shoulder again and leaned forward. "I can get that. I think, anyway. Will they come tonight, your...stepbrothers?"

*NICK!* My own screams rang inside my head. All I saw was blood. "I don't know."

She straightened. "Then we try. If not, we make a run for it. Once we get past the guards, then the fence, we can try to outrun them through the forest."

I lowered my gaze to the flimsy white negligees we were both wearing. "We'll die of exposure before morning."

"Not if we keep running." She stared at me. "What's the fucking alternative? You going to learn how to be a whore, Castlemaine?"

I swallowed hard. "Fuck no."

A slow, careful smile tugged the corners of her mouth. "Then let's find that phone and get us the fuck out of here."

I glanced behind me at the kitchen staff, then turned back and nodded. We left the glasses on the table and made our way out into the hallway. But out there we were too goddamn exposed. Double doors barred our way up ahead, the scanner blinking red. "We don't have a keycard."

"We don't need one." Viv glanced behind us, then moved to the wall and pressed a code into the keypad. "You don't think I'd let that asshole come and go without me finding out his fucking passcode, do you?"

Hope surged as the light on the keypad turned from red to green and the doors gave a *clunk*. Viv moved fast, pushing the handle, and slipping through. I followed, hurrying behind her. We turned to each other, reaching out, grabbing each other's hand as we ran.

Bare feet slapped against the floor before we turned and

stopped at the next set of locked doors. By the time we lunged through the open door and raced ahead, I couldn't hear anything other than the booming of my heart.

Viv tugged my hand, and we turned a corner. For all I knew, we could be running headlong toward our end. Still, I kept going, following her, until the resounding sound of a man's voice echoed. Viv stopped, her chest heaving with deep breaths.

I tried to listen over the loud rush of my own breathing.

"I can't have the others seeing another outburst like that." The Principal's firm tone carried. "What happens outside of the contract is not meant for these walls. I'd hate to have to readjust the terms."

"I understand," a clipped, indifferent tone followed. "It won't happen again."

I jerked my gaze to Viv as we stopped near the corner, pressing our spines against the wall. Footsteps sounded until the thud of the doors came. I waited until the panicked scream in my head was dulled enough for me to risk a peek. They were leaving, heading outside, I was guessing. I shifted my gaze back. "Viv."

She moved next to me and glanced around, seeing the door of The Principal's office open.

"Come on." She grabbed my hand and yanked me forward.

We were going to get caught...any second now, we were—

I stumbled after her into the office. Viv skirted the desk, snatched up the receiver and shoved it my way. "Call, Ryth... and hurry."

My stomach clenched. What if I'd forgotten the number? What if...fear rooted me to the spot. All I could do was stare at the phone in my hand. *Nick.* His face swam in my mind. My hands shook. I just wanted to make sure he was okay. *Please God, let him be okay.*

"You want to stay here and be fucked by strangers?"

I flinched at the words and jerked my gaze to Viv. "No."

"Then dial the goddamn number and tell your step-brothers to come and get you."

"Us," I whispered, stepping closer, and punched in the number. "Come and get *us*."

I swallowed hard as the phone on the other end rang, and rang, and rang. I needed his voice. Just one whisper, one sound.

"Yeah?" The deep growl echoed down the line.

A hard sob ripped free. *"Nick?"*

Silence..."*Ryth?*"

"Nick!" My knees shook, my spine bowed. I closed my eyes, rocking at the sound of that beautiful growl. "Nick. *Oh, God, Nick.*"

"*Princess,*" he barked, his voice growing loud. "Is that you?"

"It's me. It's me...I don't have much time."

The sound of screams and barking dogs drowned him out. "You okay, princess?"

"Yes," I answered as Viv yanked open drawers and rifled through papers, searching his office. "For now, but not for long."

"We know where you are." Desperation etched his words as the heavy *thud* of a door came from out in the hallway. "You hear me?" My stepbrother barked. "We know where you are and we're fucking coming. Just hold on, baby. *We're fucking coming.*"

# SIXTEEN
## *tobias*

I YANKED the passenger door of the Escape closed behind me and sat back against the seat. The engine started with a growl. Then we were moving, pulling away from the warehouse and leaving Nick behind. Out of the corner of my eye, I caught the steel door of the warehouse as it rolled shut. He'd be fine, as long as he didn't open his goddamn mouth. He better...Ryth's life depended on it.

Sideways looks came from the driver beside me. I said nothing, just watched the side mirror as we picked up our escort along the way.

"You're backup, got that?" The asshole behind the wheel reached across me, punched the button for the glove compartment, pulled out a Glock, and tossed it to me.

I held the thing. No doubt the numbers were filed and there was blood on the sight. There always was when it came to Amo.

Ryth's face stayed with me as we slowed. Waiting for one of the guys on the bikes to grab the gate, we hit the asphalt and accelerated. I didn't ask questions. This wasn't a fucking job interview. This was a test. One I needed to pass.

We drove through Penance, heading to some shithole that looked all the fucking same. Memories of Laz swam in the background of my mind. We'd spent nights just like this, driving, working, handling Rossi shit.

But that was a lifetime ago, before everything went downhill.

Now it was just us. Family. Not the blood kind, either.

I clenched my fist around the grip of the Glock as my father's face rose in my memory. That fucker's time was coming. The bikes pulled out beside us, flanking either side as we headed toward the nicer side of the city, where nightclubs and bars lined the streets.

Finally, we pulled into an alley that ran alongside The Viper Bar. I didn't know why we were here, didn't know who the mark was. Short of pulling a gun on my brothers, I didn't give a fuck. We pulled up behind the bikes and killed the engine. I climbed out, tucked the gun in the small of my back, and tugged out my shirt.

"We good?"

I looked across the car and nodded.

"You go with Dion to the back of the bar and wait for me there."

"Sure." I glanced at the guy on the bike who'd slid off his helmet. "Whatever."

The gun wore at my back. I followed Dion along the alley to where the back door of the club was normally closed. Only tonight, it wasn't. The hinges were silent as we pushed the door open and stepped inside. It seemed I was to be the muscle. That was fine by me. My rage was honed by every second I was away from her.

*Bring her back to me!*

My own screams rang in my head, muffled by the throb of music that spilled through the darkened hallway. Dion stepped up to a door and checked the handle. It was locked. He motioned further along the hall. I followed to the back area bar as we took seats.

The club was part restaurant and part strip joint, the expensive kind. I scanned the place, spotting Jackson standing at the back. He gave a nod, but it wasn't to me. From one of the tables, a guy rose as though on cue. He laughed, bellowed at some schmuck next to him, and motioned to the back area.

The guy next to him wiped his mouth with his napkin, then threw it on the table before rising. He was obviously the mark. Why? I didn't really care. I turned away, focusing on the bar in front of me as they passed, waiting on Dion.

But when he rose from his seat, I glanced behind me once more. Two men sat across from where the mark and his buddy had sat. One watched the mark walk toward the rear of the bar before he turned back to his meal.

I followed the guys further into the bar, lowered my gaze, and moved in. By the time we hit the hallway heading to a lap dance room, I'd dragged the gun from behind my back. Dion stepped into the room. I followed and closed the door behind me.

But there were no dancers.

There was nothing.

Just us.

"What the fuck?" The mark turned and stopped.

"Henderson." Dion stepped forward and withdrew a piece of paper from his pocket, along with a pen.

The mark glanced from Dion to me, then to his buddy at his side. "Peter, what the fuck is this?"

"They want the contract." His buddy took a step away, leaving the mark standing all alone in the middle of the dark-ened room. "Just sign it, James. Sign it and we can all make a fuckload of money from this. It's the only way. The only way they're ever going to leave us alone."

But Henderson flinched at the words, his dark eyes growing even darker. The guy wasn't used to being told what to do, that was easy to see. "And you what? Thought you'd come here with your *thugs* and force me to sign over my entire company's future?" He looked at me when he said that.

"Put it this way." Dion raised his gun. "Mr. Kendry has tried to negotiate with you. We're past that now. You either sign the contract, or there is no future...not one with you in it." He lifted the paper in one hand, and the gun in the other.

The mark clenched his jaw, not once looking at the paper in Dion's hand. I'd dealt with enough Rossi bullshit to know when a man would fold...and when he'd tell you to jam it up your ass—my hand tightened around the gun—and this guy... *yeah, he wasn't bending.*

"Fuck you," the mark snarled, then glared at his buddy. "And fuck *you*, too, Peter."

Dion let out a chuckle, one that sent a chill down my spine, before he charged forward, lips curled, lifting the gun to the mark's forehead. "Last fucking chance before *I blow your goddamn brains all over this fucking floor.*"

"*Do it!*" the mark roared. "*DO IT, AND SEE WHAT HAPPENS!*" Bad fucking move...

I sensed the movement before I saw it. Instinct kicked in, making me raise the gun and step to the side as the two beefy dudes from the table opposite the mark rushed in. Everything happened so fast. Gunshots went off. Dion was hit...someone screamed, and it was that sound that triggered me.

Something snapped...

Shattering into a million shards that all cut me from the inside. *Nick! NICK! SOMEONE HELP ME!* Caleb's desperate screams crashed through my head, mingling with my own as I spun and opened fire.

But it wasn't the beefy bodyguard I saw...*it was him...my father*. The bastard who'd done all of this.

Betrayed my mother.

Took Ryth from us.

Almost killed my brother.

*"Fuck you!"* I screamed and lunged. It was my father's shirt I fisted. My father's head that cracked back as he hit the wall. My father's eyes that widened in fear...and that's all I'd been waiting for.

*"You fucking piece of shit!"* I crashed out my fist, catching him in the nose. Blood came...and it never stopped.

The guard...

My father...

It didn't matter.

*"GIVE HER BACK TO ME!"* I howled. *"GIVE HER BACK TO ME NOW!"*

Darkness had me in a chokehold, driving my own demons down my throat. I swung...and kept on swinging. My knuckles crunched into his face as I hit him in sharp, short punches, knocking him down. He hit the floor on one knee and lifted his gun.

*Crack!* The shot rang out, my muscles howling with the movement. All the sprints, all the weights, all the fuel. They needed an outlet, and I was done running away. I drove my fingers into his eyes, grinding until the guy screamed. But I couldn't stop. Not even when the door slammed open and more men rushed in.

Two...three more bouncers. Someone grabbed me from behind. I cracked my head backwards and spun. *"YOU TOOK HER FROM ME!"*

I drove my fist into a face, and it didn't really matter who it was...not anymore.

I hit again, and again...over and over until I was nothing more than vengeance.

"Tobias!"

My name was screamed.

*"BANKS!"*

I stopped and lifted my head. My hands were wrapped around some guy's neck. A guy I didn't know...but I knew he was close to death. A stench like gasoline crammed the room. The carnage came into focus...I looked around...and froze.

"You fucking killed him," Dion gasped as he gripped his side. "You fucking killed them all." His shirt was covered in blood, his eyes wide in shock as he stared at me like I was some kind of monster.

He licked his lips, his hand wrapped around his gun. The muzzle lifted, pointing at me. "Should've stayed away, Banks. You made a mistake coming to Amo."

I sucked in a hard breath. "A mistake?"

"Yeah, *a mistake.*" Jackson's deep growl came from behind me. The hard metal bite of a gun barrel pressed against my head.

*You're just backup...*

*Go with Dion...*

The words rolled through my head. Silence settled inside me as I looked at Dion's gun. "There's no way into the Order, is there?"

"For you?" Jackson answered. "No."

There wasn't...

There never was.

I settled my gaze on Dion.

"Jack Castlemaine." Jackson pressed the gun harder against my head. "Where is he?"

Confusion moved in. "Castlemaine?"

Dion's eyes widened, fixed on Jackson behind me. The stench of blood filled my every breath.

"Yeah." Jackson moved closer. "Where the fuck is he? Our employer wants to know."

My mind was a blur, trying to piece it all together as my phone started to ring. The vibration danced against my thigh.

"See, we were coming for you anyway," Jackson murmured. "You and your brothers. But you...*you stupid motherfucker, walked right into our lap.*"

They were after Ryth's dad. They were after us, too...

But not my father, right? No...not him or Elle.

They *were the reason Ryth was in that place.*

I didn't move, just stared at Dion. Laughter spilled out of me, even though I didn't feel it. The sound rumbled, spewing out. Dion flinched at the sound and jerked his panic-filled gaze to Jackson.

The movement was all I needed. I jerked my head to the side and spun, grabbed his wrist, and shoved the gun wide. "You fucking take her from me?" I lashed out, punched the guy in the face, and grabbed the gun.

But instead of tearing the weapon from his hold, I squeezed his fingers. The gun went off beside me with a *boom!* The sound was deafening, but it didn't matter, because all I heard was Ryth's screams. *TOBIAS!* I saw her the night Nick's fucking ex had come for her. I saw what they'd done...

*Boom!*

The gun went off again, and this time Dion screamed. I twisted the gun. Jackson fought, unloading a punch to the side of my head. The blow hit me like a shotgun blast. I stumbled, then righted, curled my lips, and lunged. I snapped my head forward, hitting him in the nose. The blur of rage faded. I felt every blow this time. I hit him one blow after another until I squeezed the trigger.

*Crack!*

Jackson froze, hard breaths rising from his chest...that bloomed with blood.

"You?" he whispered as he crumbled. "You stupid piece of shit. You think you can take on the Order? *You're fucking nothing. You hear me? NOTHING!*" Laughter spilled out of him. "The bitch is fucking *gone*. Sold and fucked by a hundred different men by now. You'll never get her back...*you'll never*—"

He froze, his words dying on his lying lips.

I stood over him, his gun in my hand, his blood on my knuckles. I lifted the gun once more. "You can't take her...she was never yours to take." My finger curled around the trigger. "Because she's mine."

## SEVENTEEN

*nick*

THERE WAS SOMETHING WRONG...
SOMETHING more than the sick fucking dog fights and
foul laughter that spilled out. I didn't like that Amo fucker. Not
one bit. I stood there at the doorway of his office, watching as
he laughed and cheered when they led two more dogs into the
ring, kicking them and punching them before ripping off their
muzzles and throwing them at each other.

They stood back and watched the show. My gut clenched,
hate and acid scalding the back of my throat as I shifted my
gaze to that little puppy still on the concrete floor, cast aside
like it was nothing...until its rear leg moved. *It moved.*

I ground my teeth, my focus fixed on that movement. I
stared until my gaze blurred...then I saw it. *It breathed.* Its little
chest rose, then fell. I jerked my gaze to the others, but they
were too busy cheering and screaming under the deafening
howls and whimpers of the dogs.

Amo looked down at his phone...for the fifth time. He
glanced my way, the chilling focus making my pulse race.
Something was wrong...like *really* wrong. I broke the stare,
turning back to that barely alive pup. But he didn't care what I

was looking at. Instead, Amo turned back to the fight, unleashing a roar to pump the fight up even more. Until one by one, the guys leaned over too close and one of the pitbulls leaped, grabbed him around the arm, and thrashed.

Screams erupted. Amo and the others lunged as chaos broke out. I smiled at the asshole's screams, and instead of the blood and the panic, I turned my attention behind me...to the office. I stepped in, moving to the mess of paperwork on the desk. One swipe and a photo was revealed. A man, standing in some darkened alley, looking right at the camera.

I knew him...

My stomach clenched.

The photo was blurry, but I knew Jack Castlemaine when I saw him. I knew because I'd checked the guy out before I drove Ryth to Mitchelton Prison. This was him. I pushed the photo aside, to find Tobias' face, then Caleb's...and mine. A name was written under Jack Castlemaine's image. *Sebastian Black.* I'd never heard that name...but it was important, *somehow.* I jerked my gaze high, panic roaring. Instinct screamed as I shoved the papers back over the photos and moved, stepped out of the office, and rounded the back of the warehouse.

I had to move, had to do something. Standing there, I was a goddamn sitting duck.

I knew something was way off. They had our photos. That only meant one thing. They'd been paid for a hit and we'd just strolled right into their fucking crosshairs. "Jesus, T!" He was in trouble...big fucking trouble. I grabbed my phone, moved around some stacked crates, and punched T's number, listening to it ring.

It went unanswered. I tried again.

"Answer the fucking phone, T," I muttered, and stopped beside a wooden crate. The top was lifted. I stopped, listening to the phone ringing, and shoved the top aside. There were grenades and half a crateful of C4. "Fuck."

I hung up, grabbed three grenades, and turned.

My phone rang and I answered it without thinking.

"Nick?"

I froze...*no...this wasn't real. She wasn't.* "Ryth?"

"*Nick!*"

"Princess?" I growled, forgetting everything else for a second. "Is that you?"

"It's me. It's me. I don't have much time."

I almost wept with relief until it hit me. "You okay, princess?"

"Yes, for now, but not for long."

"We know where you are. You hear me? We know where you are and we're fucking coming. Just hold on, baby. *We're fucking coming.*"

The line went dead. I ripped the phone from my ear and looked at the screen. She was gone. I pressed the button, but found the number was unlisted. I thought of calling it back, until I stopped. If she's in trouble, if calling that number drew attention to her, I'd never live with myself.

Instead, I shoved my phone into my pocket. There was no waiting, not for T, or anyone else. Not anymore. I needed to find a way inside that compound. *Now.* I yanked the pin from a grenade as I strode around the corner of the office.

"*Hey, asshole!*" I called out, and tossed the grenade through the air.

*BOOM!*

The thing detonated against the pit...but Amo wasn't there. I scanned the space, catching movement as he stepped out from the office. His scowl flickered for a second before he lunged. My ears rang with the explosion, but his screams of rage still pushed in as he hit me.

Agony tore through my side, but I didn't have time to protect myself. I just reacted, driving my fist up as I turned and unleashing a backhand that cracked across the bastard's face. His head snapped to the side and blood spewed from his nose. From the pit, the second dog came, lunging for the nearest guy.

Sickening sounds of terror came.

"*Nick!*" I jerked my gaze as my brother came running across the space, his eyes wide, his face splattered with blood. Christ, he was a mess. He just raised the gun in his hand. *Crack!* The shot rang out, slamming into Amo.

The bastard spun away from me.

"You doublecrossing piece of shit." Tobias sucked in a harsh breath and strode forward. "You come for me? You come for my *brothers?*"

"T," I croaked, staring at him. He was a bloody mess, but there was something unhinged in his gaze, something that terrified me.

Amo just sneered and wiped at the blood blooming along his side. T just sucked in another deep breath, holding Amo's gaze. "Let's go, Nick."

I tightened my side muscles and gripped the last two grenades, stepping away. My brother looked like a stranger, harder, colder—*bloodier.* He aimed the gun at Amo as I approached. The pitbulls were gone, the two assholes who'd beaten them now silent. Blood was everywhere, splattered all over the pit and pooled on the floor.

"Come after us again, and I'll come back...and next time I won't come back alone," Tobias warned.

"I heard the word," Amo snarled. "You and the Rossis are at war."

"You think so, do you?" Tobias held up his phone and pressed the button, then put the call on speaker.

It was answered on the second ring. "T." Lazarus Rossi's deep snarl echoed.

"Yeah," Tobias muttered. "It's me. I just want to check we're good, *brother?*"

There was a second before Lazarus answered. "Yeah, we're good. You okay?"

Tobias took the call off speaker. "Yeah, sure," he said, his gaze fixed on Amo. "I'll call you soon."

Then he hung up the call, slipped his phone into his pocket, and pulled out the keys for the Jeep. A jerk of his hand and he tossed them through the air toward me. I snatched them with a hand holding a grenade. I was already moving, heading for the half-open garage door.

Until I stopped and glanced down.

The little Rottweiler puppy still lay there, eyes open, breaths shallow. I shoved the pinned end of the grenade between my teeth before I bent and picked it up. The little thing never gave a whimper, not even a yelp. I had to be hurting it as I carried it out the door and strode toward the Jeep.

"Easy, buddy," I urged as I stopped at the car, held him as carefully as I could, and opened the four-wheel drive's door.

*Boom!*

The crack of a gunshot made me turn and look toward the warehouse as my brother strode out and lipped under the door before heading my way. I tossed him back the keys, then yanked open the passenger door and placed the torn-up puppy on the floor before I climbed in.

"What happened? I thought you were leaving him alive?"

Tobias climbed in behind the wheel and started the engine. "I changed my mind." He glanced to the floor at my feet, then met my gaze. The puppy whimpered and licked my leg. "I couldn't leave him."

Tobias snorted a quiet chuckle. "You mean *her*, right?"

*Her?* I jerked my gaze down to the puppy as it lifted its leg and licked a wound. It was female...

My heart pounded as T pulled out and drove forward. The headlights splashed against a motorbike lying on the ground. We quickly left the carnage behind. I caught a glimpse of the two escaped pitbulls as we hit the asphalt and sped away.

"What the fuck happened with you?" I looked at the blood that covered my brother's face. The dashboard lights made the splatter look black.

He glanced into the rear-view mirror and tried to wipe the mess away. "Nothing good."

We headed for the city, watching for red and blue lights that were sure to come. Headlights from the oncoming cars were blinding. All I could hear was the dull hum from the traffic as we pulled up at the set of lights outside some exclusive clubs. Two guys climbed out of a Bentley. It took me a second before I realized who it was.

"Isn't that Caleb?" I muttered, drawing Tobias' gaze.

We didn't move, even when the lights turned green and horns blared behind us. Cars went around us as our brother adjusted his collar. He looked good, smiling at the asshole he was with as they headed for some expensive-looking club.

"Is he..."

"Having a good fucking time, by the looks of it," T growled, finally moving the Jeep forward.

I caught the turn of Caleb's head as T drove away.

"Goddamn bastard." T forced the words through clenched teeth. "Goddamn *selfish fucking bastard!*"

I didn't know if he'd seen us...but we'd seen him. Seen him looking just like our dad. Laughing. Drinking...hooking up with who the fuck knew, like he didn't even care Ryth was in that place.

# EIGHTEEN

## *caleb*

"WHY THE FUCK do we have to meet them here again?" Evans muttered as we climbed out of his Bentley.

I adjusted my shirt and stole a breath. "Because they don't trust us...yet."

Cars tore along the street next to us. Headlights flared, blinding me for a moment. Red brake lights caught my attention. For a second, I thought I saw Nick's face, but then the car was gone.

"Are you sure you want to do this?"

*No...*

But I didn't have a choice. I stepped up onto the sidewalk and lifted my gaze to the club. "Let's go," I growled, and strode forward. We were stopped at the door, IDs checked, phones confiscated. No one got into these places without giving up something. For me, it was my fucking soul.

"Caleb." Killion smiled as he strode forward. "I didn't think you were going to show."

I swallowed hard and winced, concealing the revulsion when he clapped me softly on the back. "We're here now."

"You are." He almost fucking beamed, that glint dying a little when he turned his head. "Evans."

"Killion," my buddy muttered.

"Shall we?" Killion motioned for us to follow.

Nearly naked strippers danced around poles in the front of the club, where a few men sat in business suits enjoying the entertainment. Evans watched, his gaze lingering, as we followed our host to the back of the club. That's where his tastes lay, in the front of the club where the murky gloom gave him all the darkness he wanted.

But I was different.

A tremor of excitement tore through me as Killion nodded to the bouncer guarding the entrance to the back. That excitement raced all the way to my cock. I kept my heart chained, my focus on one thing and one thing alone.

*Ryth...*

We stepped through to the back room, but there were no women waiting for us tonight. Instead, Killion led us to the exit at the rear of the club. Another bouncer waited at the door, opening it as we neared. In the back, a limousine waited. Killion climbed in, leaving the door open for us.

I followed, leaving Evans to step in last before the bouncer closed the door and climbed into the passenger seat. The idling limousine pulled away, making its way out of the alley and into the street. I sat back, turning my attention to Killion.

He watched me with interest, his gaze slowly moving down my body. He wanted me, that was easy to see. But I wasn't sure if it was my body he wanted, or more...

I glanced away, hoping to fuck getting to Ryth didn't come to that. But to get her back...I'd do anything.

"You seem preoccupied," Killion murmured.

"Family shit," I answered.

He just nodded. "You never told me how you are after your mother—"

"Fine," I snapped.

"And your brothers? Tobias still a hothead?"

*Fuck you, Caleb!* T's voice roared in my head from this morning. "More than ever."

Killion licked his lips. "I wonder if he'd be interested in joining us one evening?"

Cold plunged through me. I jerked my gaze back to the vile piece of shit. "No."

The smile was instant and fake. "Of course." Killion gave a nod, watching me.

But my mood was changed, hardening to something a little darker, something a little...*colder.* We headed out of the city to where the affluent houses sat far back from the street, hidden behind towering fences and thick hedges. Then the limousine slowed and turned. The driver wound his window down and reached to a keypad on a covered post. Killion watched me with interest.

"Christ, I need a drink," Evans muttered as the gate slid open and we pulled in.

I held Killion's stare. He was excited about tonight, a little *too* excited. Evans was already shoving open the door when we pulled up at the front of the house. The guard shoved open his door, rushing to hold ours open as Evans climbed out.

I scanned the house as we stepped out of the car. It was old, and disgustingly expensive. Sandstone and wrought iron. Ornate gardens led to a path to the rear of the house. Killion strode forward, knowing exactly where he was headed, and for a second, I wondered if this was his place.

But I didn't care, not really.

New money.

Old money.

They could have it all.

I followed him to a door at the side of the house. A bodyguard stood sentry just inside, nodding at Killion as he entered. He watched us as we followed Killion upstairs. There were others, three or four men and one woman, who was vaguely familiar. She was on her knees on the landing of the carpeted stairs, her mouth full of cock from one of the other partners. She met my gaze as I passed, her dark eyes glittering.

I followed Killion as we stepped along the landing. A man stood outside an open door.

"Principal," Killion greeted him, clapping him on the back.

They greeted each other like friends, but one look at this guy and I knew he was different. I glanced inside the large open room, catching sight of a woman dressed in a red negligee kneeling, legs splayed, in the middle of the room.

"She's waiting," A man called. The Principal nodded toward the room.

Killion smiled as he stepped in. "Caleb, follow me."

I didn't want to go into that room. But one simple no and the trust I was building would be shattered. My heart was pounding as I stepped through the doorway.

"C," Evans murmured. But he followed.

There were more women, all dressed in the same negligee, some wearing red, some black, and two standing against the wall, dressed in white.

"The red you can fuck, the black are for sale...but the white." Killion glanced at the two terrified looking women. "The white is view only." He turned to the kneeling woman. "Up."

She rose as The Principal entered the room. Two other men came in behind him, stopping on either side of her. A nod from Killion and they stepped forward. One reached out, grasped her neckline, and yanked, tearing it from her body. Her breasts spilled out as he unbuttoned his pants and shoved down his fly.

"On your knees," Killion ordered.

She knelt with barely more than a whimper. But her gaze never moved from Killion's stare. She knew who she performed for, opening her mouth as the guy stepped forward and grabbed her by the hair as he pushed his cock in her mouth. She opened wide, sucking, licking, giving Killion all he wanted.

"Good little whore," Killion murmured.

He didn't care about the guy. It was all about her. The degradation, the humiliation, her shame. "Begin," he instructed. The second guy worked the button of his jeans. But I'd seen enough. Killion turned his head, glanced at another one of the women in red, and motioned her over. "Come."

She stepped forward. I glanced at the others, those dressed in black and white. The same clothes the woman from last night wore. *Red you can fuck, black is for sale, but the white...*

Killion's words raced through my head. My heart pounded. That sense of knowing hovered at the edges as I strode toward them. *The red you can fuck.* I glanced back, to find Killion watching me, waiting to see which one I'd take.

No...

I didn't want to do this.

Sweat ran down the nape of my neck. If I took anyone else, then he'd know I wasn't ready—I met his stare, those dark eyes glinting—if he knew I wasn't ready, then there'd be no way I could get into the Order.

Ryth's face swam in my mind. I tried to swallow the burn of revulsion as I stepped forward, met the gaze of the woman dressed in black, and gave a jerk of my head. "Come."

*Jesus...Jesus, this felt too much like cheating.*

I met Evans' stare, desperation howling inside me. He glanced back at Killion. I knew the bastard was smiling, knew it in my writhing fucking soul. "Come with me," I forced the words through clenched teeth.

He flinched, his cheeks burning. But if he didn't...if he left me alone with her, then...

I headed for the other side of the expansive room as grunts came from behind me. The woman who was getting railed by two guys for Killion's sick pleasure gave a whimper, then a grunt, before the slaps of flesh on flesh rang out. The sounds... the smells...my cock hardened.

*Are you going to be our good little girl and keep our dirty secret?*

My own words slammed into me as I stepped into the darkened room. It was a bedroom, a sex room. The bed was placed in the middle of the room, illuminated by one bedside light, turned low.

"Master?" came the soft feminine murmur behind me.

I spun, finding her standing close...too fucking close.

The bed.

Her fucking body.

*You going to beg?* The same words I'd said to Ryth pressed against me. "Turn around." The command was husky and raw. I didn't want to look at her. Didn't want to see her face when I...

Evans hovered in the doorway. His eyes were wide, the whites almost fucking neon. All I thought about was Ryth, the way she'd trembled that night when I'd grabbed her and dragged her into the pantry. I stepped closer to this woman as she turned, giving me her back.

*You going to scream?*

I stepped closer, until the heat of her body pressed against mine. One fast movement and I fisted her hair and dragged her head back. "You going to scream?"

The past...

The present.

They collided. Only now, my body clenched with revulsion. A shadow moved in the doorway. Behind Evans, Killion stepped close. He watched me as I fisted her hair and dragged her back hard against me. "Answer me...*are...you...going...to...scream?*"

"No," she answered breathlessly.

I closed my eyes. It wasn't what Ryth had said to me. In my head, I replayed that moment.

*Yes...yes, I'll scream.*

Touch her. Just fucking touch her. It's just sex, right? Just fucking sex.

Rage burned in me, taking me deeper than I'd ever gone before. Give me a gun, and I'd unload it on her and Killion and this entire fucking place. I just wanted Ryth back...*now*.

Revulsion burned as I reached up, grabbed the strap of her red negligee, and yanked. The fabric tore, her breasts spilled out, and every nerve inside my body fired with betrayal. Evans stepped closer. Killion grinned as I looked down her body at her exposed breasts.

Her puckered nipples waited, but my hand refused to move. I pulled her harder against me, desperate for my body to override my head. Just do it...just do what he wants. I swallowed hard as the woman in front of me moaned. I shoved her over, making her bend at the waist, and reached down, snagged the edge of her panties, and ripped them free.

She jerked and unleashed a cry. But I could tell it was fake. Everything about her was fake, from her clothes to the desire in her stare. She was nothing more than a warm body for me to fuck, nothing more than someone for me to own.

The Order.

The Principal.

*You want your own private fuck toy. Someone you can control...*

My thoughts collided. My pulse raced. The thoughts that

had hovered at the edges of my mind now burned neon bright. These women were from the Order...the same place they'd taken Ryth.

*The same fucking place.*

White. I reached for my zipper and yanked it low. *The white are for view only...*They were fucking graded, from new to ready to be bought, to be used...

*Jesus fucking Christ!*

I looked down to the red panties in my hand and dropped them to the floor. Her bare breasts jiggled as she pretended to thrash in my hold. She thought I wanted to take her by force, thought that was my kink. She was waiting, bent over. Her fake fucking whimpers filling the room. I didn't want this, didn't want any part of this. I turned my head, to see Evans staring at me in horror.

But the doorway was empty. Killion was gone.

*"Fucking dirty slut."* His voice carried from that room. *"Fuck her harder."*

Cries rang out from that room, sick, real fucking cries as they railed her. Acid spilled into the back of my mouth. This wasn't what I wanted. This wasn't Ryth. "I can't," I groaned, shaking my head as I turned to Evans.

Confusion mingled with rage.

He stepped closer, stopping at my side to hiss, "Then you're fucked. You get that, right? This is why we're both fucking here."

Torment raged through me.

"You have to...fuck her," Evans insisted.

I shoved her forward. She stumbled and hit the edge of the bed. Her bare ass and pussy were on display, and my cock softened. "I can't...I fucking can't."

"You think they won't know?" Evans growled. "Killion is in that fucking room listening, right goddamn now."

I clenched my fists and nearly buckled under the weight of the knowledge. I'd lose her...I'd lose my one fucking chance to get her back.

"Get the fuck out of the way," Evans snarled as he pushed me aside.

He strode forward, reaching for his zipper. With one hand, he grabbed the back of her neck, with the other he reached for his cock. "Don't fucking look at me, you got that?"

He didn't wait for her to answer, just drove her face against the mattress, shoved his pants down, and thrust in hard enough for her to buck and groan. Only this time, that sound was real. I stood there watching as he spread her wide, his hips slamming her ass over and over. I'd seen my brothers fuck our stepsister, seen Ryth wrestle with her own demons. How she liked what Nick and Tobias did to her. That's what had turned me on. That's what had gotten me hard. Not...this...

Grunts and whimpers came from the woman. Evans clenched his jaw, biting down on his own moans in a desperate attempt to stifle them. But the groans and grunts from the next room swallowed everything else. Evans dropped his head, his fingers digging into her hips as he used her...until with a low, guttural moan, he thrust in and stilled.

Harsh breaths consumed him. "Get your fucking dick out, C," he growled, then pulled out of her.

The cries from the other room grew silent as Evans released his hold on the woman and stepped away from the bed. He turned as the slow thud of footsteps came closer. In a blinding flash of desperation, I knew what I had to do.

I moved closer to the woman, still bent over the bed, and deepened my breaths. "You fucking stay there," I commanded, placing my hand on her hip. "You fucking stay right there. Do not move."

She didn't.

Killion stepped into the doorway as I slipped my cock back into my pants and tugged up the zipper. That cold, unflinching gaze scanned the room, stopping on me standing behind her, then he lowered his gaze as I stepped back.

Her pussy was slick, the remnant of cum shining brightly.

"Well done," Killion smiled. "Well fucking done."

I didn't dare look at Evans, who faced the wall. From the doorway, it looked like he was repulsed by what I'd done... unable to look.

"Get cleaned up," Killion instructed. "We're going to the Order. Let's find you one to own."

# NINETEEN
## *caleb*

I THOUGHT I was going to be sick. Revulsion rolled through me as Killion left the doorway, heading back into the other room.

"Evans," I called, but there was nothing more than a shake of his head.

"Go." He didn't even look at me as he made for the door. "Just make sure you get her back, Caleb. Don't let this be for fucking nothing."

He left the echo of his steps behind. I stared at the doorway, wrestling with my fucking guilt. I slowly glanced at the woman still lying facedown on the bed. "Get up," I commanded. "Get up and take care of yourself." *I'm sorry. Sorry we're no better than—*

The words never made it to my lips. Remorse would need to wait.

I adjusted my pants and made my way into the next room. The woman Killion had used lay in a ball on the floor, the two men who'd used her sucking in hard breaths as they stood naked over her. And Killion...Killion fucking beamed.

He turned when I neared, his smile sickening. "A drink? Come on, we'll have one in the limousine."

I followed him out of that room and headed back down the hall before we made our way down the stairs. But there was no sign of the man he'd called The Principal. I tried to search for Evans, but he was nowhere I could see. Probably drowning himself with the most expensive Scotch he could find. Things would be different between us now...

*Very fucking different.*

I swallowed the taste of acid in the back of my throat and followed Killion out to the waiting limousine, climbing back inside.

"Evans?" Killion asked as I sank onto the seat.

I shook my head, leaving the piece of fucking shit to smile even harder. "Good, he's not like us, Caleb." A nod from him, and the car doors were closed. "He'll only hold you back."

The engine started, and we pulled out along the driveway, heading for the front gate.

"You're destined for greater places. Places I can help you get to."

A twitch came at the corner of my eye. I wanted to reach across the seat and beat him bloody. I wanted to make him just as damaged on the outside as he was on the inside. But I didn't, because this was what I'd wanted, right? This...fucking torture.

Instead, I nodded. "Yes."

"Yes?" Killion whispered, his eyes shining brightly.

That word resounded, moving deeper, making me colder. I looked out the tinted windows as we left the house behind and turned onto a main road. I wanted to track every turn and every mile we drove. But I couldn't. Darkness wrapped itself around my mind and sank its claws in deep. I was spiraling down.

Killion watched me with the kind of excitement that should have terrified me. Only, when I met that gaze, I felt nothing. No fear, no excitement...just nothing.

We drove, taking what looked like back roads until we pulled alongside a towering fence and stopped at the same gates my brother had crashed into yesterday. Only this time, they opened for us. The driver's window rolled down and he spoke to the guard. Then we were driving through, heading to the building in the distance.

The place was big...stretching quite a way across the grounds. I swallowed hard as my pulse picked up pace.

Killion watched my every move. So I forced myself to be careful, scanning the building with little interest. "Another party?"

"No." Killion leaned forward as the limousine came to a stop. "Even better."

The driver was out of the car in an instant and opening his door. Killion climbed out, adjusted his jacket, and lifted his gaze. The place was massive. A gray concrete, hostile-looking place. There was no name outside, nothing but a team of guards who headed our way.

"Killion."

The stony, careful tone came from behind us. The steel front door was open, and The Principal stood inside. He met Killion's gaze before moving to mine. "Mr. Banks." He stepped to the side. "Welcome to the Order."

Panic moved through me as I stepped inside. I fought the need to charge ahead, to throw open every door and tear down every wall until I found her. But one wrong move and this was over.

I still wasn't convinced I had them fooled. This could be a way to lure me here, then handcuff and imprison me. Hell, to even kill me to get me out of the way. So I decided to play it safe. "I still don't even know why we're here." I raised my brow and scanned the expansive foyer. "Or what this place is."

"Oh, I think you'll enjoy what we have to offer very much." The Principal smiled. "After all, you've already had a taste."

He led the way along a wide corridor to a set of double doors that were locked. My pulse raced as I watched him press a card against the scanner and wait for the doors to swing wide.

"A little intense," I muttered.

Killion gave me a careful smile as he strode forward. "Can't be too careful, can we?"

Careful...that was one way to put it. I clenched my jaw and followed, our steps ringing loud. Now where the fuck was Ryth?

# TWENTY

*ryth*

"WHAT ARE YOU DOING HERE?" The Principal stepped into the office, scanned the desk, then settled those cold gray eyes on us.

We stood pressed against the wall, as far away from the phone as possible. I didn't dare look at the receiver where I'd all but thrown it in a desperate need to cover up my call to Nick. One wrong move and he'd see it. One wrong move and he'd—

"The Teacher..." Vivienne started, her eyes wide. "Said to come for you."

There was a scowl and a flex of his jaw. He was pissed at that.

Still Vivienne kept going, her voice trembling as she spoke. "Mr. St. James caused a scene." Her fingers trembled as she reached for her jaw and the red marks that the bastard had left behind. "The Teacher...he had to step in."

The Principal crossed the room in an instant, grabbed her around the neck, and shoved her against the wall. *"Master,"* he snarled, his lips curling as he leaned close. "He is your *fucking Master and you will respect him as one.*"

Vivienne's eyes widened.

But then he pulled away, almost like he'd forgotten himself for a second...*no, not forgot himself. More like showed his true face.* He was dangerous, more dangerous than Lazarus Rossi...more dangerous than my own mother.

The Principal sucked in a deep breath, those cruel eyes flicking to me. "Let's not have this discussion again."

He flinched, then reached into his pocket and pulled his phone free. "Back to your rooms," he instructed. "Immediately."

We scurried past him and out into the hall. Her hand found mine as we raced toward the double doors. We barely reached them before movement came through the glass sections of the doors up ahead. A guard strode toward us, leaned over to press his card against the scanner, and opened the doors, heading for the one where we stood.

"What the fuck do we do?" I whispered, risking a glance over my shoulder. But The Principal hadn't followed us out.

"I don't know." Vivienne's hand tightened around mine.

The guard pressed his card to the scanner and opened the door. He didn't even need to say anything, just stood to the side and waited for us to step through.

"Our rooms," Vivienne murmured.

"You're not going to your rooms," the guard answered. Then he motioned us forward, back along the halls and toward the classroom. "We have company coming."

My heart sped with the words. I glanced toward Vivienne as her face grew pale. Company...what did that mean? But we passed the classroom and the wall where Vivienne had been held against her will and toward another room further along the hall.

Darkness spilled out of the open doorway up ahead. I

shook my head, my steps slowing as Vivienne reached the entrance.

"Move," the guard gave me a shove, sending me forward. I tried to clutch Vivienne's hand, but she was ripped from me as the guard pushed between us and into the murky gloom. "Over there."

I followed and stepped inside, taking in the steel gray blinds and long black plush leather sofas. Other women stood along the wall of the room, casting glances our way as we were pushed forward.

"Line up," the guard ordered.

I made my way toward the others, turning to stand with those wearing white. The color somehow protected us, for now. We waited in silence. Every sound sent a tremble of fear through me. Vivienne said nothing. I glanced her way, hoping for some kind of strength, but she had none to give.

The slow, heavy thud of male steps echoed. I counted one set, then another....and another.

Was it the Teacher? Did they find out about the call? I swallowed hard as shadows spilled across the doorway.

The Principal stepped into the room, those dead, gray eyes sweeping along the room, lingering a little too long on me before turning away. Another man followed, an older guy with gray hair and dark eyes that sparkled with excitement. He smiled as he followed The Principal in, his gaze scanning the rest of us. "I told you," he murmured. "Exquisite."

Movement drew my gaze as another shadow spilled across the doorway...and a man stepped inside.

My heart stuttered.

My body froze.

*It was Caleb...CALEB!* I started forward, hope surging inside me as he scanned the room, those perfect hazel eyes finding mine before he looked away. *He looked away...*

I stopped, barely half a step away. Vivienne lashed out, grabbed my wrist, and jerked me back into line as my step-brother murmured a reply. "They are stunning."

# TWENTY-ONE

## caleb

"THEY'RE UTTERLY PERFECT." Killion turned to glance back at me. "Are they not, Caleb?"

I couldn't answer, couldn't move. To see her standing there, dressed like...*one of them* was almost too much to bear. Her eyes widened, and a look of relief washed over her as our gazes collided.

She started forward, and it was all I could do not to lunge across the goddamn room and take her in my arms. But one wrong move, and *they'd know.* Doors. Guards. Men with machine guns. They all stood between us. Right now, we didn't stand a chance. I gave a tiny shake of my head, cast a careful glance toward The Principal, and forced myself to answer. "They are."

"You can choose any one you want." Killion strode toward the ones dressed in red. "You can own her, anyway you want."

"As long as the contract is complete," that sick fuck growled at my side. "With payment, of course."

I clenched my jaw and forced the words through clenched teeth. "Of course."

The woman next to Ryth grabbed her hand and yanked her

back into line. The movement drew Killion's attention. Like a hunting shark, he narrowed in, looking past the others to Ryth. "Who do we have here?"

*No...Jesus, no.*

He left those dressed in red and black behind...until he reached the white. "New recruits?" He glanced at the bastard behind me.

"Some," The Principal answered. "One is under contract already, but only as a ward. She's not yet...broken."

Killion turned back to Ryth, standing last in the line. Panic thrummed in my head, the sound booming. I cleared my throat and kept on walking, heading to the opposite end of the line. I didn't see them. I *couldn't* see them. All I saw in the corner of my eye was Killion as he moved one girl closer. "This one." He stopped in front of Ryth and reached up, grabbing her face cruelly. "Is ruined."

The pink birthmark reddened under his grasp.

*No...not ruined.*

*Special.*

"She's...perfect," Killion murmured as he yanked her closer. "I want her."

"*No!*" She shoved away from him, jerking her gaze to me. "*Get the fuck off me!*"

"Ryth is new," The Principal declared as he stepped closer. "She doesn't yet understand."

"But she will, won't you, little one?" Killion spun her around and pressed her against the wall. "I'll make her."

Rage punched through me with an icy fist. I took a step. "He said she's not for sale."

But the bastard barely heard me. He yanked Ryth's negligee up and kneaded her ass with his filthy fucking hand. "I don't care."

"*Fuck you!*" She bucked, driving him backwards. She was so

goddamn small, dwarfed by his size and power. Killion liked that. He liked them small and weaker. But she wasn't weak— not when she was with us.

The image of her and Nick came roaring back to me. Her words echoed in my head. *Get on your fucking knees, Nick. Just get on your goddamn knees.* She was ours. She was...*mine.*

My past and present collided. Her and us. Our forbidden torment, then the brutality in this room. Killion grabbed her wrists with one hand, and lifted to pin them to the wall.

"That mark on your face looks like the mark of a hand," Killion growled in her ear. "Like you've been beaten." He moaned, pinching her nipple. "You like to be beaten?"

She moaned in agony and that sound was a knife to my fucking chest. *I'm going to kill him! I'm going to tear his fucking—*

Something had to be done. I had to — "This one." I grabbed a woman in red at the far end of the line.

Killion stopped mauling my fucking stepsister and watched me.

"She is beautiful," The Principal murmured, and stepped closer. "Olivia is quiet and vulnerable, trained in all the ways a man might require her to be."

She's trained...

That alone should sicken me. But it didn't. I grabbed her around the back of her neck and pulled her forward.

"*No. Don't do this,*" my stepsister moaned, betrayal etched in her tone. I knew who her words were meant for. She'd rather be at the mercy of a fucking monster like Killion than to see me touch another woman. I was hurting her...*this was hurting her.*

I had to force that out of my head. I had to focus. I was so close now. So *fucking* close. Couldn't she see what I was doing? *Couldn't she see this was just a game?*

Killion watched me as he pushed my stepsister against the wall. She struggled, his hand around her throat, the other sliding over her ass to yank the white lace negligee higher. "Just a taste. Surely you can allow me that."

I grabbed this woman, my fingers clenched tight, finding the taut tendons that ran alongside her neck. "I could press this right here." I dug my fingers in. "Make your entire world turn to darkness. Would you like that? Slipping in and out of consciousness while I fuck you?"

"Dear God," Killion murmured. "You really are just like me, aren't you?"

She let out a whimper, filled with shock and desire. That sound vibrated through my fingers and permeated the room. The thought of us being the same made me sick to my stomach. Killion was a weak, pathetic piece of shit. A sick fucking sadist who didn't give a fuck about pleasure, he was all about pain.

He had no idea what it meant to deny and give all at once. How her pleasure was a fucking playground, how you could be so fucking tender and brutal all at the same time. How you could give and give, and all the while, the moans were for you. Those tiny gasps *were for you*. How this was as much for *her* as it was for me.

*For Ryth, you mean...*

I closed my eyes as her name filled me.

It was Ryth I spoke to. Ryth I felt against my body. Ryth I wanted more than air to breathe. I tightened my fingers, feeling the frantic throb race. "Have you ever been licked as you pass out?"

The woman moaned against me.

As hunger rose inside me, I pushed against her. I leaned down, my breath dancing across her ear. "I'm going to ride this sweet, young body, princess. Gonna fuck you hard and slow and as you scream my name. I'm going to tighten just a little as I suck your clit and eat your pussy." I pressed against the vein in her neck, making her buck in fear, then eased my hold. "Then I'll release as you come. We're going to do that over... and over...*and over, princess*. By morning, all you'll manage is a whisper, from all the fucking screaming you'll do. I'll bruise you, and you'll love every goddamn minute of it."

In the corner of my eye, Ryth's chest rose with a breath. But Killion was no longer pushing her against the wall. I turned until I faced him, desperate for him to see what he could have right now.

*Come on...come on, you fucking bastard.*

I held his stare, those dark eyes shining with excitement. I pulled this woman against me, this woman who was nothing more than a fucking diversion. My gaze wavered, but I tried to hold his focus. I couldn't look at Ryth, couldn't see tears shimmering or her look of fucking betrayal. Not yet...because I wasn't done with my deception.

Not yet *FINISHED BREAKING HER FUCKING HEART*.

"You will be mine. You understand me?" I hissed, tightened my hand around her neck, and lifted until her body stretched taut. "You'll be fucking mine until I'm done with you."

Killion released his hold around my stepsister and moved closer. "Olivia, you said her name was?"

The woman nodded meekly, but it wasn't her submission I wanted. Fuck, I was rock hard, my cock driving against my zipper. The fantasy of Ryth was almost painful. "Yes," she whispered, just like she'd been trained.

My focus slipped...I met Ryth's stare, my cock twitching, desperate for release. I wanted her...I wanted her so fucking badly. I wanted to kiss her, to taste her. To have her back in that pantry once more. Only this time I wouldn't stop, not even with her mom mere feet away.

This time I'd fuck her against the canned foods. I'd fuck her until her legs shook and her pussy throbbed.

This woman moaned, driving her ass against me, her warmth pressed against my shaft. I wanted to come...wanted to —

"Can't be tender," I growled. "I'm going to be a beast to you. You'll fucking hate me and want me at the same time."

"No." Ryth stumbled backwards. "No..."

"I'll take her." Killion strode forward, stopping in front of us. In the howling desperation of the room, no one heard Ryth as she cried. No one but me.

I sucked in a hard breath. "You want her, Killion?"

His chilling smile grew wider. "I do, do you have a problem with that?"

That's what this had come down to, wasn't it? It was all a game for men like him, always a fucking game. I dropped my hand from around her neck and pushed her forward, leaving her to stumble toward a monster. "No, not at all."

My body screamed for release, but it was my soul that was trapped in that pit of darkness inside me. A place I knew I'd never come out of.

"Draw up the contract," Killion instructed. "I'll take this one tonight."

"Very well," The Principal murmured.

I tore my gaze from my stepsister to his. That stony focus never flinched, not once. He gave a jerk of his head and the guards moved forward, taking the rest of the women from the room. Ryth was the last one to leave, the last one to walk past me, and as she did, I turned my gaze toward her as she spat.

Spittle flew through the air and landed on my cheek.

I wore it.

I deserved it.

*No, I deserved more.*

Agony filled those blue-gray eyes of hers as she was led away. Killion and The Principal stared, but they said nothing, waiting for me to call for her to be beaten. After all, she was a nobody, right?

The anguish that filled my chest said otherwise.

"Let's go," I murmured. "I want out of here."

Killion nodded, his gaze turning to his prize. "I couldn't agree more."

# *caleb*

I WAS numb when we walked out of that place. Empty when we climbed back in the limousine, and broken when we drove away.

"You are lovely, aren't you?" Killion tugged Olivia's negligee down, exposing her breasts as we drove through the gates. "Pity you missed out on this one, Caleb. I'm sure there'll be others."

I nodded and felt nothing. "I'm sure there will be."

A low, sickening chuckle spilled from the piece of shit as he fondled her. "Although, I am sorry I cut you out. Let me make it up to you." His dark eyes were fixed on me. He truly was a sadistic sonofabitch. "You name it and it's yours, anything you want."

My heart thundered. *Then turn the car around and take me back there. Give her back to me.* I held his gaze, the words screaming in my mind. But would he? Would he really or was he fucking playing me? It was just his style, tease me just enough to have me desperate, then snatch it all away.

If I showed my hand, he'd know, and this would all have been for nothing. I had to remain in control for Ryth's sake. I swallowed hard and turned to stare out the window. "I'll let you know," I murmured.

My mind raced, on one hand, desperate to have her back, and not fuck it all up on the other. I lifted my hand and touched the remnant of her rage on my cheek as a whimper sounded in the car. But it wasn't a sound of desire—it was one of pain. Acid burned in the back of my throat. I was going to be sick, vomit all over this nice new leather like a fucking kid.

Every mile was agony.

Every second, torment.

Every whimper from the woman across from me was a nail in my coffin.

"I need to get back to The Black Room for my car." The words are strained so much, he'd barely be able to hear me.

"Swing by the club, driver," Killion demanded. "I think our guest has had enough of our company for one evening."

Bright lights of the city sparkled up ahead. I didn't have to lift my gaze to know he was watching me. I couldn't meet that gaze, not anymore. Instead, I closed my eyes and tried to keep my shit under control. A hurricane howled inside me, one that needed to get out.

I opened my eyes to faintly familiar streets before the limousine pulled into a side street, and turned, stopping at the rear of the club where hours ago I'd met Evans and climbed into his Bentley. Hours ago. I yanked the handle before the car pulled to a stop. It may as well have been a lifetime.

"Caleb."

The night air was rushing in as Killion murmured. As the door cracked open, I stopped. "I had fun tonight. I hope we can do it again...*soon.*"

Soon...

Revulsion burned in my gut as I shoved the door closed behind me. My gaze fixed on the blue shine up ahead, like it was my last hope for salvation. That hurricane roared as the limousine pulled away. I shoved my hand into my pocket and pressed the button on my key fob, all but lunging for my driver's door.

Lights flashed before I slumped behind the steering wheel and yanked the door closed. *No,* her voice resounded. The betrayal. The pain...*the look in her eyes as I left, knowing I'd failed her.* I lashed out, punching the steering wheel. *"FUCKING PIECE OF SHIT!"*

I'd done that to her.

I'd done that...*to*...*her.*

My hands shook as I stabbed the button, starting the engine. Then it all hit me. I shoved open the door and fell forward and remnants of top shelf Scotch burned in my throat as I heaved and retched.

*No.*

Ryth whimpered.

*No.*

*No.*

*No.*

Shadows moved across the concrete in front of me. Someone yanked the door wider, tearing it from my grasp before I was grabbed and dragged from the car. I lashed out, but all I hit was steel before I was slammed onto the concrete. Agony carved through the side of my face as the cold and stench of my own foulness hit me. I was lifted, hauled upwards, and slammed against the side of my car.

"You fucking *disgust me!*"

I jerked my gaze up, staring at my brother. "Tobias."

He was wrath in that moment, his dark eyes even darker than I'd ever seen before. Haunted, frightening. I shifted my gaze behind him, to find Nick standing there, staring at me.

"You're out here partying, brother?" The disgust in Nick's

voice was wounding. "You're out here while *our fucking sister is in that awful place?*"

I shook my head, but the words wouldn't come.

Faint parking lot lights glinted off the steel as Tobias lifted a gun. My knees buckled, my brother's hold no match for Hell's pull. I crumbled, hitting the asphalt beside the car. "Do it." The words burned. "I deserve it. I deserve it all for what I did to her tonight."

The night stopped cold.

"What did you do, brother?" There was no trace of my kin in Tobias' voice. The bite of the muzzle pressed against my head. "Tell me. I really want to know."

"I betrayed her." I lifted my head, meeting that stare. "I fucking left her in that place."

Nick flinched and took a step closer. "What the fuck are you talking about?"

I opened my mouth to tell them, trying to find some resemblance of hope in what I'd done tonight. But there wasn't any. There were just the screams of the women I'd betrayed to do what?

*Nothing.*

*I'd done absolutely nothing.*

"I tried. I fucking tried." I clenched my fists. "Don't you see that? *DON'T YOU FUCKING SEE THAT?*"

My scream rebounded in the night. I lashed out, grabbing Tobias' wrist and pressed the gun harder against my head. "Do it. *Just fucking do it!*" My screams echoed in the night. I slumped against the car, defeated. *"I can't live like this. I can't not see her in that place. I can't..."* Not see what Killion did to her.

"You saw her?" Nick whispered.

The gun wavered, pulling away. "No." I yanked Tobias closer, holding that hateful stare. *"No!"*

"I think you'd better start talking, C," Nick demanded. "And you'd better do it now."

They hated me. Fuck, they hated me. Tears blurred my brother's face. But it was nothing compared to Ryth's empty stare that burned in my mind. "I failed her. I failed her and I don't know what to do."

Tobias leaned down, his body moving into the wash of light. There was blood splatter all over him, flecks of red so dark they looked black on his skin. I glanced at his hands and winced. They were bloody...and not just a smear. I jerked my gaze to his eyes. I wasn't the only one wearing sin this night.

"Let's get one thing straight," my little brother growled. "I don't give a fuck about your conscience. Hold out on us again and I'll blow it all over the hood of your nice fucking car. Got that, *brother?*"

He would, too.

My breath wouldn't come. But I forced the words, anyway. "She's alive," I started. "But she's in danger."

"She called me," Nick stated. "Said the same thing."

I shook my head. "We have to get her out of that place. We have to get her away from..." *The Principal.*

"What the fuck are they doing to her?" Tobias demanded.

*Get the fuck off me!* Her screams resounded. "Nothing good."

"Get the fuck up," Nick growled. "We're going home."

"Straight home, C." Tobias punched the muzzle of the gun into my side. "Don't make me come after you."

I gave a nod as Tobias scanned the parking lot and tucked the gun away in the small of his back before both of my brothers left, striding toward the front of the club. They were strangers to me in that moment. But maybe that wasn't it... maybe I was the one who had strayed from our bond. I was the one they didn't know anymore. I was the one they didn't trust.

My arm shook as I pushed off the car, stepped around the open door, and slipped behind the wheel. The Lamborghini jerked and jolted under my heavy-handed shifting of the gears as I pulled out of the parking lot and headed home.

Part of me dreaded seeing my brothers again, another part was relieved, desperate to shed the weight of this burden. I clenched my hands around the wheel, carefully driving the streets all the way home. The lights were on inside the house when I pulled into the driveway.

Funny, I'd never felt this goddamn alone, not even after mom died, and yesterday when I'd almost lost my brother. Those moments paled in comparison to this walk of shame. I pushed the door open, hearing a pained whimper, then my brother's gentle voice. "Easy, sweetheart. Easy now. I'm not going to hurt you."

I walked into the kitchen and found Nick shirtless, cradling a wounded puppy. "What the fuck happened?"

Nick shot me a glare over his shoulder. "You weren't the only one who had one helluva night. Grab that towel there." He nodded to a dish towel. I strode forward, desperate for some kind of purpose. "Hold it to her wound."

"What the fuck happened?" I pressed the towel gently against her side and a faint smear of blood soaked into the white. "Whose dog is this?"

"Mine," Nick muttered, his focus fixed on the task of checking her entire body and wincing at every whimper. "We need to get her checked over by a vet."

"Later," Tobias insisted behind me.

I straightened at his icy tone, and turned.

"Right now," Tobias started, tugging a clean shirt over his head as he stopped at the other side of the counter. "I want to hear what our brother has to say."

Nick stopped tending to the puppy and instead cradled her

159

against his body, stroking her head. "Start talking, C, and it better be good."

I gave a nod, not knowing where to start. How the fuck could I tell them what I'd done...*no, what I was.* "We needed a way in to that place, so I found one." I broke Tobias' stare.

"How?" Nick demanded.

I shook my head. "Does it matter?"

Tobias gripped the counter, the movement drawing my gaze. There was dried blood between his fingers and in the beds of his nails. I didn't have to ask what had happened. It was all there in those dark, unflinching eyes. "Yes," he forced through clenched teeth. "It does."

"I went to a sex club, a sadistic, vile fucking sex club with a man I wish I'd never fucking met, to gain entrance to an exclusive club. The kind of club that buys women from places like the Order."

Tobias went still. So still, he didn't breathe.

"What the fuck are you saying?" Nick stepped closer, his hand falling from the pup. "They traffic the women?"

I nodded, my stomach sinking. "Yes. That's exactly what they're doing."

*No...no, get the fuck off me!* Ryth screamed. In my head, I replayed Killion's hands roaming over my sister.

"Ryth is in that place?" Nick's voice was a whisper.

I stared at Tobias. "Yes."

"Has she been..." My youngest brother started and stopped, his face turning a shade of gray as he looked away.

"I don't know," I answered. "I just don't know."

"But you saw her, right?" Tobias met my stare. "You saw her tonight."

*Get the fuck off me!* She raged inside my head. I couldn't tell them what Killion had done to her, couldn't tell them, I'd stood by and watched it all. "Yes, I saw her."

"Then you know how to get in." Nick moved closer, holding my stare. "You know how to get in."

I nodded. *Anything you want, Caleb. Anything at all,* Killion urged. "Yes, I know how to get in. But we need to be very careful. If they even *think* we're there to get her out, they'll kill her and us."

"They won't," Tobias snarled. "We won't let them."

*ryth*

WHITE WALLS BLURRED AROUND ME. The thud of my steps sounded distant and strange. But the thrashing sound of my heart was a deafening, terrifying roar consuming my head.

Vivienne glanced my way as we left that room behind. Spittle dried on my lips. My stepbrother hadn't come here to save me. He'd come here...*to buy one of us for sex.*

My knees buckled at the thought. I fell and hit the floor hard. Agony carved through my knees.

"Easy, now," Vivienne whispered as she grabbed my arm and hauled me to my feet.

*He wasn't here for me...*

*He wasn't...*

A sob tore free as I stumbled forward.

"Keep moving," the guard snapped as we slowly stumbled past.

Vivienne shot him a glare as we moved with the others. But my steps slowed again, my feet refusing to move. I wanted to go back there, to tear through the door and slam into him. I wanted to beat him until he was bloody. I wanted to hurt him how I was hurting. I wanted to...

I wanted to...

*Touch him, to hold him. I wanted him to hold me and tell me everything was alright. That he was here to take me from this place.* That he wasn't like all those others. But then that would be a lie.

I'd seen it in his cold eyes when he'd grabbed that woman, as he'd held her against his body and whispered the same things in her ear that he'd whispered in mine.

He was a fucking player. A goddamn *piece of shit!* No, he was worse than that. He was the kind of man who saw me as property, to use and discard whenever he wanted. I couldn't believe I'd felt something for him. I couldn't believe I'd —

"Ryth," Vivienne hissed, and cast a panicked glance further along the hall.

Out of the shadows came the white-haired guard, his hungry steps eating up the distance as he scanned the line of us and stopped at me.

"We have to move," Vivienne whimpered, and yanked me forward. "Now!"

I let Vivienne pull me along with the others through the set of double doors, but the moment the savage guard neared, he cut across the hall and grabbed me, driving me backwards into the wall. "You have something to say to me?"

I lifted my gaze, seizing his. He was pissed, and it didn't take a genius to figure out why. We'd broken into The Principal's office and used his phone. I clenched my jaw, jutting my chin upwards. "How about, *fuck you?*"

His lips curled back as rage ignited in his eyes. Behind me, the faint sound of male voices spilled out.

*This one is ruined...*

Those words rose. I could still feel his hands on me, my

face, my ass...my breasts. My stomach clenched, recoiling from the memory.

"Try a goddamn stunt like you did in that room again and you won't have to worry about being sold to the highest bidder." He pushed against me until the warmth of his breath blew across my cheek. "I'll take you for myself."

I clenched my jaw, biting down on a whimper, and turned my gaze away.

He leaned harder, crushing me against the wall. "I'm coming for you, Castlemaine. I'm fucking coming—"

"Please," Vivienne whispered, yanking my hand. "She didn't mean it."

Desperation flared in her wide, terrified eyes. The weight of the guard's glare was heavy, but he made no move to stop Vivienne as she wrenched me free. My bare feet slapped the hard floor as I staggered away.

"Meal room." Another guard motioned along the hallway. "Now."

I followed, feeling nothing but the icy sting of betrayal. I had no room for pain or fear, no room for anything other than the burning rage boiling inside.

"Come on," Viv hissed, yanking me harder as we followed the others inside the dining room. She pushed me toward a table, making me take a seat.

I slumped down on the seat, just sitting there, staring at the table. "He betrayed me," I whispered.

Vivienne leaned close, watching the others as she hissed, "What the fuck are you talking about?"

"Caleb." I lifted my gaze to hers. "I thought he came for me, but he didn't."

She stiffened as the realization dawned. "That man..." she froze, mouthing the words. *That man was your brother?*

I could only nod, the words too brutal to speak.

Her chest rose hard. "But you just." *Called him.*

"It was the oldest." I shook my head, my shoulders slumping forward as tears pricked my eyes. "Caleb."

She sat back, watching from the corner of her eye as the other girls moved along the counter, grabbing food and drink. I had no idea what time it was, if it was day or night, or if I'd been in this place a week or a lifetime. Right now, I didn't care.

"You need to eat something," Vivienne urged.

My stomach clenched. The thought of food was sickening. I shook my head. "I can't. But you...you need to." I really looked at her for the first time, saw how she was fearless, tearing me away from that guard, even if it drew attention to herself. "Why are you helping me? Why do you care?"

She swallowed and glanced at the others sitting across the room before she answered. "I told you."

"I don't believe you," I whispered. "There has to be more."

Her cheeks burned as she looked away. "If you're not going to look after yourself, then that's your concern. Me, I'm going to eat, because I need the energy." *To run.* She didn't need to say the words. Still, she cut me a glare that said just as much as she rose and made her way to the counter.

I stared at the table, feeling that stab of agony move deeper. He was out there, walking down these halls, leaving me behind like I meant nothing to him.

Slick tears slipped free, gathering momentum as they rolled down my cheeks. I flicked them away as Vivienne returned with two cut sandwiches and two containers of juice. She slid one plate across the table my way, then followed with the drink. We said nothing, just like the others. But that empty quiet drew my focus. I glanced across the dining room, catching sight of one of the others dressed in red watching me with interest.

There was nothing comforting in her stare.

Nothing that looked like Vivienne's at all. She didn't eat, didn't drink. Her dark eyes watched my every move. I forced myself to take a bite of the sandwich and swallow. But the bread stuck like a hard wad in the back of my throat, hurting as I washed it down.

"You need to keep your head down."

I glanced at Viv as she carefully observed the other girl. "You need to be careful here, Ryth." Her words were stony. "More now than ever before."

Shadows spilled across the doorway. I lifted my head as three men stepped inside. The Principal, the Teacher...and the Priest. My cheeks burned as I stared at him. I hadn't seen him since he'd had me abducted from that warehouse, leaving Nick bleeding.

*Nick...*

A pang tore across my chest when I thought of him. He was alive and coming for me. But when he found out about Caleb and what had happened tonight, he'd be savage...and he wasn't the only one. Tobias. My breath caught as he filled my mind. His rage-filled eyes lingered in my mind. He'd kill Caleb. He'd kill him and not think twice about it.

After he came for me.

*Please, God, let it be after he came for me.*

"You need to stay quiet tonight," Vivienne insisted as The Principal and the Teacher strode across the dining room.

Their cold gazes swept through the room, The Principal's stare lingering a little too long on me as his voice filled the space. "Classes will begin tomorrow. Some of you will attend a more *intense* level of training."

A more intense level of training.

That sinking feeling made me regret the bite of the sandwich.

"For now, you'll be escorted to your rooms." He stared at us...waiting.

Others were the first to rise, watching him as they skirted the tables and hurried toward the doorway. I rose along with Vivienne. But I didn't scurry around them like the others. Instead, I held The Principal's stare.

"Ms. Castlemaine," he murmured.

I wanted to lunge across the room and claw his fucking eyes out. I wanted to scream and rage, but my anger would do me no good. The tracking monitor smacked against my ankle as I walked. I was still a prisoner, either way.

*We're coming, Ryth!* Nick's words haunted me as I made my way out of the dining room and into the hall once more. We headed back to the dark, empty cells, each guard stepping close as we stepped inside. The doors closed, locking behind us with a thud.

The silence was the hardest part.

Because that's where the memories waited.

Memories of a time when I'd felt truly alive.

When Caleb wasn't the monster he'd been tonight. And my life had meaning other than to be sold like a piece of meat to the highest bidder. Lights dimmed outside in the hallway, leaving me to sit on the side of my bed in the dark.

Maybe every single moment I'd been with them was a lie? I pulled my feet up and wrapped my arms around my knees. Nick's desperation filled me. That kind of pain couldn't be faked. "He'll come," I whispered out loud. "He'll come."

I sat like that for a while before I lay down and tugged the blanket higher, covering the ugly fucking thing they made us wear day in and day out. I trembled with the cold and closed my eyes, willing myself to sleep.

Something clamped over my mouth. A bass voice growled quietly. "I told you I was coming for you, bitch."

I jerked open my eyes, my heart pounding as the hand across my mouth drove me into the mattress. In the washed-out light that spilled in from the hallway, I caught the shine of white hair...and I screamed.

The sound barely ripped through the room, muffled and raw, burning in the back of my throat. I slapped him away, but he was too strong, his other hand wrapping around my throat as he yanked me from the bed. Agony cleaved through my head as I hit the concrete hard. Sparks detonated behind my eyes, shocking me for a second. He cast a careful glance toward the door and dragged me onto the floor and out of sight from the door.

Before Nick's roar ripped through me...*and I fought.*

"*NO! NO! GET OFF ME!*" I struggled, clawing his face anywhere I could. He didn't care, turning his head as I went for his eyes, and yanked my negligee, tearing it from my breasts.

He was an animal. Cold. Mute. His determination glinting in those dark eyes. I kicked and screamed as his hand mauled my breast and pinched my nipple. But it didn't matter. He held tight and clawed, pawing me as he grabbed my panties and yanked.

I bucked, terror moving deep. Outside, a shrill alarm sounded.

"Fuck!" The bastard jerked his gaze toward the hallway, then returned it to me. "I'll just have to be quick, won't I?"

His fist was a blur before it cracked against my face. My head snapped to the side. Agony bounced through my skull and for a second, I couldn't move. He took those seconds, fumbling with the button of his pants in a frenzy. In that dullness, I knew what was happening and what was about to happen. *Please, no!* Fear punched through my shock. I bucked and kicked, driving my knee up until I caught him in his side. He gave a grunt, his dark eyes squinting with pain. I punched and clawed, raked my nails down his cheek, and went for his eyes.

In the darkness, my aim was bad, but I hit something warm and soft. Something my nails sank into.

*"OW!"* he roared. *"Fucking bitch!"*

I kneed him again, driving even harder this time, and was rewarded with a grunt. Seconds were all I had. I kicked and shoved, driving him backwards, and scurried out from underneath him. My panties were gone. My lace negligee was in tatters, and out in the hallway, that piercing alarm continued to sound.

A dull glow came from the guard's pocket before his phone rang. I stumbled backwards, my breaths punching through my chest as I howled, *"Get the fuck away from me!"*

Thunder approached out in the hallway.

Shouts came next as doors were thrown open and slammed against the walls with a *bang!* The guard shoved upwards as my door was opened...and two guards rushed in. The overhead lights were flicked on, the glare harsh.

"What the fuck, Tig?" One guard looked at my attacker, then at me.

"What the hell is going on here?"

I glanced at the doorway as The Principal stepped into my room. He took one look at me, then at the bastard he called loyal. "Tig? The fire alarm is sounding."

But the white-haired bastard didn't answer, just glared my way. There were bloody marks down his cheeks, and one of his eyes was dripping, the slick still coating my nails. I sucked in a harsh breath, my body trembling and shuddering.

"Ryth!"

I jerked my gaze to Vivienne as she tore from a guard's hold outside my room and lunged through the doorway.

"Peter, escort Ms. Castlemaine and Ms. Brooks to the infirmary."

"Yes, sir," the guard muttered, then with a jerk of his head, he snapped, "With me."

But I couldn't move...my feet were frozen. Until The Principal stepped closer, headed for my bed, and yanked the blanket free before striding toward me. Warmth closed around me as he dragged the blanket over my shoulders and wrapped it across my front, those dark eyes piercing. "Now, Ryth. Don't make me tell you again."

I took a slow step away from him...then raced toward Vivienne.

# *caleb*

"GO OVER IT AGAIN," Nick demanded as he tended to the damn dog.

I stared at its shaved body and its sad eyes as it sat on Nick's lap, looking at him lovingly.

"We went over this already," I protested. "I think I'm good."

"Then we go over it again." Tobias strode from the kitchen carrying two bottles of electrolytes. I lifted my hand, reaching for mine...but it never came. There was just a savage stare from my youngest brother as he handed Nick one bottle, then cracked the top open on his own.

The tension between us was brutal. After last night, it was going to take a miracle for them to trust me again—if ever. I lowered my hand and started talking, replaying the same details over again. It was the fifth time we'd gone over it. Once last night, twice more this morning while we waited at the vet's office, and once again when we came back home.

It didn't matter how many times I went over it. There was still that element of doubt...because anything and everything could go wrong. "I call Killion. Tell him I want to go back in."

"Demand," Tobias snarled. "You *demand* to go back in. That sick fuck owes you. So you make him pay, anyway you damn well have to."

I swallowed the bitter tang of anger and held Tobias' stare. "I demand."

He gave a slow nod, then turned away. Something had broken in my brother. Some innate part that made him the kid I knew. Maybe it'd been worn away for a long time...and maybe it'd never been there all along.

"I demand to go back in there."

"He won't let you drive in," Nick said as he petted the mutt. "That place isn't open to just any visitors. He'll want his driver to take you."

"And if Killion decides to come with you?" Tobias watched me.

He didn't think I had the balls to carry through with this, didn't think I had the *stomach* to do what needed to be done. Only he didn't know about the things Killion had done to our sister, or the depraved depths I'd sunk to, to stop him going any further. I glanced at Nick, then back. "I'll kill him, along with the driver."

"Good." Tobias gripped the gun he'd had since last night. A gun I hadn't seen before. He stepped forward, handing it over. "Take out as many of those fuckers as you can."

I took the weapon and reached around, tucking it inside the waistband of my jeans.

Nick rose and eased the wounded puppy down on a pile of blankets he'd dragged from the closet upstairs. He winced when he straightened, his hand pressing against his own wound. "We'll be waiting at the fence. All you have to do is get her there...and we'll take care of the rest."

"Make the call," Tobias growled. "I want this night over and our sister back."

I gave a nod. "As do I."

I grabbed my phone, scrolled through my contacts, and pressed Killion's number.

He answered on the third ring. "Caleb."

"You said whatever I wanted, right?" I glanced at Nick when I spoke.

"Yes." Excitement turned his voice husky. "Do you have something in mind?"

"Yes," I answered, my pulse racing a thousand miles an hour. "I want back in...I want one of them for myself."

I could almost hear him smile. "That's my boy."

---

I shifted nervously, adjusted my jacket, and glanced around the parking lot of the nightclub. It was already well past nine. A perfect time for the streets to be busy and for Killion to already have plans. He didn't say if he'd be accompanying me, even when I pressed him. That made me nervous. Almost as nervous as the gun at my back and the knife strapped to my leg.

Headlights washed over me, blinding for a second until they passed. I winced and turned my head as my eyes adjusted and the limousine pulled up alongside me.

"Mr. Banks," the driver called, rounding the rear to open my door. "Nice to see you again."

I just nodded and stared at the opening door as it revealed an empty seat. Relief washed over me as I slid inside and the door closed behind me.

He was behind the wheel in a second, putting the car in gear.

"Are we to pick Killion up on the way?" I asked.

"Sorry, Mr. Banks. Mr. Killion said to say, please forgive

him, but he had other plans for tonight. A night at home, he said, and he knew you'd understand."

I thought of Olivia and winced. I did understand, only too well. I sat back in the seat, sickened and thankful all at the same time. We pulled away from the nightclub and headed through the city, leaving the Lamborghini in the secure parking once more.

Every mile was excruciating. The gun dug into the small of my back, making me shift against the seat. The movement drew the driver's gaze. Fuck. Every second I was in here, I felt nervous. I swallowed and tried to breathe, but under the suit, I was sweating. I yanked my collar and leaned forward, aiming the vents into my face.

"Did you need the temperature adjusted, sir?"

*Shit.* I straightened.

I was drawing too much attention to myself. "No, it's fine... thank you."

The driver just nodded, sneaking glances my way as we headed out of the city and left the bustle behind. I tried to focus on the road ahead and forced myself not to think about what was about to happen. Every second was torture. I was torn between the desperate need to see her once more and the gutting betrayal I'd seen in her eyes. I turned my head and looked out the window as darkness swallowed the car.

Shortly, the familiar sight of the towering fences appeared outside my window. The limousine slowed at the gates, and the driver rolled down his window. I was thankful I was accompanied, even though I knew what I had to do to have that security. The driver spoke to the guard for a brief moment before the window rolled back up and the gate opened.

We were through in an instant, soon rolling up to the front door. My pulse was booming. The sound was so loud, I knew they'd hear it. *Just keep calm...don't fuck this up.* Thoughts raced through my mind. The fantasy of me openly firing at everyone and everything that stood between me and Ryth played out in my head as the limousine came to a stop and the driver climbed out.

I swallowed hard as the door opened. There was a guard there, waiting for me with a stony expression.

"Mr. Banks," he said as I climbed out. "The Principal has offered his regrets at not being able to meet you tonight. Unfortunately, he was otherwise engaged."

I adjusted the button on my jacket and tried to keep calm. "I understand," I murmured.

"He asked me to escort you to the dining room. You can take a closer inspection of the assets."

*Assets...*

I winced at the word. Heat rose inside me. Still, I forced myself to nod. "Fine."

The driver stayed behind. I glanced over my shoulder, then followed the guard inside. The thud of our steps rang out in the quiet. I should've felt a sense of relief when I stepped through the door. But I didn't. If anything, it made this all the more real.

"Sorry we haven't made more of an effort. We weren't really expecting anyone," the guard murmured.

He was fishing, waiting for me to say something. I kept my mouth shut and followed him to the double doors, watching him like a hawk as he stepped close and pressed his access card against the scanner before pushing through.

I counted three doors before the piercing wail of what sounded like a fire alarm rang out.

*"Fuck!"* the guard barked, and jerked his gaze upwards to the blinking red lights on the sensors. He jerked a panicked gaze my way. *"It's been going off all night and all damn day. There's no fire!"* he yelled over the noise.

I just stepped closer. *"If you need to go, that's fine. Just point me in the right direction!"*

*Please...PLEASE! Just leave me.*

He looked uncertain for a second, wincing as we stood under the shrill sound, then lifted his hand and unclipped his access card, and my heart all but stopped. *"Through those doors, turn right, through the next set, and you'll find them!"*

I took the card and nodded before I started walking, leaving him behind. My head thumped with the sound of the alarm as I hurried to the set of double doors, then glanced over my shoulder, catching sight of the guard hurrying back the way we'd come with a second card in his hand.

I pressed the card to the sensor and waited for it to turn green before pushing open the door. The sound didn't stop, if anything, it grew worse. I lifted my gaze, catching the biting scent of something electrical burning and fought the urge to smirk. I needed to hurry...*now*.

The muscles of my thighs tightened as I lengthened my stride. The plan was too fucking vague. Get Ryth and get her out of here as fast as I could...without getting either of us killed. I winced and kept walking, my heart booming as I stopped at the next set of doors. The hallway waiting for me through the glass section of the automatic doors seemed empty.

Movement in the glass drew my gaze. An icy touch slithered along my spine. Instinct punched through me as I caught a blur behind me in the stainless steel shine of the doors. A hand clamped over my mouth before I was jerked backwards.

I stumbled and threw out my arm, my fist driving through the air. *Fight!* That need inside me surged to the surface. But the surrounding hold was weak...and not a man's.

"You want to see your sister?" a feminine voice hiss filled my ear. "Then don't fucking fight me."

I jerked my gaze to the familiar face of the woman who'd protected Ryth last night. "You?" My voice was muffled under her hold.

"I saw the way you were last night. The way you looked at her, the way you fucking want her," she hissed. "You made that sick bastard leave her alone. So, the question is, Romeo. Are you here to fuck her, or fuck *with* her?"

Anger burned as I leaned toward her ear. "I'm here to get her *the hell out of here.*"

She searched my gaze for the lie, then gave a nod and released me. "That's what I was hoping for." One glance at the glass panel of the door and she turned back to me. "We don't have much time. You need to do exactly as I say, Romeo. You got me?"

"Whatever it takes."

Her smile was slow and chilling. "That's my dirty step-brother...now this is what you do..."

# caleb

I PUSHED through the door and glanced behind me. A flicker of movement disappeared around the corner of the hallway and the sound of Vivienne's steps faded as she hurried away. *That's it...run now.*

My pulse slowed, that hate moving deeper, all the way to my icy fucking heart. Vivienne had given me her instructions, all panic and fear. I didn't blame her. But I'd come with an agenda of my own.

My brothers were all fists and fury. But that wasn't me. I wasn't hot rage and bestial brutality. I was cold. Stony. Frigid all the way to my fucking core. I wasn't human. Not anymore. I needed information and there was only one man who could give it to me.

The Principal.

I lengthened my strides, heading into the belly of this beast as the fire alarm continued to spark and wail above me. She'd said the office was just up ahead. I scanned for guards, caught sight of the closed door further along the hall, and shifted my gaze to the electronic reader on the outside the door. The kind of lock no other door had.

A twitch came in the corner of my eye as I focused on the tiny blinking red lights. They were all I saw. *No.* Ryth's whisper came back to me. *Caleb, no.*

"I'm coming, princess," I whispered, then reached into my pocket, dragged out the illegal card reader, and set to work.

I slipped the end into the lock and pressed buttons as that heavy thud in my chest resounded...never once speeding. *You fucking get her out.* Tobias' words rang in my head. *Or you don't come back, understand me, brother?*

I understood...*perfectly.*

It wasn't his not-so-subtle threats that had made me stiffen. It was him. His brutality and his determination to do whatever it took to get Ryth back, regardless of how many damn laws he had to break. So here I was, breaking a few laws of my own.

Memories came back to me and that same single-minded focus I'd honed returned. I focused on the numbers on the screen of my device, watching as they scrolled. "Come on," I growled.

The harder you hid something from me, the more I wanted it.

Just like Ryth.

And all the secrets mom had held behind the locked doors of her office. Secrets we weren't to know about. Secrets about women and the men who used them. I was just a kid breaking into her office with a screwdriver before I was busted.

She upgraded her security to something tougher, more...electronic.

So I became smarter. I became colder and more fucking determined to find out what was behind those locks.

*Beep.*

The reader stopped scrolling. The tiny red blinking light turned green as the locks disengaged with a *click*.

I rose from my crouch, shoved the door open, and invaded the bastard's space. Papers littered his desk. I rounded the corner and grabbed a handful, hunting for what I needed. There had to be something here, something I could use to figure this all out. *Contract between London St. James and The Hale Order.*

I stopped, my pulse spiking. Contract? I lifted my gaze to the cracked open door, then returned it to the paper in my hand. My gaze scanned past the legal bullshit to the real details. *London St. James is hereby awarded Vivienne Brooks as his own personal ward for the purpose of preventing unauthorized disclosure of Confidential Information as defined below.*

It was a nondisclosure contract...but one like I'd never seen before.

His silence, bought and paid for by the degradation that was sure to come.

No wonder Vivienne wanted out. But what was one life worth to these bastards? And what the hell did this London St. James know that was so fucking important?

I scanned the contract again, then searched the rest of the papers on the desk for anything else I could use. The computer sat there, filled to the brim with their secrets. There was no way I'd be able to get access to their files, not without spending hours trying to find a way past their damn security. No doubt a place like this, trading in people's sin, would have the very best you could buy. If I'd had more time...

I grabbed my phone and laid the papers out on the desk, taking photos of all I could. Anything could be important. The wail of the fire alarm stopped. But my ears still rang with the sound.

*Thud...thud...thud.*

The sound wasn't my heartbeat. I pushed the papers back

into the pile and quickly stepped around the desk, taking a seat in a leather armchair, with a look of bored distaste.

Darkness filled the doorway before he froze, noticing me. The voice was deep and dangerous...and fucking familiar. "Excuse me. I didn't realize we had company."

I lifted my gaze to the black shirt and white clerical collar. It was *him* the fucking Priest who'd stood at the end of the altar and married my father to Ryth's mom. I met his stare. "I did have an appointment."

One brow rose as he scanned the room, his gaze shifting to the stack of papers. I unnerved him sitting here alone.

"You did?"

I rose, unleashing a sigh. "Maybe another time then, for the introductions," I muttered, and stepped toward him.

"Introductions?" He gave me a chilling, sinister smile. But there was no hint of recognition in his eyes, no hint that he recognized me at all.

I almost smiled. Instead, I held his stare, daring the bastard.

"I know you, don't I?" he said finally.

"Do you?"

I stepped closer as recognition bloomed in his gaze. "Banks," he murmured.

He barely got the word out before I reacted. I lunged, driving my body into his. But I didn't stop. I was already caught in this...until the end. In that moment, I didn't fight for my life...*I fought for Ryth's.*

I unleashed a roar that was primal and drove my fist into the side of his head. The Priest let out a grunt and stumbled to the side. But if I'd thought he was weak and cowering, then I was wrong. He turned, his lips curling as he lunged, hitting me hard enough to drive me onto the desk.

The gun bit into my back, the pain stabbing into my spine. I kicked out, punched my boot into the middle of his stomach, and drove him across the room.

There was no way to stop this. No way out that didn't lose her for good. Not now. My heart was in the driver's seat as I shoved off from the desk and lunged. I drove my fist into his jaw, watching his head crack to the side. There was a second where his eyes rolled back before his stunned expression gave way to rage. He unleashed a roar, *"GUA—"*

He never finished the word. I drove my head forward, slamming my forehead to his nose. Blood spurted, splashing against my cheek as a sickening crunch filled my ears. I drove my fist into his face once more. He stumbled, stunned, then fell to his knees.

I sucked in a hard breath, standing over him. "You took her away from me." My fists throbbed...I curled my fingers tighter. "And that cannot stand."

He lifted his gaze, his face a bloody mess as I cocked my fist and drove it down once more, connecting with his temple this time. He slumped to the floor in an instant, falling silent and unmoving.

I didn't even stop to check if he was breathing, just pulled out my gun, gripped it by the barrel and smashed it against the asshole's head. Hard breaths punctured my words. "Stay down, motherfucker."

I stepped over his body and pulled the door closed behind me as I tucked the gun back in place and walked back along the hallway. I moved faster now, lengthening my strides, then looked down.

Blood splattered my shirt. I winced at the sight and reached for the buttons. My fingers pulsed, barely working, as I opened my shirt underneath my jacket as far as I could and hurried for the front of the building, praying to God Vivienne had made good on her promise...and gotten my damn step-sister out of here.

*ryth*

I WINCED as I looked at the bruises on my side. Cramps gripped my stomach like a fist—like *his* fist, the bastard who'd done this to me. The ache drove deeper the longer I stayed still. I bit down on a moan as I shifted on the bed, earning a stabbing glare from the nurse before she strode to the office at the far end of the infirmary.

They'd had a doctor come. He'd checked my bruises and my face. His cold eyes were emotionless as he probed the split on my lip, then left. That was this morning, yet they'd left me here...and Vivienne and I had this sinking feeling it was for a reason.

There were no classes.

No visits from old men who pawed my body and shoved their cock against my ass...and no visits from stepbrothers who watched it unfold and then left, like it didn't matter. Like *I* didn't matter. I snuggled into the pillow and closed my eyes. White hair and cruel hands loomed behind my eyes, and panic ignited in my chest. But it was Caleb's cold stare that hurt me more. I turned over, curling my knees to my chest, and swallowed the pain.

"Wake up."

I opened my eyes and turned my head as Vivienne rounded the bottom of the bed. "What?"

She scanned the rest of the infirmary, finding only empty beds and the biting stench of antiseptic, then yanked the sheet back from my body. They'd given me cotton boxers to wear. White, of course, the same as the replacement negligee I wore. They were worried that the white-haired bastard they called Tig had raped me...

He almost had.

Viv leaned in, staring at me intently. "You don't look so well." She lifted her head, jerked her gaze toward the office at the end of the room. "Right?"

"What are you talking about?" I hissed.

Viv stepped closer. "You want out of this fucking place, then you're sick...*right the hell now, got it?*"

Panic rushed through me. There was desperation in her eyes...a reckless determination. She cast a glance toward the cabinets that ran the length of the infirmary, her gaze stopping on the stainless steel shine of one nearby.

I followed her focus, then froze. The tranquilizer gun sat near the edge, within easy reach. My insides clenched at the sight. It was the same gun they'd used on me the first night they brought me here...and would use again.

I unleashed a moan at the sight. A small nod of her head, and Viv took a step backwards. My moan grew louder before I clutched my belly. I knew now. It was now or never...now...*or be fucking sold.*

"That's it," Viv whispered.

I deepened my moan and clutched my belly, drawing the nurse's gaze from across the room. *"Please, help me."*

Viv stepped backwards, moving toward the counter as the

nurse rushed forward, unwinding the stethoscope from her neck. "What's wrong?"

"My stomach." I whimpered and glanced to Viv. "Something is really wrong. My heart is racing."

The nurse pushed me back against the pillow. Cold metal from the stethoscope pressed against my skin. Confusion furrowed the nurse's brow as she opened her mouth to speak... but the words never came out. Vivienne lunged, grabbed the tranquilizer gun, and turned.

The nurse was too slow, her focus fixed on the panicked thudding of my heart. Viv grabbed the gun and turned, then strode up behind her, grabbed her around the neck with one hand, and pressed the gun to the other side.

*Pfft.*

The shot was almost silent. There was a second when the nurse's eyes widened. She fought for a moment, but I knew from experience it was useless. All she was doing was driving the drug harder through her system. I kicked out from under the bed sheets and lunged upright. *"Vivienne! What the fuck are you doing?"*

I threw a panicked gaze at the doorway—any moment the guard would come.

The nurse kicked and bucked, her mouth opening wide as she tried to scream for help. But there was no sound...just a hiss of air, until her eyes slowly rolled backwards, showing the whites, and her entire body slumped and was still.

"Finally." Vivienne sucked in hard breaths and dropped the nurse to the floor.

We were dead...we were so fucking dead. I looked from the nurse to Viv. "What the fuck have you done?"

She was slow, stumbling as she rose, then snatched the nurse's access card from the belt loop at her waist. "Like I said, Ryth. We're getting the fuck out of here."

Terror and desperation detonated through me as she staggered a step forward, grabbed my hand, and yanked me toward the door. We were moving before I knew it, slipping out of the infirmary with panicked looks behind us.

My pulse thundered, drowning out everything else around me. There was no way I'd hear the guards' steps if they came. Viv grabbed my hand and pulled me after her as we raced to the first set of locked doors.

She slammed the access card against the scanner and shoved through the doors.

We were through in an instant, and lunging toward the next set. My bare feet slapped against the floor until they stung. "Where are we going?"

"I told you." She forced the words through clenched teeth. "The fuck outta here."

Still, I yanked on her hold. "Viv...*Viv!*"

She stopped, turning to me with wide, panic-stricken eyes. *"What?"*

"Where the fuck are we going?"

Her chest rose, then fell. "Out of here."

I risked a glance over my shoulder. "How?"

"I have a plan. Trust me."

"I'm all for getting out of here, but if they catch us...if they catch us, Tig will be the least of our worries."

"They're not gonna catch us."

I winced at the words. Trust was hard to come by for me, especially now. But I let her grab my hand again and yank me toward the next set of doors. "Tell me this, why the fuck do you want out so bad, and don't give me any bullshit about liking what that man does to you! What's got you so freaked out...*Viv, tell me.*"

Viv stopped, and for the first time, I saw true fear in her

eyes. "I have my reasons, okay? Let's just say I want nothing to do with what's about to go down."

*What's about to go down?*

The words rose in my head, but I didn't get a chance to speak them. I shoved forward, racing to what looked like an access door to the outside. Steel barred our way.

"What's about to go down?" The words punched through gasping breaths.

She pressed the nurse's card against the sensor, waiting for the light to change from red to green. "Nothing good." But the sensor didn't change. That red light still flashed.

My mother...my father...*my brothers.* We were all caught up with this. "Tell me...tell me now."

"Murder, arson. An entire range of shit I want to be far away from. I overheard London talking on the phone the last time he took me out of this place."

"Wait...*he takes you out of here?*"

She turned and met my gaze. "Yes. That's beside the point, Ryth. Something bad is about to happen," she insisted, glancing behind us. "Something even worse than this. They had a man abducted from prison, for Christ's sake, and that's just the start of it. There's a war between the man who runs this place and someone else." She shoved the card against the scanner again and again. "Now, come *on!*"

Crimson blinked...taunting us. Shock tore through me.

"Abducted," I whispered. "What do you mean, *abducted?*"

*Boom!* The door vibrated with a thud...from the other side. I flinched and stumbled backwards, terror racing through me. This was wrong...this was all wrong. She had someone out there...*someone who was about to get us killed.*

I took another step backwards, desperation burning inside me. Turn back...*turn back now, before it's too late.*

"*SPREAD OUT!*" The roar came from behind us. "*I WANT THAT BITCH FOUND!*"

Fear spread through me like poison. Vivienne glanced back at the sound as a *thud!* came from the other side of the door.

"Who is that?" I whispered. "Vivienne...*who the fuck is that?*"

I wanted to get away from this, to fall to my knees as the guards rushed us and pray I was killed in the onslaught. But deep inside, that savage part of me still fought that white-haired guard who'd attacked me. She still screamed and punched and kicked, clawing at his eyes like someone possessed. She still fought to return to those who loved me.

*THUD!*

Vivienne stepped back and grasped my hand as she stared at the door. "Get ready."

But I couldn't move.

Viv jerked her gaze my way. Worry flared. She spun and grabbed me by the shoulders. "Snap out of it, Ryth! You want out of here, right? Then this is our only way."

"Who..." the word slipped free. *Man abducted from prison... man abducted from prison.* It was all I could hear in my head. "Who was the man, Viv?"

But before she could answer, the door burst open...and Caleb was there, his chest bare under his unbuttoned jacket. His dark hazel eyes were wide and fixed on me. "What the fuck is going on here?" I whispered.

Misery carved through his gaze as he glanced behind us and stepped forward. "There's no time to explain, just hurry."

But the pain of betrayal was a bitch, kicking through my chest. I wrenched my hand out of his grasp. "Get the fuck off me, Caleb."

Behind us, the heavy thud of footsteps sounded. Caleb

189

lunged, grabbed my hand again, and wrenched me against him. "We don't have time for this, Ryth."

I fought his hold. "Get the *fuck* off me, Caleb!"

He unleashed a desperate roar and hauled me over his shoulder. "Kick and scream all you want, little sister," he snarled. "But you're coming with me."

He turned and lunged, carrying me out into the night, where the back doors of a limousine waited.

*Boom!* Gunshots rang out, splintering the door jamb behind us...and I didn't care about fighting him anymore...*I cared about saving his life.*

"Let me down, Caleb!"

He didn't answer, just shoved me through the open door of the limousine. "Get in, Vivienne."

Secrets and lies glinted in her gaze as her focus fixed on me. She jumped in after me and yanked the door closed with a *slam!*

Caleb was already gone, racing around the rear of the car until he all but threw himself behind the wheel. Glass exploded behind us with a *BOOM!* I let out a scream and ducked, throwing my arms over my head as the limousine shot forward.

*Boom! Boom!* Bullets smacked the rear of the car. Still, that desperation to know why Vivienne was willing to risk her life for me surfaced again. I jerked around and grabbed her shoulders as she crouched on the floor. "Tell me!" I roared as the limousine's engine howled and we skidded sideways, hurtling toward the bank of trees up ahead. "The man they took from prison...*what was his name?*"

Her eyes were huge. Her desperation had nowhere to go as the limousine's engine screamed. Lights flared through the darkness, heading for us. Everything happened in a blur. One second, we were both huddled on the floor, the next we were in the air.

Glass shattered again.

Metal shrieked as they hit the limousine from the side. We tumbled, flipping over. My arms flew out and smashed into the ceiling. My head followed with a *crack*, then we crashed back down...and there I stayed, dazed, numb, swallowed by the darkness. Pain throbbed in the back of my head, making me moan. Until, with a shriek of steel, the door beside me was yanked open.

"Come on," Caleb grunted, reaching in to pull me out.

Vivienne lay against the seat...but she wasn't moving.

"Vivienne," I moaned as Caleb pulled me from the wreckage. Headlights blinded me.

"Leave her," Caleb snarled, trying to yank me away.

But I couldn't, not after all she'd done. I jerked my hand from his. "No. We can't leave her."

Caleb spun to face me. Headlights of the oncoming vehicle splashed over the blood covering him.

"Oh, Jesus...*Oh, Jesus,*" I stumbled forward.

"We have to go," he moaned, wincing, and I knew we were in serious trouble.

I flung myself backwards, reached through the door, and grabbed her am. "Viv!" I forced her name through gritted teeth. *"Get the fuck up now!"*

She let out a wounded sound, then opened her eyes.

*"We have to MOVE!"* I roared as those headlights became blinding, turning the ruined limousine into a whitewashed blur.

She seemed to understand. Kicking her feet against the seat as I yanked, she fell backwards out the door. She hit the ground with a *thud,* then turned over and lunged upwards..

*"Come on!"* Caleb cried as he raised his arm. The darkness

blurred before a *boom!* The gun kicked in his hand, hitting something behind us. A roar followed, pained and brutal. And in stunned shock, I realized this is what he'd planned all along.

He'd *always* been coming for me.

He took a step, grabbed my hand, and pulled me forward. We ran, heading for the trees in the distance.

*"Get to that fence, Ryth!"* Caleb screamed, dragging me along. *"DO YOU HEAR ME? GET TO THAT GODDAMN FENCE!"*

*Get to the fence...get to the fence.*

Steel glinted through the trees...and behind it came the small beam of a flashlight shining from the darkness. *We're coming, princess. Hold on, we're coming...*Nick's words pushed through the agony in my head. Hope exploded. I punched my bare feet into the ground, driving myself forward.

"Go." Caleb pushed me forward. "Go, Ryth...*go!*"

I charged forward, slapping away branches in my way as that glint of steel came closer.

*Crack!*

The shot exploded behind us and a *thud* hit the ground. I tore a panicked gaze over my shoulder, finding Caleb on the ground. A punishing wave of fear slammed into me. I stopped, my breaths burning like fire in my chest as Viv tore past me.

"Go!" I screamed. "I'm right behind you!"

I lunged for Caleb, grabbed his arm, slung it over my shoulders, and yanked him to his feet. *"RUN, RYTH!"* he bellowed, shoving me away as, through the darkness, the blur of white came. Heavy steps sounded like thunder as Tig came roaring through the trees.

And Caleb stiffened, holding himself still.

He lifted the gun, desperation shining brightly in his eyes.

And opened fire.

*Crack. Crack. CRACK!*

The guard dropped, hitting the ground hard. Caleb wasted no time, grabbing my arm and shoving me forward. He'd been trying to buy me time. Enough to get to the fence. Dark blurs cut through the trees all around us as we were swarmed by the guards from the compound.

I ran...terror roaring through me.

Viv unleashed a scream, the sound shrill and terrified. *"Get the fuck off me!"*

Panic moved through me. We weren't going to make it...*we weren't going to make it...*

"Move!" Caleb drove his hand against my back, propelling me forward. *Crack!* The gun kicked in his hand. Bullets smacked into trees all around us. Through the blur, I caught sight of Vivienne as they hauled her away, kicking and thrashing like a wildcat.

*"Let fucking GO NOW!"*

Her white negligee was stark in the darkness...until it was gone. Her screams faded, and the sounds of that fucking brutal struggle. Tears blurred my eyes as dark shapes shifted behind the fence.

*"Princess!"* Nick roared. "Over here!"

I ran to him, thrusting my fists and feet through the air, driving me forward. Steel glinted under the shine of torchlight. There was a hole in the fence...all I had to do was make it.

*"NO!"* Caleb roared behind me as I ducked my head and *threw* myself through that hole, leaving me to stumble, my feet skidding until I hit something hard.

Something warm.

Something that wrapped powerful arms around me.

"I have you, princess...*I have you.*"

Caleb roared and grunted. The blur of pale hair was above him until, from the corner of my eye...movement came. Tobias leaped through the air and slammed into the bastard who'd tried to rape me, unleashing a sound that was terrifying as he descended, violent and brutal.

"In the car, Ryth..." Nick whispered. "You don't want to see this."

*ryth*

"GET IN THE CAR, RYTH!" Nick shoved me toward the Lamborghini.

The doors were open and the engine was running. I stumbled to it, flung myself through the open door, and scurried across the back seat. Gunshots rang out. I flinched with every *crack,* my heart clogging the back of my throat.

Tobias' screams cut through the night, making me shove forward to grab the door.

*Crack! Crack CRACK!*

I unleashed a cry as shadows swarmed the car. But I couldn't see who they were. I whimpered, shoving backward in the seat as the driver's door was grabbed and Nick slid behind the wheel. "Hold on, princess."

He gunned the engine. "Come *ON!*" he roared at the others.

The passenger door wrenched wide, and Caleb lunged inside, closing the door in the same motion, as movement came just beyond the door.

"*Go!*" Tobias roared as he flung himself onto the seat, the door closing behind him with a *bang! "GO!"*

I was thrown against the door beside me as the tires of the sports car spun, then caught. *Crack!* A bullet hit the rear of the car.

"Get down!" Tobias bellowed, and shoved me to the floor.

His body was heavy, pressing over me as the engine screamed and Nick worked the wheel like a professional.

"Are you hurt?" Tobias' hands slid over my back. "Ryth...*are you hurt?*"

"No," I whispered, my words muffled against his leg.

Still, he had to see for himself. The car spun and the engine's howl grew deeper. The headlights were almost a blur as they speared through the trees. Behind us, the faint crack of gunfire came again.

"Show me, baby," Tobias growled, pulling me up onto the seat.

I met his gaze, and froze. His eyes were black pools in the dim light. The hard planes of his cheeks were even more chiseled than they were before. He wore a mask of cold, seething rage. His gaze fixed on me as he ran his hands over my shoulders, my breasts, and my stomach, searching...feeling. Anyone else and I'd be screaming and fighting. But I knew them...*I wanted them.*

Except for Caleb.

I cut a glance at the passenger seat and that pain of betrayal cut deeper. Caleb was quiet, his hand shoved against the dashboard. *"Go,"* he urged Nick. *"Fucking punch it!"*

The car lunged forward even more, the howl from the engine like a battle cry in the night. Still Tobias had me, his hands moving slowly, sliding over my breasts before he cupped the back of my neck and pulled me close. The warmth of his body pressed against me.

"Thought I fucking lost you, little mouse," he croaked, his tone husky and strange.

Still, I was numb.

All the way to my core.

Tobias was my anchor, holding me as the car skidded side-ways and a *crack* sounded as we hit something.

"Just get us home, Nick!" Caleb barked.

"Thought I lost you..." Tobias moaned again as he clung to me.

His warmth, his voice, the scent of him. They invaded me, pulling me back to the person I once was. Headlights washed through the car, flashing across his face, making him look haunted and enraged.

"Nick," Caleb growled.

"I see it." Nick worked the gears and babied the wheel.

The oncoming headlights grew brighter, washed over us, then were gone. Bright city lights sparkled in the distance. Nick's handling of the Lamborghini was masterful, hurtling us toward the crowded streets.

"Get rid of them." Tobias released his hold on me and turned, lifting the gun in his hand. "Or get me close enough to take them out."

Nick spun the wheel, tearing us around the steady stream of cars, and gunned it through a yellow traffic light as the rest of the cars braked.

"Easy." Caleb braced as we veered around a slow car then braked hard, spinning into a side street and disappeared into the darkness.

We turned hard again, taking street after street until I lost all sense of direction. Then finally we turned again, tearing past a familiar entrance. It was the park, the one where Nick had taken me. An ache bloomed as I remembered how he'd tackled me to the ground, all lust and desperation. That felt like a lifetime ago.

"We're in and out," Nick growled and turned the wheel. "They'll be coming...and fast."

The Lamborghini shuddered as Nick braked and pulled the car into the driveway. Tobias' Jeep was parked near the house. Fear moved through me as I searched for Creed's car. "Where are they?"

"Dead, hopefully," Tobias muttered as Nick pulled up to the front door and shoved open his door.

"Five minutes!" Nick barked. "Grab whatever you can, then we're out of here."

Tobias and Caleb raced ahead. Nick moved more slowly, watching the street, then motioned me closer. "Hurry, princess." It was only then I saw how he pressed his hand to his side. *RYTH!* His screams still roared in my head as I hurried forward.

"You're hurt."

He met my gaze. That look of sadness made my heart ache. "Don't worry about that now. We need to get you out of here."

I followed him inside. Heavy steps echoed from upstairs, moving like thunder through the house. A bag sailed over the stair railing, hitting the ground with a thud.

"What do you want?" Tobias yelled.

*"My laptop and charger. That's all!"* Nick shouted, and headed for the kitchen. "Princess. Give me a hand, will you?"

Whimpers came from behind the laundry room door. He opened it and stepped in, crouching in front of me. "Easy, girl."

"Nick?" I questioned as he picked up a whimpering black and tan bundle, then handed it to me.

My heart melted at the sight of the poor little puppy. One leg was bandaged and there was another around her neck. "Oh my God, she's beautiful. Where did you get her?"

She stretched her neck to give my hand a lick as footsteps thudded down the stairs.

"We're out of here!" Tobias barked.

"Later, princess." Nick grabbed my arm, urging me toward the door.

"Here!" Tobias threw a sweater through the air, leaving Nick to catch it as T glared at the sheer negligee I wore. "No one looks at you like that, little mouse. Unless it's us."

Nick took the puppy from my arms, placing the sweater over my shoulder. "We're out of here, *now.*"

"No." Tobias stopped, staring at me, then shook his head.

A pang tore through my chest and flickers of betrayal rose as he lifted his hand. "Not until we get rid of *that.*" And he pointed to the tracking bracelet around my ankle.

Nick lowered his gaze, his brow furrowing before there was a clench of his jaw. "Those *fucking* bastards." He stepped closer, the puppy in his arms. Then he knelt in front of me, lifted my leg, and placed my foot on his thigh. He lifted his gaze to mine. "They fucking tracked you like a goddamn animal?"

My pulse sped at the words as I nodded. I swallowed hard, recoiling inside when I thought of the tattoo carved into my body.

"Cut the damn thing off." Nick jerked his gaze to Tobias. "I don't want a fucking thing of theirs touching her."

Tobias strode around the kitchen.

"Bolt cutters." Caleb stepped closer, not daring to look me in the eyes. "That's what will get it off."

"The garage." Nick slipped my foot back down and rose, still cradling the puppy. "Hurry."

Tobias took off, racing through the house, his heavy steps like thunder that disappeared into the garage. Nick glanced at me while I glared at Caleb. Then C turned away and hauled the bags out to the car.

I was grateful when Tobias raced back in, carrying massive bolt cutters. "Up on the counter, little mouse." He gripped me around the waist, lifting me easily. My white boxers rode high under the sheer negligee. Tobias looked...no, he *stared*. Then he set to work, slid the opened jaws under the clasp, and bore down.

Muscles strained as he cursed, then tried again.

Then with a *clunk,* the anklet broke and fell off. I leaned forward, my hand moving over my bare skin as my throat tightened.

"Let's go, princess," Nick urged, nodding to Tobias. "You're free."

I hurried along with them and headed out the door to the car. "Ryth, you're with me," Nick urged behind me as we raced outside.

I opened the passenger door as Nick came alongside me and placed the puppy in my arms. "Where is the Mustang?"

Nick raced around the front of Caleb's car and slid back behind the wheel. "It's a long story."

He started the engine and shoved the sports car into reverse, making a Y-turn before peeling out of the driveway. Brake lights flared from the Jeep. But I couldn't let the Mustang go. "Tell me," I urged, holding on to the puppy as the Lamborghini shot forward.

He cast a careful glance my way. "It's in the shop."

In the shop? He kept that car perfect, gleaming and purring. There was no way it'd be in the shop, not now. I rubbed the puppy's ears and was rewarded with a warm, wet tongue between my fingers. "I don't believe you. Tell me. Tell me what happened to the Mustang and what they did to you... in that warehouse."

"They stabbed me." The words were cold, painful. "They stabbed me and I crashed the Mustang into the gate of that place, trying to get you out."

"You did?"

He glanced my way. "Yeah, I did."

I swallowed the ache in the back of my throat. *RYTH!* I flinched, my hand methodically massaging the puppy's neck, drawing my focus. "And this little one?"

"That's a whole different story, one I don't think I'm ready to wrap my head around." He glanced in the rear-view mirror when he said that, his gaze moving to the glare of the round headlights behind us.

We headed back into the city. I shivered, then balanced the puppy, dragged the sweater free, worked my hands into the sleeves, and yanked the belt down to work the sweater into place.

"Talk to me," he said carefully. I caught the wince in the headlights of an oncoming car. "Only if you want to."

I looked away. I couldn't think about that place without seeing Caleb.

Now it was my turn to wince. "It's a whole different story." My words were stony. "One I don't think I'm ready to wrap my head around."

He didn't push and for that I was thankful. We headed to an apartment building before Nick pulled the car over.

"We know someone here?" I asked as I looked up through the windshield.

"You can say that." Nick pulled into a parking spot, leaving Tobias to slip in beside us. "Me."

"This is your place?" I pushed the door open, holding the puppy with my other arm.

He killed the engine, climbed out, and closed the door, taking his time to walk around the car and stop outside my door. "Yeah, princess, my place."

I climbed out, carrying the puppy, shaking my head when he moved to take her from me. I needed her. The warmth, the feel of her against me. Without her, I was lost, shaking, falling apart at the seams. I followed Nick after he grabbed his things from the back seat and headed for the building.

We took a rickety old elevator up to the top floor. From the outside, the place looked grungy and old. But the moment we stepped out and headed for the top-floor apartment, it turned sleek, industrial...and expensive.

He punched in a code for the front door, then pushed it open. "There's clean clothes in my bedroom, some food in the cupboard."

"Dibs, first shower," Tobias called as he strode around us, scanned the place, and disappeared.

"You hungry?" Nick asked.

I shook my head. "No." I doubted I'd ever be hungry again.

"Cold?"

I shook my head.

"Thirsty?"

Caleb let out a snarl, then headed for the living room and the expansive glass windows that overlooked the city. He didn't want to look at me, didn't want to hear me, didn't want to listen to me speak.

"Want to tell me what went down between you two?" Nick murmured, staring after him.

Pain carved through me. I couldn't look at C, couldn't watch the way his body moved as he walked away. Whatever Caleb and I had had before, we'd never have again, that I knew in my heart.

"No," I answered and turned away. "I don't think I can."

# TWENTY-EIGHT

*ryth*

TOBIAS STRODE out of the bedroom. His hair was still damp, his chest bare. A towel was precariously wrapped around his waist, leaving his thigh flashing as he walked.

He headed for me, and I could see the need in his eyes, a hunger that burned in the darkness, one I felt in the depths of my soul. He wrapped his arms around me, drawing me against his chest. I buried my head in his neck and inhaled his carnal, masculine sent. One I once loathed.

"I thought I'd lost you, little mouse." His words were a moan in my ear, sending my pulse racing.

I couldn't get enough of them. I couldn't get enough of him. I tightened my arms around him, flattening my body against his. "Never."

"We can stay here tonight," Nick announced as he opened the refrigerator behind me. "But then we need to think about leaving. We need someplace secure, someplace where they wouldn't dare come for us." He glanced at Tobias. "Not unless they want a war."

Tobias scowled. "You really want to hole ourselves up in a Rossi safehouse?"

"You have a better idea?" Nick responded. "Then I'm all for it."

But no one did. Even if it was the last thing Tobias wanted to do, he'd ask his enemy for one more favor. And he'd do it for me.

He stared down at me with those bottomless dark eyes that were utterly terrifying to anyone else. His fingers curled as he brushed a strand of hair from the side of my face. "But we have tonight, right?"

I shivered at the words.

"No."

I jerked my gaze to Caleb as he stood staring out the window. Tobias' lips curled when Caleb turned and regarded him with a savage glare. "Not until she's ready."

Tobias dropped his hand and took a step toward him. "Not until she's ready?" Rage seethed under the surface of his words. "Got something you want to share, C?"

Caleb's brows furrowed with a wounded look. But not once did he look my way. He just held Tobias' stare, that detached look growing even colder. My stomach tightened. Would he tell the truth? Or would he pretend what happened in that place had never happened at all? In the end, he curled his lips in a snarl and headed for Nick's bedroom, yanking his shirt free as he went.

Tobias stared after him. So did Nick.

He was jealous and petty, wanting to ruin the moment, and he'd succeeded. Tobias lifted his arm and motioned me under. "Come on, little mouse. Surely you must be starving."

But food was the last thing I wanted. "No." I didn't think I ever wanted to eat again, or sleep, or be alone.

"What did Caleb mean, princess?" Nick inquired, looking at me.

"What did they do to you?" Tobias' words were strained. "That's what C means, right?"

"Don't push her," Nick snapped at his brother. "You don't have to tell us, not unless you want to."

I didn't want to. I wanted to forget that place and everything that happened within those walls ever existed. I wanted to pretend we were back in the days before I'd been taken. I wanted to pretend it was just us.

"Or we can forget all about that shit." Tobias gave me a way out. "We start fresh, right now, in this moment. What do you say about that?"

I forced a smile. "I think I'd like that."

"Then food." Nick pulled a bunch of food out of the refrigerator and opened a cupboard. "I don't have a lot to work with. But it could be a while before we have anything decent...and you need to make a phone call, right?"

He cast Tobias a sideways glance. There was a mutter and a pissed-off growl before my moody stepbrother turned and stalked away.

Nick busied himself with ingredients, pouring stuff into a saucepan. There was stock, some frozen chicken, and some type of frozen dim sum. I watched while I rubbed the puppy's ears. "Where did you get her?"

"A dogfighting ring. They thought she was dead." He looked up at me. "She fought and survived. I guess she's tougher than she looks."

I didn't know if he was talking about the dog or if he was talking about me. Maybe it was both. Maybe that was the whole reason he'd saved her in the first place. Whatever that was, I was glad. "Does she have a name?"

"I was hoping we would pick one together, seeing as how she's going to be ours."

Ours...

While Nick cooked, I thought about a name for the dog. Nothing came to me, not at first. She was kind and sweet. Those big, sad, shimmering eyes made her look even sweeter. But under the gentle nuzzle of her cold nose and that happy spark was the heart of a fighter. "A dog fighting ring?" I whispered.

"Two full-grown pitbulls attacked her, and she survived." Nick continued to stir the soup. "Even when those bastards threw her out like a piece of trash."

A fighter...*just like me.*

"You're a rebel," I whispered to her. "Aren't you?"

Nick lifted his head from stirring the pot that now had the most delicious salty scent. Even if I'd said I wasn't hungry, my belly still grumbled.

"Rebel, that's what I want to call her."

Nick smiled and stepped closer. "Rebel, huh?" He looked at her. "She looks like a damn rebel to me. Nice one, Princess."

"The shower's all yours." Caleb strode out of the bedroom, his hair and bare chest still damp, wearing a pair of Nick's gray sweats.

My pulse raced at the sight, betraying me as I took in the muscles of his chest and hard stomach.

*Can't be tender.* The memory of those words surfaced. *I'm going to be a beast to you. You'll fucking hate me and want me all at the same time.*

That was the truth. I hated him...and wanted him still.

"I'll find you some clothes," Nick growled, glancing from me to Caleb before he disappeared into the bedroom.

"Are you ever going to forgive me?"

It was the first time he'd spoken to me, the first time he'd even acted like he saw me. "After what you did to me?" I stepped closer, staring into his eyes. "After what you let *them* do *to* me?"

"And what was that?"

I flinched at the dangerous tone in Tobias' voice as he came closer. "Because I'm dying to fucking know, brother."

I didn't answer. Instead, I stepped closer, placed the puppy in Tobias' arms, and muttered, "I'm going to take a shower."

I couldn't deal with Caleb right now, or the bloodshed that was sure to come. I stepped into Nick's bedroom as he cast a pair of sweatpants and a T-shirt onto the bed. He rose and looked at me. "What is it?"

I shook my head. "Nothing."

But out in the kitchen, Tobias wouldn't leave it alone. "You going to tell me, brother? Or do I have to beat it out of you?"

Nick flinched at the threat, but he didn't move. It wasn't just the Hale Order destined to destroy us. We were doing a perfectly decent job on our own.

"I'll leave you, then," Nick declared when the front door to his apartment slammed shut with a *bang!*

I grabbed the clothes and hurried into the bathroom, desperate to get the stench of that place off me. And my memories scrubbed clean, but the water wouldn't be hot enough for that. I closed the bathroom door behind me and tugged off the sweater, then the negligee and the boxers, casting them onto the floor in the corner of the room. I'd never wear fucking white again.

My gaze went to the mirror, and to the tattoo on my abdomen, that was still red and painful, before I stepped into the shower and turned on the water. The spray was hot and stinging. I welcomed the heat, lowering my head as the faint sound of raised voices drifted in.

I tried to push their anger and rage to the side for a moment, and instead...I cried. Hard shudders wracked my body as I slowly crumpled to the floor. I'd left her...she'd protected me, tried to save me...*and I'd left her alone in that place.*

They'd hurt her. I knew that without a doubt.

They'd hurt her, use her, and break her.

All because I'd left her behind.

I wrapped my arms around my knees, drawing them up tight to my chest.

My chest tightened and pain flared in the back of my throat. I'd left her...*I'd left her.*

Agony turned to a scream. I bit down on my fist, rocking and moaning.

*They had a man abducted from prison, for Christ's sake.* Viv's voice echoed in my head. *There's a war between the man who runs this place and someone else.*

I pulled my fist out of my mouth. The man they'd abducted had to be my father. Shudders tore through me at the thought. I shoved upwards, my knees shaking as I switched off the water and stepped out. Wet towels were discarded on the bathroom floor, and it was almost like everything was normal...except I knew it wasn't.

I grabbed one that was still folded, using it to dry my body, then wrapped it around my hair.

"Princess." Nick's voice intruded as he opened the bathroom door and lifted his head. "I know you said you weren't hungry—" he froze.

His gaze was fixed on the mirror...and the black tattoo inked into my skin.

There was a second when he didn't understand what he was seeing. Until I turned around and lowered my hand to cover the marking.

"Those fucking bastards..." The words punched through on a harsh breath before he drew a lungful and roared, *"THOSE FUCKING BASTARDS!"*

*ryth*

I FLINCHED at his roar and stepped backwards until I hit the vanity. But there was no stopping Nick, not when his gaze was riveted on my stomach. He stepped into the bathroom. "They...*they tattooed you...*" He jerked his gaze to mine, his eyes iridescent with rage. "Like goddamn *property*?"

I dropped my other hand, hiding my shame. Tears came, slow and thick, sliding down my cheeks as a wounded sound tore from the back of my throat. That's all I was to them. Someone they could own, like I was nothing.

The sound of thunderous footfalls neared, tearing through the bedroom before Tobias was there in the doorway behind his brother.

That merciless stare slowly slid down my body...until he stopped. "Drop your hands, Ryth," he demanded.

I shook my head, my hands trembling in front of me.

Nick stepped closer, trying to take the cruel edge off his tone. "Show us."

I shook my head again, my tears blurring their faces. "No."

"Princess," Nick urged, stepping closer until he stopped

right in front of me. His hands were so gentle, pushing mine to the side. "Let us see."

I couldn't look at them, not when they saw my body no longer belonged to them. It was ruined...no, *I* was ruined. I turned my head, my body trembling with the weight of their stares.

"What the fuck is that?" Tobias snarled.

"H and O," Nick answered, his curled finger finding my chin. "For Hale Order, I expect."

"Those motherfuckers." Tobias forced the words through clenched teeth. "Those goddamn motherfucking bastards. They hurt you. They fucking hurt you and they're going to pay for that. I swear on my fucking life, princess, they're gonna pay."

"It doesn't matter." My words were painful.

"Yes, it fucking does." Nick held my gaze, and it swallowed me in his sadness. "I'll get the tattoo removed. Whatever the cost, princess. I'll get it removed, okay?"

He was desperate for me to know that, as though somehow the memories would disappear with the ink. But they wouldn't...they never would. Tobias stepped closer, sliding his hand underneath Nick's and turned my head. "Never again, you hear me? Never a-fucking-gain will they lay their hands on you."

His voice was husky and needy as his mouth inched closer to mine. I closed my eyes, knowing what was coming but still unable to stop it from happening.

He kissed me...slow, hard, all teeth and lips and tongue, until I broke away and winced. "I don't need your pity, Tobias."

He reached up, grabbed my hand and pulled it lower until I cupped his erection. "This feels like pity to you, little mouse?"

He'd always been savage and demanding, always the hard edge to the Banks's blade, cutting away my resolve.

"You tell us to back off and we will, Ryth," Nick reassured me. "You want space? We'll give you space. But if you want us to show you how much we missed you and how this fucking mark or anything else that happened to you in that place means fucking nothing to us, then we want to do that, too."

Tobias' hand splayed out over mine. There was no force there anymore. No demands...just the warmth of his hand on mine. They wanted to fuck me...wanted to make me forget everything else existed.

"You belong to us, princess," Nick urged.

Tobias' dark eyes sparked. "And we belong to you."

My hand pressed against his erection...this *male* who'd fought, who'd bled...who'd raged—for me.

Hands all over my body. My face pushed against the wall. The memory of that room pushed to the surface and shame followed. I wanted to tell them what they'd done to me.

*Ryth is new.* The Principal's words surfaced. *She doesn't yet understand.*

*But she will, won't she?* Revulsion rose as that man's voice returned. The man who'd come with Caleb...the one he'd let put his hands all over me. I tried to shove the memory aside. "They..." Movement drew my gaze toward the doorway of the bathroom.

Caleb stepped across Nick's room, stopping on the other side of the doorway. Anger punched to the surface, turning icy and terrifying. *You fucking bastard!* I wanted to lunge across the room and scream at him. There was no escaping what had happened in that place, because everything we had now was stained with the memory. To cut that out meant to ruin *us*.

And I hated him for that.

211

An ache flared through my chest, forcing me to shove the pain away.

"Fuck that place," I snarled, but my stare said something else. I turned into Tobias, cupping my hand harder against him. *And fuck you, Caleb.*

"That's my girl," Tobias murmured.

I held Caleb's stare as Tobias slid his hand along my ribs and cupped my breast. I wanted to hurt Caleb more than I wanted anything else. His stare was so fucking cold as he watched us.

"Christ, I missed this." Tobias licked my nipple, drawing my gaze. He lifted his head. "I fucking missed you."

I slid my fingers through his hair, driving his mouth back down. He obeyed...Christ, he obeyed, kneading my breast as he took it into his mouth and slipped his other hand between my legs, dragging his finger along my slit before plunging in.

"Oh." I rolled my head backwards, meeting Nick's mouth.

The memory of them returned. Lips and tongues sliding in my pussy and my mouth. Desire bloomed inside me, pulling me back to them...to *this*. Nick broke away to drag his shirt over his head. "To the bed, T."

But I froze, my gaze fixed on the large bandage, then I met his stare. "Wait, we can't."

Tobias lifted his gaze, his brow furrowed. "What?"

I shook my head. "You're hurt, Nick."

"You think that'd stop him?" Tobias chuckled. "The man escaped the hospital after fucking surgery...to find you."

My breath caught. "You did?"

"I did," Nick acknowledged as he shoved his sweats lower. His cock sprang against the waistband of his pants. "And I'd do it again, in a heartbeat." He sank to the bed and laid flat on his back. "Now, you gonna make me fucking wait, princess...or you gonna let me give you what you crave?"

Caleb was cold as stone as he stepped backwards away from the bed. But he never left, not even when Nick patted the bed beside him. "We still have to be careful. So, backwards, princess."

Backwards? To take my weight from his body, of course. I nodded, lifted my leg and straddled his hips, making sure I stayed away from his wound.

"Higher," he urged.

I shuffled back, moving up to his stomach. He wanted to touch...

"Higher."

I glanced at Tobias as he watched, his bemused smirk alien with those dark, dangerous eyes. I shuffled backwards again, moving to Nick's chest. He pressed one hand to his wound and the other slid under my thigh. His fingers stroked me. I stilled. My hands braced on either side of his body as I trembled.

Callused fingers plunged into my heat. I closed my eyes, fighting the urge to rock against him.

"Higher."

I opened my eyes and my feet slid over the pillow as I shifted back once more.

"Now fucking sit."

A charge of adrenaline tore through me. I shook my head, looking down. I hovered over him...open, exposed. He could see *everything*. Tobias was breathing hard. Caleb's dark gaze was riveted as I lowered my body on my stepbrother's face.

His tongue slid along my crease and, Jesus, I was back there, floating the way only Nick could make me feel. His hand went to my thigh, then my hip. That high hand drove me down until there was nothing but the warmth of his mouth.

"Ride him, little sister. Just like you did the night of the wedding," Tobias growled.

I leaned forward and fisted the sheets, but instead of rising up, I rocked. His tongue dove inside, only to find my clit...over and over. I wanted more...*more*. His cock throbbed in my line of sight, the head beaded with a tiny, single tear. Such a beautiful waste. I reached up and fisted his length, and Nick moaned under my pussy.

"Fuck me, that's the way, little mouse," Tobias urged, his own hand diving inside the waistband of his pants. "Suck him."

I opened my mouth and leaned down, sliding my tongue around the bright red head of Nick's cock. A growl from him reverberated along his tongue, sending the vibration against my core. I unleashed a moan of my own, grinding against him as that heavy tension built. I closed my eyes, sliding his cock along my tongue as I clenched tighter and sucked.

Nick's hips jutted off the bed. "Oh, fuck...do that again," he moaned, pulling me higher to suck my clit.

I did, taking even more of him as I licked and sucked, my focus torn between the plunging of his tongue and my own desperate need to make him come in my mouth.

It was a race.

An agonizing, animalistic race. *I was going to come...I was going to—*

I sucked and fisted as the climax hit me, making me drive down until I smothered him. I wanted to come in his mouth, wanted him to suck and swallow me. He did, unleashing a growl. His cock twitched, that thick vein pulsing as warmth splashed the back of my throat.

Deeper, *more*. I sucked, swallowing the salty taste as my body shuddered with release. I rose as he softened, lifting to his heavy breaths.

"Jesus Christ, princess," Tobias groaned.

I panted and lifted my gaze, seeing his cock in his hand. My movements were slow as I lifted my leg over Nick and turned to kneel on all fours. "Tobias," I ordered. "Fuck me...*hard.*"

I leaned down, tasting my own desire on Nick's lips. He smiled and reached up to cup the back of my head as the bed dipped behind me. I wanted them...I wanted *this.* My body used the way I needed it to be used, but by *them,* my step-brothers.

Tobias' big hand slid over my ass, then along my back, before he shoved, driving my face into the mattress. He pushed one knee between my legs and gently shoved, splaying my knees wider. One hard thrust, and he was inside, driving all the way to the hilt. I whimpered as that howl inside me screamed, *yes!*

"This the way you want it, little mouse?" Tobias thrust again, the slick sound of our bodies colliding loud in the air.

*"Harder,"* I demanded.

The pressure eased on my back. He reached under my arm, his hand sliding over my breasts until he gripped my neck and lifted me. Nick stared at us, his eyes widening as his brother lowered his head to growl in my ear. "You remember I love you, right?"

The thrust of his cock had me whimpering. "Yes."

"Good. 'Cause I'm about to fuck you like I don't."

His hand gripped tighter, the pressure sending panic shooting through me as he punished me with his hunger. But I could still suck in air. His own breaths were heavy and hot against my ear. "Jesus, Ryth," he growled. "You. Will. Be. The. Ruin. Of. Me."

I fumbled to hold on, gripping his arm as he forced my knees even wider, until I had no balance. He became my support, his cock driving deep as he fucked me hard.

He was savage.

The way only Tobias could be savage.

*Mine,* his hand around my throat screamed. I whimpered as my body took over.

"I would kill the fucking world for you," he snarled.

I stared into Nick's gaze, watching panic spark inside him, and in that moment, I knew the truth—Tobias would, and he'd still rage after it. The thought of that drove me even closer. His brutal hold around my throat, his ruthless thrusts. Both sent me over the edge. I reached my arm around behind him, pulling him even harder against me as I groaned, climaxing hard.

His hold eased instantly, moving to my hips as he thrust one more time and let out a guttural moan. My body couldn't hold my weight, not anymore. I collapsed, crashing to the bed beside Nick. Spent. Safe.

Hard breaths consumed me as I slowly lifted my gaze to the spot where Caleb was.

But he was gone.

Pain moved through me as the word rose *good.*

I knew I didn't mean it. As much as I wanted it to be true. Tobias collapsed beside me. "You okay, princess?"

I nodded and reached for him, pulling his body hard against me as I curled up against Nick's side and closed my eyes, whispering, "Now I am."

# THIRTY

## *caleb*

"OH, JESUS..." Tobias growled.

The heavy sound of their breathing punctured the air. It was all I could hear. Them. *Her.* I stood outside Nick's room, unable to watch them a fucking second longer. My balls ached. My cock was hard, throbbing in my fucking pants. I dropped my hand, fisting the length in my sweats, and braced my other hand against the wall. *You will be mine. You understand me?* My own words echoed. They were the words I'd said to another... but they'd been all *hers.* Everything I had was hers.

"Ryth," Tobias grunted her name as he came.

*You'll be fucking mine, until I'm done with you.* I clenched my grip as that ache built and built and built.

Low whimpers from the puppy somewhere behind me shattered the hold Ryth had over me.

For a second, at least.

"C?" Nick called my name. I closed my eyes. He expected me to fucking join them...one look in her eyes and I'd known that would never happen. Not now. Not after what I'd done.

If only they knew...

I dropped my hand and took a step away from the door, the need now as empty as my fucking heart. If they knew what had happened, they'd kill me. I knew that.

The puppy whined once more, drawing me away from the room. I strode over, yanked the front of my pants loose, and knelt down, rubbing her forehead.

*Beep.*

The volume on my phone was low, but still too fucking loud in the quiet of this place. I grabbed it and rose, finding a message from Evans. *What the fuck have you done?*

Panic rushed through me as I stared at the screen, then glanced behind me to Nick's bedroom. They were quiet... asleep? I walked over, shoved my feet into Nick's runners, and went out the door. Cold rushed in, hitting me like a blow. Goosebumps raced along my arms as I closed the apartment door quietly behind me and strode to the elevator, yanking the gate down before I punched the button.

The old thing shuddered and shook as it dropped lower, stopping at the ground floor. I waited until I was sure I was far enough away before pressing the button on my phone. "Evans."

"What the *fuck,* Caleb?" He was panicked, strung out. His tone was about three octaves too high. "What the fuck did you do?"

"What are you talking about?" My pulse raced.

"You take her back, for fuck's sake," he demanded. "You hear me? *Take her fucking back.*"

"You know, and I know, that's never going to happen."

Silence echoed through the speaker. Then the faint sound of heavy steps thudded.

"Talk to me. What's going on?" I urged.

"What's going on?" he hissed. "You fucked me, you get that, right? You *fucking fucked me.*"

"Has Killion said something—"

His hard bark of laughter made me flinch. "Has he said something?" Evans repeated shrilly. "He came to my office and closed the door. He threatened me, Caleb. *He fucking threatened my goddamn family!*"

I swallowed hard as my stomach sank.

"You realize how bad this is, right?" Evan's tone turned stony. "You understand the kind of people you're dealing with. You took what belonged to them. You took it...and now you need to give it back."

*Give it back...*

Like she was their goddamn property. Those footsteps resounded in the background again, only this time *they echoed.* My mind was racing, trying to piece things together that my gut was screaming about. "Thanks for the heads up, Evans," I said carefully and hung up the call.

Lights glinted in front of me, the city still busy even in the dead of night. *He threatened my family.* Evan's words resounded as my phone vibrated in my hand. I glanced at the caller ID and saw his name before I hit the button sending the call to voice-mail, then I switched the damn thing off.

*Get on your knees.* Killion's sadistic fucking growl slipped through my mind. I glanced at the phone in my hand. *Lick it... fucking lick it.* That hunger rose inside me once more.

The depraved, sick hunger I needed to fight.

I closed my eyes, my breaths moving deeper. It was more than sex, more than desire. It was the total control I craved. The way she was with Tobias, his hand around her throat, his cock driving inside her. He'd used her. *Christ.* He'd used her. My cock hardened at the thought. I lowered my hand once more, only this time I slipped it inside the waistband.

*Lick it...that's a good girl.* A moan ripped free, hurting and hard at the back of my throat. I worked my cock, desperate to feel a fraction of what I'd had with her before. In my head, we were back in that kitchen pantry, my hand over her mouth, my fingers deep in her pussy.

I dropped my head, driving my hand all the way to the base of my cock then back up again. I turned and leaned my hand on the concrete wall of the apartment building.

*When I take you, Ryth...I'm going to take you all fucking night. You're going to be my favorite fucking toy...my wet, perfect plaything.*

In my head, her breath caught and her throat moved, trapping a moan that built. I moaned for her now as my cock kicked in my hand. Warmth spurted between my fingers, slick, desperate with need. I sucked in a hard breath and opened my eyes. Still that need filled me. That hungry fucking need. My hand was a poor substitute for the real thing.

I wiped my hand on my pants and headed back inside. But those echoing steps in the background of Evans's call worried me. He wouldn't talk, I knew that. It was the reason I'd gone to him.

So what if Killion made idle threats?

Evans didn't really know a goddamn thing, only what I'd told him, which was minimal. The elevator shuddered as it stopped. I lifted the grate and walked out, punched the code Nick had given me into the digital lock, and made my way inside.

The place was quiet when I eased the door closed. The heavy, rhythmic sounds of breathing came from my brother's bedroom. I kicked off Nick's runners and walked barefoot to the bedroom doorway. The room was dark inside, the bathroom light off, the three of them sound asleep. Still, the moonlight spilled through the large floor-to-ceiling window, caressing her skin.

She lay in Nick's arms, using his bicep as a pillow. Tobias

faced her, one arm over her waist. They were perfect, just the three of them. My own fucking heart was gnawing and pulsing, driving that unbearable hunger through my veins.

I looked away...I had to. It was either that or go insane.

I'd never have that. Not again. Not with her. I knew that. I left them and headed to the second bedroom. The puppy limped over, her nails clicking on the floor as she followed me inside, then carefully jumped up on the bed as I yanked the bedding down and slipped between the sheets.

But sleep didn't come. Not for a long time.

I tossed and turned, unable to shrug off the ache and that nagging voice in my head that told me this was going to end badly. I closed my eyes, forcing myself into the darkness. When I woke to the brightening room, my eyes stung and watered.

Soft snores came from the puppy curled at the foot of the bed. I shifted, dragging my feet around her, and was rewarded with an exhausted and annoyed loud sigh. "Sorry," I muttered.

The rest of the apartment was still quiet. I yawned, rubbed my eyes, and stumbled from the bedroom toward the kitchen. Last night's dinner had been shoved into the refrigerator, still in the pot. But the thought of food made me sick to my stomach. I needed coffee...

And to think.

Footsteps. Echoing footsteps. I couldn't shake the thought of it from my head. I searched the cupboards, finally found the coffee in the freezer, and set to work brewing a pot before I headed back into the bedroom and grabbed my phone. I switched it on and was rewarded with a whole slew of missed calls and messages. The last one snagged my attention.

*Davis: Have you seen this? What the fuck?*

My pulse skipped as I clicked on the link, which took me to an online news article.

*Distinguished Attorney at Copeland Law, Michael Evans, was found murdered in his home this morning after an apparent home invasion.*

"*Jesus,*" I croaked, my fingers fucking shaking as I expanded the article, searching for any more information before I moved back to the calls.

There was one more...one more call and message. My stomach clenched as I pressed the button and logged into my account.

"*We want her back, Mr. Banks. Deliver the girl or the next one will be you...or maybe one of your brothers, how about that? Like the little fucking punk who blindsided me. I think I'm going to enjoy paying him a visit.*"

A scream followed, guttural, etched with pain. "*Please don't...I DIDN'T KNOW! I DIDN'T FUCKING KNOW!*" The howls of desperation made me sick to my stomach. Then it ended. Silence followed, terrifying, ending silence. I closed my eyes, my hands shaking. They'd fucking killed him...

*They'd fucking* killed *him.*

I jerked my phone away and killed the call, then just stared at the doorway. We needed to get out of here...*now.*

I forgot about the coffee...forgot about everything else, strode out of the kitchen, and headed for Nick's bedroom. They were still entwined and asleep when I charged in. "Nick" I walked around to the side of the bed, giving him a shove. "Wake up. We need to get out of here."

My brother cracked open his eyes, staring at me with a bleary gaze. "What?"

Ryth opened her eyes, her gaze finding me. Her hate for me burned bright. But I couldn't worry about her anger right now, not when I was too preoccupied with saving her life.

"They're coming and we need to get out of here."

"What the fuck?" Tobias groaned.

They didn't believe me...they didn't believe me. I lifted my phone, logged back in, and hit replay....and the sounds of Evans begging for his damn life echoed through the room before I hit pause. "Get the fuck up...we're getting out of here."

THIRTY-ONE

*ryth*

"PLEASE DON'T...I *DIDN'T KNOW! I DIDN'T FUCKING KNOW!*" I shoved up as screams filled the bedroom before Caleb pressed the button, ending the sound. Still, they rang in my head, terrified, tortured cries. My breaths turned shallow and my pulse raced.

"We need to go." He glanced my way, those dark eyes etched with pain. "*Now.*"

Nick shoved up, kicking off the sheets. "T."

"On it," Tobias snarled, and rolled to the other side of the bed. In their absence, I grew cold.

"We need to get as much stuff from the apartment as we can, princess," Nick urged as he yanked on his clothes and glanced my way. "Can you do that for me?"

I nodded, sliding my way to his side. He turned, grabbed my face in his hands, and kissed me, before breaking away and staring into my eyes. "I'm going to get us a ride, one they can't trace, then we need to look at getting rid of our phones and anything else those bastards can trace us with. I'll be back as soon as I can."

That thunder in my chest flared into an ache. *No, please don't leave me.*

I wanted to stop him as he shoved on runners and headed for the door. "Stay with her. No one gets inside without you taking them out, got it?"

"I'm not going anywhere," Caleb muttered as he left.

I could hear Tobias grumbling outside the bedroom, his growl sounding desperate and pissed. I could only guess he was talking to Lazarus.

"Tobias told the truth last night." I jerked my gaze to Caleb as that ache in my chest radiated. "He would indeed kill the world...for you." He turned then and headed for the door, muttering, "And that includes his brother."

He left me standing naked in Nick's bedroom, his words mingling with those tortured screams in my head. I moved, yanked on my clothes, and turned to the bathroom. Take everything. That's what Nick had said. I yanked open the cabinet, searching for a bag and found one in the back, finding perfumes and female deodorants, as well as shampoo and conditioner.

They'd been Natalie's...they had to be. I swallowed down a flare of jealousy and shoved it all into the bag. I was past caring about ex-fucking girlfriends. Right now, all that mattered was staying alive...*and together.* My stomach tightened as I emptied the bathroom of all I could, even taking towels and washcloths before dumping it all on the bed and turning my attention to his closet.

By the time I was done with Nick's room, Tobias came looking for me. "Nick's back, and we have a place to stay. We gotta move fast, you understand, princess?"

I nodded, glancing at the kitchen. "I need a few minutes."

"You have ten, then we're out of here," he threw over his shoulder.

Rebel gave a whine, drawing my focus. "It's okay." I rushed forward, yanked open the freezer, and started pulling out the contents. "I'll make sure you're fed."

My hands were burning with the cold when Nick shoved open the door and strode back in. "Ready?"

I gave a nod. "Bags are in the bedroom."

"T," Nick barked.

Tobias strode in, wearing jeans and a black t-shirt and tucking a gun behind his back. He looked dangerous in that moment, more than he'd ever looked before. Caleb's words resounded in my head. He hadn't spoken as though the idea of Tobias killing for me was a fantasy...more like a reality.

"Ryth?"

I jerked my head up, meeting Tobias' dark brown eyes. "Yes?"

He lifted his hand and brushed a strand of hair from my cheek, his gaze fixed on the birthmark. "You ready?"

I swallowed hard. "Ready."

"Car's downstairs," Nick announced. "We're out of here. T, you got the address?"

"Got it." Tobias dropped his hand, stepped around me, and grabbed four of the shopping bags, filled with as much food as they could hold, then strode toward the door.

We were out of there in a heartbeat. Nick grabbed Rebel and carried her to the elevator. We rode down in silence. I shivered even though I wore one of Nick's sweaters, walking barefoot as we carefully made our way to the car. Tobias was first, his gun in his hand, scanning the area before he glanced over his shoulder and nodded.

The car was older, a blue Ford with the engine still idling. Caleb moved forward. "Stay behind me, Ryth," he whispered, glancing around before he yanked open the back door and motioned me inside with a jerk of his head.

I hurried to climb inside, pushed aside two full shopping bags, and held out my arms for Rebel.

"Okay, princess?" Nick asked. I nodded. "There are clothes and shoes in those bags for you. We'll get more when we arrive at the safehouse."

Clothes...shoes? I gripped the puppy to my chest and glanced at the bags as Nick closed the door and slid behind the wheel. Caleb climbed in beside me and Tobias settled into the passenger seat. Then we were pulling away from the apartment building, leaving it all behind.

"Here." Caleb reached for a bag, pulling out a pair of brand new runners.

"I've got them," I snapped, eased Rebel into the gap between us, and grabbed them from his hand.

He flinched, my anger stinging, but I couldn't help it. I wasn't about to pretend what had happened in that place didn't happen. The old Ryth who'd put up with shit like that was long gone. This one was just as savage as the men she loved. I leaned forward, glanced over Nick's shoulder to see the ignition on the Ford a mess of twisted wires, before I focused on sliding the runners on and tying up the laces.

"Head north on Eastgate, then take Montview all the way up to Morningside."

"You mean their warehouse? Fuck, T. I wanted safe. I didn't want to be camped out in their fucking backyard."

"You wanted a safehouse. Then this is a goddamn safehouse," Tobias snarled and glanced over his shoulder. "Freddy'll meet us there."

Nick exhaled hard as he drove through the streets, taking the long way around as we avoided early morning commuters...and cops, seeing as how we were in a stolen car. By the time the sun beamed hot through the windshield, we

227

were driving past warehouses enclosed with eight-foot fences topped with razor wire.

There were no people lingering in the streets here. It was... quiet, real damn quiet, and eerie as hell. A car sat at the corner of the street we turned into, the shadowed outline of someone behind the wheel. Tobias looked right at the guy, holding his stare as we turned in. I realized with chilling clarity that this was where my father had worked, where he'd lived mostly, because he was hardly ever at home and when he was...he argued with my mom.

More like she argued with him.

"Take the third on the left," Tobias motioned. "Then it's the fifth house on the right."

Nick braked and turned hard, then glanced into the rear-view mirror, but he needn't have bothered, one look around at the barred windows and massive dogs that patrolled the fences of these compounds told us no one came and went from these places without the Rossis knowing about it.

I'd had no idea...

Not how powerful they were, nor how dangerous.

Nick turned the car, then again, pulling into the driveway of a small, nondescript brick house. A black Explorer was parked at the curb, the paintwork gleaming. Nick left the engine running as he pulled up. The front door opened and Lazarus Rossi's bodyguard stepped out.

Freddy...

That was his name.

Black sunglasses glinted as he turned his focus to me. He stood back, leaned against the brickwork, and crossed his arms. Tobias, Caleb, and Nick climbed out first, leaving our things in the car as they walked around the car and headed up the stairs to meet him.

Rebel gave a low whimper. I scratched her head and shoved

the door open. Words were exchanged without the greeting of a handshake. Freddy just glared...at me, as the others stepped inside the house. Nick came out a second later, bending down to lean into me, his voice low. "Ready?"

"Sure," I answered, grabbed the bag of clothes Nick had bought me, and followed.

The house was quiet and plain, but fully furnished. Nick carried Rebel inside and placed her down on one of the soft cushions on the sofa.

"Nice dog," Freddy muttered as he followed us inside.

"Ryth, you're in here with me," Nick called.

A surge of excitement filled me as I followed him into one of the bedrooms. Tobias and Caleb had already dumped the bags from Nick's apartment on the bed, then walked back into the living room. The moment I followed them out, I felt Freddy's gaze fixed on me.

"Everything good?" the bodyguard asked, staring at me. But I knew the question wasn't aimed at me.

"Yeah," Tobias answered as he lifted a gun he hadn't had before and placed it on the counter. "We're good."

A nod, and the bodyguard stepped closer. Only it was closer to me.

"Good, we want to make sure you're all safe and sound," he muttered, staring at me through those dark sunglasses. "Where's your dad, Castlemaine?"

Heat rushed to my cheeks. I scowled, then glanced at Tobias and back. "I don't know. Why are you asking me?" The longer I stared at him, the more pissed off I became. "I told Lazarus before, I don't have his damn money."

Freddy just smirked and let out a sigh as he straightened.

"We don't have it." Tobias stepped closer.

Freddy just cut him a stare. "You really think this is just about fucking money? Time to grow the fuck up, T. I taught you better than that. Just make sure you hold up your end of the bargain here. The first number you call after contact better be fucking mine."

He turned then and met Nick's stare, then Caleb's, before heading out the front door.

Nick strode after him, locked the door, and peeked through the blinds as the thud of a car door sounded, followed by the growl of the Explorer's engine

"What the fuck did he mean?" Nick turned back to us. "I thought they were after the damn money. What's more important than that to the damn Rossis?"

There was silence before Caleb spoke. "Information, that's what."

"Information?" I murmured, and one by one, they glanced my way. "Information on what?"

"On the bastards who're chasing us." Nick dragged his fingers through his hair and turned away. "I can't believe I fucking missed it. It's not about money."

"Whatever your father has on those people is dangerous," Caleb muttered. "Which is why we need to find him...and fast."

## THIRTY-TWO

SO, that's what this was about...it wasn't about money at all, was it? *It was about goddamn information.* I dragged my fingers through my hair as my mind raced, stuck on that open folder in the warehouse. One filled with details of the hit on Ryth's father. I tried to piece it all together, until I slowly became aware of Ryth.

She was the center of it all.

Her dad, her mom...that goddamn place.

She trembled standing there, her eyes wide and filled with shock. Fuck if she didn't look like she'd bolt from this damn house any goddamn second. *Do something.* Tobias just scowled at the damn door, oblivious of her. But I wasn't. Not in the fucking slightest. "Princess." I moved closer, commanding her softly. "*Hey.*"

She jerked those wide eyes to me, panic igniting.

"It's all going to be okay," I murmured.

Her lips trembled, drawing me to her. I didn't see the kid who'd moved into our house anymore. I saw the fighter, the one who ran from that place, desperate to get back to us, just like we'd fought to get to her. We had more history together in the past month than Natalie and I had had in years.

I wanted to protect her, wanted to love her. I wanted to give her the kind of home she hadn't had, one filled with loyalty and love. I stepped closer, tilting her gaze to mine with the tip of my finger under her chin. I'd tasted her and fucked her, and Christ, if I didn't crave more. "Stay with us, okay?"

Her panting breaths were out of control. Shit, I needed to get her out of her head. So I did the only thing I could think of. I lowered my head and kissed her. Still, she was stiff and unresponsive. Desperation surged as I moved closer, taking more. Warmth caressed my mouth. She trembled, but those breaths slowed, moving deeper. I cupped the back of her head, spearing my fingers through her hair. And slowly, so damn slowly, she drew away from those panicked thoughts and into me.

"They won't come." Tobias spoke as I deepened the kiss. "They can't trace us, not now. They won't be able to do a damn thing, we'll make sure of it. And when they realize that, they'll leave us alone."

His words were meant to be comforting, but they just drew me away from the feel of her. I gently broke away, lifting my gaze to hers and found that glint of fear now dulled.

"Stop talking and kiss her, Tobias," I murmured. "She needs to feel and not fucking think."

But Tobias just glared at the door. "I need to run or fuck, but if I do fuck you, little mouse, it won't be something you need. It'll be a goddamn punishment."

He headed to the door, yanked it open, and left. I clenched my jaw. Selfish fucking asshole. I glanced at Caleb, who just scowled. "Well?" I barked at my older brother.

But he just winced as Ryth turned away. "I don't need

anyone kissing me, for fuck's sake." She tore away from me... no, she tore away from Caleb. "Least of all *him.*"

*Least of all him...*

I looked from her to him. "What the fuck is going on with you two?"

Caleb just looked cold and detached.

*Bang!*

Ryth slammed the bedroom door closed behind her. I stepped close to Caleb and jabbed my finger into his chest. We didn't have time for this. As if we didn't have enough enemies at our goddamn door. "We *all* agreed to do whatever it took to get her out of that place. I know you had to do some fucked up things to get close to her. But whatever it was, whatever happened between you two, you need to flip the switch back, C. Get back on the right team. Fix it, or you'll lose her forever."

I winced at the stab of pain in my side, then lifted my hand and braced the wound. But I was unable to shake that goddamn folder from my head. The last thing I wanted to do was leave, but if I stayed, neither of them would speak.

They needed a catalyst. A reason to bring whatever this was to the surface. And they needed to find it without me being here. I headed for the bedroom at the end of the hall. On the single bed sat a duffel bag filled with weapons that Freddy had left us. I didn't need to look too closely to see the numbers had been filed off. Don't ask, right? That was one of the perks of belonging to the mafia. Right now, I'd take every weapon I could get my hands on.

I shoved a gun into the waistband of my jeans and walked out, cutting Caleb a glare before stopping outside her door. I lifted my hand, wanting to knock and offer words of comfort. But what comfort could I give?

In the end, I just left, closing the front door quietly behind me. I climbed back into the running Ford and backed out of the driveway. I needed another ride, one that wasn't fucking stolen.

I made my way through the Rossi neighborhood. The streets were damn quiet. No one caused trouble here, not unless they wanted the damn Mafia after them. I headed west, unable to shake that fucking folder from my thoughts. If I could just find where her damn father was...then I could stop this.

I'd stop it all, and I'd save her...

It's all that drove me.

# THIRTY-THREE

*caleb*

FIX IT...FIX *it?* I clenched my jaw and stared at the closed bedroom door. How the fuck could I fix this? I turned, running my fingers through my hair. The damn pup stared at me from the cushion on the sofa. "What the fuck are you looking at?" I snapped and let out a pent-up breath.

Purpose filled me, for a second, at least. I strode into the kitchen, yanked open a cupboard, and grabbed a plastic bowl, then filled it under the running tap and returned to the corner of the living room. "No shitting on the carpet, right?" I placed the water bowl down where she could get it. "You need to go outside, come and get me. I'm sure I can at least manage that without fucking it up."

Then again...

I yanked my phone from my pocket and stared at the message on the screen. I wasn't stupid; I knew they'd try to track our damn phones. Which is the reason I'd turned off my location the moment we'd hauled ass out of that damn place and made sure the VPN was switched on.

I planned to get rid of it, just as soon as I figured out these screenshots. I pulled up the images and expanded the view, narrowing in on every damn word. There had to be something in those contracts I'd snapped in The Principal's office, some piece of information I could use that'd get those bastards off our backs.

*Thud!*

I jerked my gaze toward the sound that came from the bedroom.

*Boom!*

"What the hell..." I dropped my hand and took a step.

*THUD!*

I moved to the door, lifted my hand to the handle, and stopped.

*BOOM!*

"Ryth?" My voice was cold. I licked my lips, *try harder.* That fucking voice drove me to turn the handle and open her door. "Are you—"

She was on the bed, her shoulders hunched, her body shuddering as she wept. I took a step closer, agony coursing through me at the sight. I watched her stiffen and lift her head. Her voice was husky. "Get the fuck out, Caleb!"

"Ryth," I started, not knowing how to ease her pain.

She shoved to her feet and spun, tears shining on her reddened cheeks as she grabbed a desk lamp beside her and hurled it across the room. *"I said, GET THE FUCK OUT!"*

I lunged, narrowly missing the damn thing as it crashed against the wall.

*Fix it. Fix it. Fix it.* Nick's fucking voice haunted me. Every time I looked at her, I wanted—*have you ever been licked as you pass out?* My own words pushed through. *No.* I tried to shove them away.

She spun back around, grabbed a book that'd been next to the lamp, this time aiming it at my head. I ducked, letting it hit the wall behind me and fall.

"*Stop!*" I commanded as she turned, desperately searching for anything else she could get her hands on. She was going to hurt herself and destroy Rossi's goddamn house if I didn't do something. I took a step, reaching for her. "Ryth, *I said stop.*"

With a savage exhale, she spun, those wide eyes fixed on me. "*Fuck you!*" she screamed, and wrenched her hand back before lashing out.

*Slap!*

My head snapped to the side. I froze with shock for a second, until the beast inside me roared for retribution. But I leashed it and turned back to her.

"*Did you tell them?*" she screamed, her eyes wide and wild. "Did you tell them how you just stood there watching him...*touch me?*"

She lashed out again. Only this time, her blows were feeble, leaving me to grab her wrists and yank her against my chest. *Fix it...fix it...fix it.* "No," I answered, staring down at her. "I didn't."

Pain flickered in her eyes. "You fucking *bastard.*" She sucked in a deep breath. "You cold, unfeeling, sick piece of shit! I should tell them. Tell them what you did..."

*Do something, or lose her.*

"Go right ahead," I snarled. "What do you think would've happened if I hadn't distracted him?" She tried to yank her hands from my hold, but I held her, wrenching her hands back to my chest. "Hate me all you want, because what *you* saw as betrayal was a fucking necessity in my world. I did what I had to do, little sister, and I'd do it again. Because in the end, I got what I came for, regardless of the cost."

"*You'd do it again?*" she said coldly. "You want your hands on her, don't you? You want her."

*That* was the real reason, right there. She was jealous. A surge of satisfaction burst to the surface and my cock hardened at the thought. I drove her backwards until her legs hit the bed and she fell.

Jealousy shifted in her eyes as she looked up at me. "I *fucking hate you!*"

I was on top of her in an instant, grabbing her hands as I shoved her back against the mattress. *"You hate me?"* I roared. *"Is that it, Ryth. YOU FUCKING HATE ME?"*

She bucked. *"Yes!"*

*Fix it...fix it. Fix it.* Nick urged, the ever-desperate white fucking knight. Only I wasn't so perfect, was I? I wasn't like him. I was the one who didn't want to feed her or give her a goddamn puppy. I was the one who wanted to hold her down and fuck her until she learns her place, only letting her come when she's a begging, dripping, fucking mess. "I don't think so, princess." That hunger rose and this time I couldn't drive it back down. "I think I like you exactly right where you are— underneath me. There's only one problem," I lowered my head to whisper. "There's too much screaming being done and not enough sucking."

She stiffened at the words, her chest rising hard against mine as she panted. "You're pathetic," she hissed, but still I heard the lie in her trembling words.

She liked the way I spoke to her. She liked to be degraded.

"I bet if I slid my fingers in that sweet cunt, I'd find the truth, wouldn't I? You don't fucking hate me, Ryth, you *want* me." I pushed upwards, just enough to stare into her eyes. "That's why you're upset, isn't it? You don't want to want me, but you do."

I gripped her hands above her head with one hand and shoved the other under the waistband of her sweats. I was between her legs in an instant, finding her warm and slick. "See." I fucked her with my fingers. "You need to be fucked, don't you, princess?"

Her eyes closed as her lips parted with a rush of air. Fuck me, she was beautiful. Agony bloomed with the memory of that room. "You think I don't replay that fucking moment in my head?" I slid my fingers in and out, working her better when she widened her legs for me. "You think that's not going to *haunt* me until my last goddamn breath? I fucking *hate* what he did to you, Ryth...*But I hate that I still want to do it even more.*"

That was the truth. The sick, debased fucking truth. "You think I didn't want to be the one to push you up against that wall?" I circled her clit, slipping two fingers inside, watching her push back into the pillow. "I'm tearing myself apart every fucking *second* with this goddamn hunger for you. You drive me insane, little sister, I'm torn between wanting to protect you from me...and making you choke on my goddamn cock."

She let out a moan at the words.

I was already aching and hard. I ground myself against her, forcing her thighs wider with my knee. She opened her eyes, her lips curling as she stared up at me. That rage sparked in her, making her fight...and fuck, *I liked it.* "You going to fight me, princess?" I pinned her arms. "You going to spit on me?"

Her lips curled. Fuck, she looked savage in that moment.

Pure fucking rage.

Before I lowered my hand to her throat. "You remember what I said in that room?" I clenched my grip, pressing my fingers against her neck before I released them. "I want to lick you as your eyes flutter and that darkness rises up. I want you to lose yourself to me. Will you do that, Ryth? Will you be nothing but the pleasure I can give you?"

She gasped, sucking in harsh breaths.

I lowered my head, pressing my body against hers, revelling in the feel of her.

"You said the same thing to *her*." Her words were a harsh whisper, but I still saw jealousy in her glare.

"No," I growled against her ear. "They were all for you. Every sick fucking word." I pressed against the veins in her neck. "You're the one I see in my head. You're the one *I own*. I can't stop myself, can't control this goddamn need. I'm going to keep a leash on it, going to be as gentle as I fucking can—*if you'll let me.*"

She was still. So goddamn still. I wanted to be inside that head of hers. I needed to know what she was thinking. I pushed, hoping. "Now, the safeword, princess. Do you remember?" I repeated.

Her gaze narrowed on me, "Yes."

"Do you want..." Hope flared, and in that moment, she saw my hunger, my need...and she didn't recoil.

Adrenaline surged, even as I trembled. No one *saw* me...not even my brothers, not like this. She had all the power here, even with her small body trapped under me and my hand around her throat. She was the one in control, the one who had those slender fingers wrapped around my heart.

She held my gaze, and even though I wanted to hide behind that mask, I didn't.

"Do it." Her breaths were raspy.

My cock twitched as my pulse raced.

"Stop," I murmured, trying to catch my breath. "A safeword is no good here, so you need this."

I rose up, grabbed my belt buckle and slipped the belt free from my trousers, winding it tight I pressed it into her palm. "You drop this and I stop, you understand?"

She was silent. I lifted my head, staring into her eyes and saw the same darkness as mine. "Do you understand, Ryth? This is important."

Her pulse raced under my thumb. The thready vibration

incited that dominant craving inside me. I was like a lion on the hunt, paws pounding, hitting the dirt at full speed, my mouth open, teeth desperate for the feel of her flesh. I ground my cock against her, needing to be inside. But I wanted this more. To bring her to the edge, to...*own her.* "Say it."

"I drop this and you stop," she whispered.

I held her gaze for a second longer, then dipped lower, pressed my lips against her neck, and dragged my hand along her crease outside the sweats she wore. They were Nick's sweats, dark gray. I watched her, pressing just a little until her pupils widened, then roughly yanked the sweats down. "Feet," I demanded.

She froze for a second, her mind trapped between panic and obedience. Then she lifted one leg.

"Good girl," I praised her, releasing the pressure. Her pulse kicked with the words. "My sweet, perfect, fuck toy."

She whimpered, and I smiled at the sound as I tore off the new runner my brother had bought her and cast it to the floor. "The other one, princess," I reminded.

She did as she was told and lifted the other leg. I tore the other runner free. "Hips."

She lifted. Christ, she was good at obeying. I lifted my gaze to hers, stroking the side of her throat, drawing her focus to the touch. I yanked the sweats from her body, finding her bare underneath. My gaze moved to that tattoo on her body, the H inside the O. My brothers had raged at the sight. They'd wanted blood, screamed about revenge. But not once did they see it as her.

And it *was* her.

Every mark they'd done to her body against her will.

She'd fought them, oh fuck, how she would've fought.

Still, they'd won, ripping away her control.

She needed to find it again, to fight, and rage, and learn

how to give in, to find the power in submission...where I was concerned. She needed to be protected, to be cared for the only way I knew how.

My darkness met her rage.

I lowered my head, kissed the tattoo, and felt her stiffen. "So fucking perfect," I whispered, and opened her legs. Her pussy was gleaming. I dragged a finger along her slit and caught the tremble. She was already wet...fucking soaked.

*She fucking liked this.*

I parted her lips and slid my finger around her clit. It pulsed at the touch. I was betting right now there were butterflies in her belly...a flurry of animalistic hunger. I rose up and pressed my lips against the flutter on the side of her neck, the flutter that moved as she tried to swallow, until I licked, dragging my tongue along the artery and sank lower, keeping my hold around her throat.

I tightened my grip, felt the rise of panic, and released as I spread her pussy with my fingers and licked her core. "You're doing so well, princess, so fucking well."

A moan tore from her throat. The sound vibrated against my hand and my cock punched against my pants. I eased my hold, then pressed again as I sucked her clit and slid a finger inside her. She was so slick, dripping.

Her hands fisted the sheets. She needed to be put in her place where I was concerned. Press...release...suck...slide. Over and over, until that moan came again. She was close...so fucking close.

I pulled out and kissed her clit before easing my hold around her throat. "You hate me." I licked my lips and looked down at her slippery fucking cunt. "I can see it in your eyes. Nick wants me to fix this. He wants me to fix *us*."

I watched as that panicked rage moved back into her stare,

then lunged, grabbed her shirt, and yanked it up, exposing her breasts. "So this is me, *fixing it.*"

Her soft pink nipples puckered. I lowered my head and grazed my teeth across the flesh, biting just enough for her to flinch.

"Caleb..." My name was a fucking snarl, a spit with words.

I ignored her plea. "Turn over."

That pissed-off gleam in her eyes was there, burning with such ferocity. I lifted my head and met that stare. Dominance, fight. Control. She needed to learn...*with me, she had none.*

She didn't need any.

I rose, watching her body tremble. She thought she could demand, like I was...*Nick.* I held her defiant glare. "Now."

With a curl of her lip, she did as I'd instructed. "On your hands and knees."

Her breasts swayed as she turned, then pushed up on trembling arms. I bit my lip and looked at her. "Look at that perfect fucking hole." I grazed the sensitive flesh, stopping at her ass. "So fucking tight, aren't you?" I pushed my finger in. Her body fought, clenching at the invasion. *Jesus fucking Christ.*

"Such a good little whore," I murmured. She dropped her head at the filthy words and drove back against my finger, pushing it in deeper. "This ass is mine," I declared, and lowered my head and slid my tongue into her core. "This cunt...*is mine.*"

She whimpered. I drove in and out, fucking her ass and her pussy, just how she needed. "Legs wider, princess."

But she didn't obey, too entranced by my finger, knuckle-deep in her ass, and the tip of my tongue curled, licking her clean. I pulled my head away and slid my finger out, giving her a second before she understood the rules. "Don't make me tell you twice."

She shifted then, widening her knees, giving me all the access I wanted. The image of her riding Nick's face rose in my mind. She'd liked that, being in control...being on top. I shoved my pants low, and a flare of punishing ache tore into my balls with the movement. I was painfully hard, desperate to come as much as she was.

But this was our moment, our time to make sure we set the bar. I leaned over, worked the spit into my mouth, then unleashed, splattering her ass with saliva. Slick warmth coated my fingers. I pushed it in deep, working that tight ring of muscle, feeling her desire take over. And slowly she relaxed, impaling herself all the way up to the hilt.

"That the girl, that's the good fucking girl," I murmured, watching my finger slide all the way inside. "Look at the way you take it." I rose over her, sliding my hand around her throat once more.

This time she moaned with the sensation. She knew what was coming. The thud of the door sounded and the familiar heavy gait of Tobias came closer. He stopped at the doorway, his chest heaving in deep breaths—just like hers.

"Fuck me," he growled.

But I ignored him. This moment was all hers...*no*, it was *ours*. I slid my thumb along the artery, then pulled my finger from her ass and gripped my cock instead. *Press*...release. Her throat worked as she swallowed. I pushed against her hole, feeling her body fight. *Press*...release.

She moaned as the head slipped in, stretching her. Christ, I loved to stretch her. She dropped her head, her arms shaking. I swore there was a whimper, but I was too focused on the feel of her fighting my cock. I clenched my grip, just enough for the panic to start, and her body gripped me tight. "Breathe, princess."

Tobias came closer, watching as I drove inside. He bent down low, gripped her chin, and lifted her gaze to his. "Look at me while he fucks you." There was an edge to his tone as he watched my hand grip her throat, one I knew only too well. "That's it, princess, take his cock."

I growled at my brother's praise. My balls clenched, tightening with the need to come. The wet slaps of our bodies were audible, the sound driving me to the edge...until I pulled out and released my hold. Her ass gaped, slowly closing as I pulled away. She gave a whimper, her entire body shaking now.

Harsh breaths punctured my words. I tried to keep control, but it was fucking hard. "Tell me how much you want to come, princess."

"Please..." she panted, and whimpered.

Her arms buckled, sending her face first onto the bed. Tobias straightened, looking down at her as she rolled onto her back and opened her legs, her body a quivering fucking mess. She lowered her hand to her pussy.

"No," I barked, and she stopped, her eyes wide.

I pounced, grabbed her hand, and yanked it over her head with one hand, while I pressed inside her thigh, opening her slit. "Does she need to come, brother?"

Tobias rounded the bed, kicked off his shoes, and yanked his shirt over his head. "Fuck, yes she does."

"Together," I demanded.

Her eyes widened as I yanked her forward, grabbed her around the waist, and lifted her in front of me. Her ass was mine, her cunt, my brother's. Tobias grabbed her hands as we stood and wound them around his neck. "Hold on, baby," he urged, looking down.

I grabbed my cock as he lifted her leg winding it around his waist. One thrust and I was deep in her ass from behind. I couldn't hold back and released a moan.

"Breathe, Ryth," Tobias demanded as he slid into her pussy.

Pressure pushed against me as she took both of us.

I gripped her jaw, turning her glistening, unfocused gaze to me. "That's my perfect princess. Take it all."

Tobias grunted, lowering his head as he thrust. I timed his brutal blows, thrusting deep. She moaned and whimpered, clawing hold of my brother as we fucked her.

"Going...to...use...you." I slammed home, thrust after thrust. "And...you're...going...to...*fucking love it....*"

She let out a cry and dropped her head backwards. I closed my eyes as my orgasm hit, tearing through my body like a blade. I wanted to say the words...to tell her how I felt.

But no word encompassed this. Warmth spilled around me as I filled her.

"Mine." Tobias branded her. "You're fucking mine. Just like this...just...like...this..."

Her body bounced, held upright by us alone.

"Come, princess," I urged as she whimpered and slammed her eyes closed. "That's it, come."

Her body clenched and pulsed, which drove Tobias to the edge. He dropped his head against her shoulder, his fingers digging into her hips as he thrust one last time.

She shuddered and panted as I gently slipped free. Tobias was next, sliding out. And all three of us fell onto the mattress. My mind was numb, my body spent, my soul and my heart sated enough. When I finally found the ability to speak, I whispered against her ear. "You know my depths now, little sister. You know my depravity. I can't let you go, not now...not ever."

*ryth*

CALEB GRIPPED MY CHIN, tilting my gaze to his. "You understand what I'm saying, princess?"

His breaths were hard, heaving. Still, there was power in his eyes. A well of untapped carnal need...all for me, and I wanted more.

My body trembled. My pussy throbbed with its own heartbeat. I was mindless and numb, but still felt everything. "Yes." I finally grasped how he loved me. "I understand."

He leaned forward and kissed me softly before he tilted my head, staring down at my throat. I didn't need a mirror to know he'd left marks behind. His hands...his hunger. I couldn't seem to catch my breath at the thought, and in the wake of that desire, the memory of Vivienne came back to me. The way she'd looked at that man who was old enough to be her father...it was exactly like this.

*She liked it.* The control. The degradation.

I stared at Caleb, feeling that heady sense of power once more, as the front door opened and closed with a thud.

"You need to see this," Nick called out. The sound of a television filtered in.

"What the fuck?" Tobias muttered and rolled out of bed, pulling up his sweats as he walked around the end of it. He bent and snatched his t-shirt from the floor, the muscles along his back flexing with the movement before he turned his head and cast a ravenous glance my way.

My breath caught with that primal power in his eyes. He'd liked what we'd just done together. He'd liked it a lot.

Caleb followed, grabbing my sweats, t-shirt, and bra from the floor before he turned back to me. That dark carnal need was just as dangerous now as it was before.

He moved closer, bending to hold open my sweats for me. "Princess." His cock swayed as he bent, and my gaze was riveted by his body as he moved. God, my brothers were going to kill me. I slid one foot in, then the other, took my bra and t-shirt from his hold, and froze...as the sound of my mother's voice cut through the air.

*"We're terrified for her safety. We just want Ryth to come home."*

Caleb jerked his gaze toward the door, then moved fast, grabbed his own clothes from the floor, and rushed through the door. I followed, stepped around the mess on the floor, and rushed into the living room, seeing my mother on the TV.

She stood next to Creed, dabbing her eyes with a handkerchief, and stared directly into the camera. *"We fear she's being held hostage by her stepbrothers. They're dangerous, very dangerous. We've had reports they've assaulted one of my husband's employees and set fire to our family home. We don't know what they'll do next, and we're afraid for my daughter's safety. We're so upset it's come down to this, but we just want her found. Please, if anyone has seen my baby, we've set up a dedicated number through the Hale Order Ministry."*

"That fucking bitch!" Tobias barked and jerked his gaze to Nick. "That *motherfucking bitch!*"

Nick just stared at the screen. "They're setting the goddamn city on us, like fucking hounds."

Tobias stepped closer, but it wasn't my mom he looked at, it was Creed.

"Every fucking cop, every fucking mercenary," Nick muttered, turning away until he saw me.

But I couldn't tear my gaze from the man standing behind them...a man I'd know anywhere. *The Principal.* "It's them," I murmured, and met Nick's stare. "It's the goddamn Order behind all this."

A phone rang, drawing my focus. We all turned to Caleb, lowering our gazes to the pocket of his sweats.

"You didn't get rid of your goddamn phone?" Nick jerked his gaze to Caleb's.

"No," he answered, staring at his caller ID. "Don't worry, they can't track us." He pressed decline, sending the call to voicemail. Barely a few seconds later, his phone dinged with a message. He glanced my way and took a step backwards.

"Who is it?" Tobias snapped.

Caleb turned around. "No one."

But T wasn't hearing it. He stepped forward and grabbed Caleb's arm, stopping his brother cold. Caleb just looked down. "Take your fucking hand off me, Tobias."

There was a tense second where I thought T was going to push him, until he slowly let go. Caleb's phone rang again, the shrill sound making me flinch.

"Who is it?" Nick demanded. "C, who the fuck keeps calling?"

"Killion," Caleb answered carefully.

He didn't move, didn't look my way. But I knew he wanted to. My breaths deepened as the name conjured memories of that room. I could still hear his rasping breath in my ear, still feel his hands all over me, pinching my nipple before dropping between my legs.

"Why is he fucking calling, C? And why the hell haven't you gotten rid of your goddamn phone?"

Caleb just shook his head, turning to glance my way before answering. "Because he thinks I'm fucking broken, that's why."

"Broken?" Tobias' snarl was frightening. "Why the fuck would he think you're broken, brother?"

Caleb didn't answer, not for a long time, until he did. "Because he had someone killed. Someone I knew...someone who was a friend."

A friend...

I swallowed hard. "Because of me, right?" I whispered.

Nick shot me a glare. "No, Ryth. Not because of you." He strode toward me and forced my gaze to his. "None of this is your fault. I need you to remember that."

*Not my fault?* Maybe not. Still, it didn't change the fact that if I hadn't walked through their door with my mom that night, that guy would still be alive—I lowered my gaze to the bulge of the bandage under Nick's shirt— and Nick wouldn't be hurt.

"What's so damn important on that phone, Caleb?" Nick asked even as he lifted his finger to my chin, forcing my gaze to his. "Better be damn good."

"Contracts," he answered. "Disguised by sick fucking deals, where they trade women for silence."

"Silence?" Nick's gaze darkened as he turned to his brother. "For what?"

Caleb just held his stare. "That's what I'm trying to figure out."

"And you haven't yet, which means there's nothing there, not enough, at least." Tobias strode toward the TV and hit the button, killing the image of my supposedly weeping mother.

"They killed a man," I whispered. "They killed him."

"And burned everything to the ground." Nick glanced at Tobias. "I went back to those mercenaries, trying to find more information on the hit they have out on Ryth's father, and it's all gone."

His words stopped me cold. "There're mercenaries after my father?"

"Yeah," Nick nodded. "So this is about more than just you, princess. It all comes back to that fucking place."

Hale Order.

"Whose name is on the contract?" Nick asked.

Caleb lifted his phone. "London St. James."

*St. James...Vivienne.* "I know that name."

All my brothers swung my way. Heat rushed to my cheeks, and the room came into focus. All I could see was his grip around her jaw as he snarled, *Fifteen days. I'm going to enjoy stretching you out, Vivienne.*

My mouth turned dry. "The man who owns Vivienne."

"Owns?" Caleb murmured.

Darkness glinted in his eyes with the word. Even in the wake of terror, what we'd just done together, he wanted more. Control. Dominance. *Owned...*I now knew what that meant to Vivienne. My pulse raced as I answered. "That's what she called it. She's his ward. Contracted by the Order."

"As a payment to keep quiet." Caleb pulled up the details on his phone, handing it first to Nick who passed it to Caleb, then Tobias and finally to me. *Hereby awarded Vivienne Brooks as his own personal ward for the purpose of preventing an unauthorised disclosure of Confidential Information as defined below.*

I scanned what the *'as below'* meant, but all it read to me was a whole lot of nothing. "Before we ran, she told me she overheard this bastard who owned her on the phone. She said they were talking about taking a man from prison."

"Your dad..." Nick raked his fingers through his hair. "Jesus, they have him. They have your dad."

I swallowed hard as my heart gave a squeeze. If they did, then there's no way he'd be alive now. Maybe that's why they were after me. Did they think he'd told me something? Something which was *confidential...*

I handed Caleb's phone back, wanting to never look at it again.

"Then we find this London St. James and we make him talk." Tobias glanced at the others. "Then we find Ryth's dad and we get the fuck out of the city."

"And go where?" Caleb met his stare. "Where do you propose we go?" He lifted his phone. "If you think these guys are just going to let us go, then you're fucking delusional."

"Then we go after them." Nick's words were chilling. "And we start at the festering heart of this."

*Festering heart?*

"Who?" Tobias snapped.

Nick held his brother's stare and answered. "Haelstrom Hale."

## THIRTY-FIVE

*tobias*

"WE START at the festering heart of this." Nick looked at me, knowing what needed to be done.

I just nodded. I was ready. Ready to finish this once and for all.

"What?" Ryth glanced from Nick, to Caleb, then me. "No." She shook her head and stepped toward me. "No fucking way. Do you have *any* idea what that will mean?"

"Yes," I answered, holding her stare. "We force them out into the open."

"And get yourselves killed in the process," she snapped, her blue-gray eyes darkening with a scowl. Fuck, she was cute when she was pissed. "No. I won't allow it."

Caleb's stare was steely. "It's happening, princess. Whether you like it or not."

She turned, throwing her hands into the air. "You're all fucking suicidal, you know that?"

"More like homicidal," I answered carefully.

She stilled at the words, her chest rising a little harder. Nick stepped closer, captured her chin, and tilted her gaze up to his. "There's nowhere that's safe for us, not anymore." He nodded toward the TV. "Sooner or later, someone's going to spot us and they'll take you...again."

"Not going to happen," I growled, that cold hunger burning inside me. "Not now, not fucking ever. I'll take that sick piece of shit out before I let him put his hands on you."

She thought these were just words, just a threat with no ability to follow through. She didn't realize that there had been a hole in me in the seconds, and the minutes, and the goddamn hellish days when she'd been taken. Did she think I'd paced the floor, wringing my goddamn hands, bereft with her loss? She'd learn soon enough.

"I know where he is." Caleb lifted his head, scowling at the phone in his hand. "According to this, he has a standing lunch reservation at an elite restaurant in the city."

My pulse jumped a little as I muttered, "Then let's fucking go."

Caleb lowered his hand. His gaze was stony as he headed for the bedroom. We left her behind, staring at our backs, as Nick and I followed Caleb to the bag of weapons which had been courtesy of Lazarus. I changed clothes, yanking on black jeans and a black t-shirt, then strapped a double harness around my shoulders and stowed two black Glocks in the holster.

"There's no going back after this. You get that, right?" Nick glanced my way as he adjusted his shirt, tucking his own weapon in the back of his jeans. "If this doesn't work, then we need to think about running."

Running. I shook my head. "Not an option, brother." I met his stare. "People like Hale won't give up, and if you think he will, then you haven't been paying attention." I glanced at the doorway and listened to Ryth as she paced in the living room, while the drone of the TV still echoed in my head. "They were on the fucking TV, Nick. You think they're just gonna make that go away?"

He didn't answer.

"They exposed themselves. That's how desperate they are to get her back."

"But why her?" my brother muttered.

Movement came in the corner of my eye. I didn't have to turn my head to know she was there. I felt her like a goddamn magnetic hum in my soul. To me, she was a gravitational pull.

"Why her?" Nick repeated, shaking his head. "I can't work it out. Why the fuck *her*?"

I didn't answer. Because the truth was, I didn't fucking know either. It was all I thought about, all that drove me. Why her? *Why her?* And how could we end it?

I shook my head, knowing she was listening to every word and tearing herself apart in the process. "It doesn't matter." I adjusted my holster and grabbed my leather jacket, yanking it over my weapons. "They want her and they're not about to stop, not unless we make them...so we make them."

Nick gave a slow nod, determination burning in his gaze.

"Ready," Caleb added from the doorway.

My focus found Ryth as I turned and strode toward her. Nick was kind and comforting. I was hard edges and bloody knuckles. She was safe because I was savagery. I strode past her, headed for the front door, and the others followed.

I climbed into the back seat of the dark grey sedan Freddy had left for us after he disposed of the stolen car. Nick slipped behind the wheel, leaving Caleb to slump into the passenger seat. But Ryth didn't come out, just left us sitting in the damn car to wait...until finally she stepped through the door of the safehouse and headed for the car.

She slammed the car door behind her, glaring my way. But

we were already moving, pulling out of the driveway and heading for the city in icy silence. She wrung her hands, twisting and bending her poor fingers in ways that looked fucking painful.

A twitch came in the corner of my eye...*she's hurting herself... she's hurting herself...she's hurting herself.* I clenched my jaw and lashed out, grabbing her hand. Her breath caught. Surprise flared in those damn beautiful eyes. Harsh breaths felt too fast as I stared back at her. I wasn't like this, wasn't comforting or caring, *and yet, here I was.*

She made me uncomfortable.

Made me feel skinned and raw and not like the bastard I really was. I lowered my gaze to my fingers curled around hers, and knew this was love. We drove into the city like that, me in the back seat holding her hand, trying to stop her from ruining her goddamn knuckles.

It worked until, under C's directions, Nick pulled us into a darkened alley and parked the car. My hand was sweaty when I let her go, but I didn't swipe it across my thigh as I climbed out. I clenched it instead, turning my focus to my brothers as we rounded the rear of the car. Ryth climbed out, leaving Nick to pull her close to his side. "I want you to hang back a bit." He brushed a strand of hair from her face. "Stay in the open where you're seen. But if shit goes south..."

"If it goes south, then I'm fucked either way," she answered.

He pressed the car keys into her hand. "In the glove compartment, there's an envelope. You'll find details there for an account I set up in your name. One they won't trace, not for a while anyway, and enough cash to get you set up somewhere."

Pain flashed across her face as she shook her head. "That's not going to happen."

"No," I agreed, finding Caleb's gaze. "It won't." I'd kill the motherfucker right in the middle of his prissy fucking restaurant before it came down to that.

"You'll be fine, as long as you're out in the open so there're witnesses. We aren't planning on doing anything rash." Caleb cut another glance my way. "We just want to have a...*discussion*. That's all. Help him see we aren't backing down, no matter what bullshit he throws at us."

"So, you're calling his bluff?" she questioned.

*"More like giving him an ultimatum,"* Caleb answered.

That seemed to appease her a little, and the fear eased in her eyes.

"Okay, princess?" Nick murmured.

She gave a nod. There wasn't much else she could do, was there? This was happening whether she wanted it to or not. I looked over my shoulder, then turned back and checked my weapons one last time.

"Let's do this." I headed for the street, then along the pathway to the expensive-looking restaurant. Caleb and Nick fell in line behind me as I pushed through the glass doors and climbed the stairs.

The maitre d' was stationed at the front and smiled for a second, until he glanced from me to my brothers and stuttered, "Do you have a reservation?"

I didn't answer, didn't even slow, just kept on walking, scanning the tables until I caught sight of the bastard in the distance. He sat with three other men, casually sipping from his cup. Two discreet security guards stood toward the rear, dressed in black, with the bulges of a weapon under their jackets. One fucking move...and I'd lunge across the restaurant before they even had a chance to react.

"Uh-uh," Nick snarled softly, meeting the closest asshole's gaze.

"Mr. Hale," Caleb called, drawing the bastard's attention.

Cold, black, beady eyes shifted our way. Muscles flexed in a carved jaw, one that looked like it'd been chiseled from stone. There wasn't a hint of emotion as Haelstrom Hale glared from my brothers to me.

"I'm sure you know who we are," Caleb said carefully.

The problem was, my brother was too fucking polite. I leaned down, braced my hands on the edge of the table, and stared into the black pits of Hell. Recognition shimmered under the surface. Fuck, this guy was cold, all the way to the fucking core. There was something rotten inside him. Something festering that seemed to swell behind those black pits as he looked away, searching the restaurant beyond us. But it wasn't his security he looked for...no, it was Ryth.

In the corner of my eye, I saw her. She waited in the middle of the restaurant, standing between the tables like we'd told her. I knew instantly when he saw her. His breaths deepened, his pupils blew wide.

"You don't fucking look at her," I snarled, and leaned down, drawing his focus. "You hear me, you piece of shit? You don't fucking look at her at all."

"Haelstrom." One of his buddies stared at the gun as my jacket gaped. "What's going on here?"

"Nothing," Hale answered.

"Call off the hounds, Hale." Caleb was calm beside me, far more than I was. Rage seethed inside me.

One of his guards moved toward the table until he lifted a hand, stopping him cold. "It's fine, Gregor."

"Yeah." I met the guard's glare. "It's fine."

"How did you find me?" Hale asked.

But no one answered. I knew Caleb had been talking to Freddy behind our backs. Hale wasn't the only one with scouts in the city.

"We are here to tell you to stop coming after her," Caleb

continued. "Pick someone else, *anyone* else. Ryth doesn't belong to you."

There was a twitch in the corner of Hale's lips. A tell I didn't like at all.

"We don't give a shit if her mom doesn't want her with us," Nick added. "We don't give a shit what our father has to say. We're telling you now, Ryth won't be stepping foot inside that place *ever again*."

Caleb waited until Nick finished before adding, "Unless you want the world to know *exactly* what goes on there."

And there was that fucking twitch again, the one that pinched the corners of those beady eyes. Eyes I wanted to close, permanently. "That sounds an awful lot like a threat, Caleb."

C gave a shrug. "Threat. Promise. Call it what you want."

I looked at the pompous pricks he sat with, seeing each of them turning their heads as they looked away. They knew exactly what kind of monster they sat with...and they were afraid of him.

Spineless pieces of shit.

Hale gave a slow sigh and uncrossed his legs. "Tell me, what exactly do you think you can do here, Mr. Banks?" He glanced at Ryth, who'd crept closer. "Ryth is a troubled young woman, running away from an environment that offered stability and safety, one her mother contractually chose over something that encouraged reckless criminal behavior. She's emotionally unstable and extremely vulnerable. It concerns me she will be even more so when she finds out exactly what kinds of things her *step*brother entertains. Particularly the debased private parties where he entertains his exhibition fantasies."

Caleb froze. His face turned ashen. Tendons stood out along his neck until his pulse was visible.

"Caleb?"

I winced at her small voice as Ryth stepped closer. Hale never looked her way, just held C's stare.

*Motherfucker.*

"What is he talking about?" she asked.

"Would you like me to show her the recording?" Hale offered. "I'm sure it's available to view, even if it is only forty-eight-hours old. I thought after that night your...*tastes* would be sated." He glanced at Ryth. "Then again, maybe not."

The wounded sound that ripped from her throat was instant and punishing. Ryth stumbled backwards, then turned and tore past the other diners as she raced for the door.

"Nice talk," Hale murmured. "Maybe we'll have another one...soon."

*Soon...*

That one word was more of a threat than the fucking ammunition we'd come with. I glanced at those filthy fuckers at his side and committed their faces to memory.

My brother jerked his gaze to her, then unleashed a roar and charged after her. *"Ryth!"*

Hale smirked as C raced through the restaurant, leaving me and Nick behind.

"You ready for the afterlife, motherfucker?" The words slipped out. I expected the smile, but I wanted the *rage*.

Hale turned that icy stare my way. I knew the kind of man we were dealing with now. He was the fucking devil, a devil dressed in fucking Calvin Klein with an army of the corrupt all around him.

## *caleb*

"RYTH!" I roared as I hit the front door of the restaurant. But she didn't stop, just hurtled down the front stairs and ran for the alley. *"Stop, for fuck's sake!"*

"Get the fuck away from me!" she screamed, lunging for the car. The moment she sank into the gloom, she spun, her eyes shining with tears. "I fucking *trusted you!*"

"I didn't do it!" I barked, pouncing on her the moment she hit the end of the car. I grabbed her arm and spun her to face me. "Do you hear me? *I didn't fucking do it.*"

Her fist drove through the air, landing on the edge of my jaw, and we were back there once more—all rage and fury and I was consumed by her pain. I grabbed her, not caring about her blows or the brutal fucking throb in my jaw, and pulled her against me. "Why do you think I'm so fucking destroyed?"

Footsteps thundered in the alley behind us. I knew it was Nick without even looking. "It was Evans. He did it to save me from destroying myself by betraying you. He did it all, and they killed him anyway."

"Get the fuck off me, Caleb." She beat at me with her

pathetic blows. But I took them all, every single flare of pain, because I deserved it. "Get the fuck off me now."

I released her and let her stumble and fall against the rear of the car. She looked up at me with those eyes filled with betrayal. "I fucking *believed* you."

"Don't you think I know that? *My friend is dead because of me.*"

She froze, her breaths racing. "What?"

"That recording you heard before. They killed him, and it was all because of what we did that night." I glanced over my shoulder at Nick. "It was fucking betrayal and a goddamn message. Nick said before that we'd all have to do some sick shit to get you back, so this is mine. This is mine, okay?"

Tobias strode rapidly into the alley and motioned to the car. "Whatever it is, we need to do it later. Get in the car. We're out of here *now*."

He was right. Nick pressed the button to unlock the car and we all climbed in. This time, I took the back seat. "Better start talking, brother," Nick snapped as he shoved the car into reverse and punched the accelerator.

We were driving back through the city within minutes, heading back to the Rossi safe-house. I looked at Ryth, who sat as far away from me as possible, almost hugging the car door. Then I started talking. "There was only one way I could get into the Order and that was through Killion."

I caught her shudder at the name and she jerked her gaze to me. Tears shimmered on her cheeks, making me feel like more of a bastard than I felt already. "To get in, he wanted me to have sex with women the Order provided."

She swallowed hard, and pain ignited in her eyes before she looked away. There were feelings involved here, more than I'd ever expected. Her heart and mine were on the line. "But I couldn't go through with it. Evans saw that, and it came down to do it or lose you. So, while I stood there and watched, he did it for me."

"Jesus..." Nick shot a glare at the rear-view mirror.

My voice was raw and husky. I felt that burn all the way down into my chest. "It fucking destroyed him to do what he had to do in that room. Still, they killed him for it anyway."

The silence inside the car was deafening until Ryth spoke. "Did he hurt her?"

I flinched at the words, biting down on the rage inside me. "No," I answered as I looked her way. "But I can't speak for the others."

She wrapped her arms around her ribs and shivered. I knew the last thing she wanted was for me to touch her, but I couldn't stand to see her in pain. I slid across the seat and pulled her into my arms. She resisted for a moment, then turned and buried her head against my neck. "I wouldn't lie to you about this. I know what's at risk. I promise you on my life, and my brothers' lives, that I didn't touch that woman."

She lifted her head, and I knew in that moment I was utterly intoxicated with her. I leaned down and brushed her lips with mine. "Do you know me now? Do you know me better than anyone? I might do a lot of things, Ryth, but I'll never lie to you."

I kissed her once more, slid my finger under her jaw, and tilted her lips to mine. Her mouth was hard and unforgiving until the heat between us took over. Inch by inch, she gave into me, until her arms went around my body and pulled me against her. Desperation drove my mouth harder against her. I lowered my hand and cupped and kneaded her breast until she moaned.

My brothers were silent in the front seat as I lowered my hand and pushed her shirt up and over her breasts. I tugged down the bra strap, releasing her nipple. "I would've risked my life rather than betray you. Do you know how fucked up that is?"

Her response was to arch her spine to give me the heat of her body and not the sting of her rage.

"Christ, C. You can't wait until we get back to the house?" Nick muttered.

I couldn't wait, not for one more fucking second. This was more than sex, more than lust and desire...this was a carving out of my soul. This was a promise, one I needed her to understand. I gently pushed her back on the seat as my hands moved to the button of her jeans and yanked down her zipper.

She lifted her ass and let me slide her jeans and panties down with one hard yank. By the time we turned onto the freeway, my fingers were inside her, sliding deep. I couldn't get enough. I lowered my head and kissed the top of her slit. "There's no one else. You get that, Ryth? There's no one else for me."

Her fingers slid over my head and fisted my hair as she lifted her knee and spread her legs as far as she could. Tobias reached around and gripped her thigh, supporting her as I dragged my tongue along her crease and sucked.

"That's it, little mouse," Tobias urged. "Let our brother exorcise his goddamn demons."

His words only drove me harder, because that's exactly how this felt. This wasn't asking her forgiveness, this was demanding it. I lifted my gaze to hers, splayed my fingers on either side of her slit, and widened it. I licked her like my soul was on the line, driving her closer to oblivion.

She was so fucking wet, her pink pussy was so fucking ready for me.

"Eat her," Tobias snarled. "Fucking eat her, C."

Her body twitched and she raised her feet higher, but they were still entangled in her jeans. The pressure on the back of my head increased and urged me harder against her. God, she was close, so fucking close. Tiny whimpers coincided with a clenching of her ass. She bucked, then turned slick and warm against my mouth and let out a guttural moan.

"That's it," my brother praised. "Christ, that's it, princess."

Hard breaths consumed me. She clenched her thighs and her pussy pulsed against my mouth as I gave her one last lick and pulled away. "No one else, Ryth. I promise you."

She looked up at me, the birthmark blazing on her cheek as I slipped my fingers inside my mouth and sucked. Fuck, I never got tired of seeing her like this, all pink and flushed. I lowered my gaze to her pussy, all swollen and wet.

"We need to find this London St. James." Nick broke the spell, drawing my focus to him behind the wheel. "Whatever he has on Hale, we can use. Maybe then the bastard might listen to our threats."

He was right. London St. James and Ryth's father were the key to all this. "I go after him, find a way to make him break his allegiance. We give him what he wants."

Ryth lifted her head as she reached down and slid her jeans and panties back into place. "You mean Vivienne, don't you?"

"Do you have another idea?"

Her brow furrowed until she closed her eyes and shook her head.

"Then that's it," Nick answered. "We get her out of that place and lure St. James to give her whatever information he has."

But Ryth wasn't so sure. She was quiet, opening her eyes to find mine. She was scared, and it wasn't just for herself. I knew what Vivienne had done to protect her in that room, knew what she'd done to help her get free. To Ryth, this would be a betrayal. "The moment we get what we need, we set her free. You have my word," I urged. "I promise."

265

"I know if I were her, I'd rather take my chance with us, than stay a fucking second longer in that place," Tobias muttered, turning back to the road. "Especially now."

After we'd left her behind. That's what he meant. Christ. I clenched my fist, still feeling the ache from what I'd done to the Priest. They'd take it out on her, I was sure of that. "We get her out, get what we need, then we hide her," I added. "Somewhere they won't ever find her."

"Where?" she asked. "Where can she possibly go where Hale won't find her?"

"I don't know," I answered. "But we'll find somewhere."

We drove back to the safehouse and pulled into the driveway. The more I thought about it, the more I knew Killion was deeper in this than I'd ever realized. He'd been my way in, but he was more than that. He was at the festering heart of that place. Maybe he was even just as much in charge as Hale was.

Evans' screams merged with Ryth's in my head.

I climbed out and lingered behind the others as they went into the house. Tobias scanned the street, then grabbed his phone and punched in a message. By the time I walked inside, I saw the sleek black Explorer creep past the house. Freddy was behind the wheel. I knew we were safe for now, but I didn't know for how much longer.

I walked into the living room and heard the bathroom door close. A quick scan of the rest of the house, and I headed for the back bedroom and the bag of untraceable weapons.

"Going somewhere?" Tobias hovered in the doorway.

I shot him a glare as I grabbed two of the filed down Sig Sauers and a spare clip. "Out."

He stepped closer. "Want some company?" It wasn't really a question. Maybe Tobias didn't entirely trust me after all. As brutal as my younger brother was, this was something I had to do alone.

"No." I pushed past him. "Keep her safe."

I went to the kitchen and held out my hand to Nick. "Keys."

He shot me a look, then glanced toward the doorway. "Where are you going, Caleb?"

I shook my head. "Keys, Nick."

With a deep sigh, he slapped the keys into my hand. "You get yourself killed, brother, and she'll never forgive you."

I strode toward the front door as I muttered, "Then that'll make two of us."

# THIRTY-SEVEN

## *caleb*

DON'T GET KILLED. Sounded simple, right?

Although it didn't *feel* simple. Not with what I planned to do. I climbed into the car, started the engine, and backed out of the driveway, feeling more dangerous than I'd ever felt in my life.

I took the back streets to the other side of the city, replaying the moment I'd met Halestrom's stare. Steely dark eyes and a chiseled jaw. The man was a predator and always calculating. A machine pretending to be human.

The threat hadn't exactly gone to plan. I assumed he'd want to do anything he could to keep his sick facility a secret. But instead of hiding behind his bribes and money, he seemed to almost dare us to expose him. After all, the Hale Order was, in his eyes, above reproach, hiding behind its prison-like structure for troubled young women.

Only that place offered no fucking counselling. It was nothing more than a front to traffic women to the elite. I licked my lips, tasting salt and pleasure, and my pulse raced at the memory of what had just happened with Ryth.

I'd almost lost her today, almost pushed her too far. The

image of her standing there with that fucking look of betrayal hit me like a fist to my chest. She'd cried...*because of me.*

My breaths raced as I shifted my gaze to the rear-view mirror, scanning the cars behind me. I'd almost lost her...*I'd almost lost her.* *"Fucking idiot!"* I yelled, and punched the steering wheel.

That weighed heavy on my soul as I headed for Evans' apartment on the upper west side of the city. He lived in the penthouse suite of a sleek, expensive apartment building his family owned, complete with onsite security and state-of-the-art camera systems. It'd been months since I'd been there. But before all the shit with mom and Ryth blew up, I'd spent my weekends there drinking and partying. That time felt like a lifetime ago. I winced and turned the wheel, pulled into the back entrance of his building, and switched off the ignition.

This whole thing was a goddamn mess.

I parked the car, climbed out, and strode to the entrance. Evans had been a friend, a better one than I'd deserved. He was lonely, and awkward, an heir to a fortune that weighed heavily on him, and deep down, I'd taken advantage of that, using him to find my way into the kind of debased parties that now haunted me.

Evans had opened doors for me and introduced me to the kind of men I now wished I'd never laid eyes on. Men like Killion. Maybe it was my fault this had happened? Like I'd somehow drawn their attention to Ryth...like blood in the water enticing a pack of frenzied sharks.

The idea of that was almost too much to bear. "No. It can't be that simple."

I fixed my gaze on the building and stepped up to the keypad, then punched in the number Evans had programmed for me. He'd wanted me to come and go without him having to worry about security. I never thought I'd be using it for this.

*He threatened me, Caleb. He threatened my fucking family.*

Those words resounded as I waited for the lock to release. I pushed in, scanned the foyer, and headed for the elevator. The code was needed one more time to take me to the tenth floor where Evans' penthouse apartment waited. Cold, empty eyes met me in the reflection of the stainless steel elevator doors as they closed.

I looked unaffected on the surface, while inside, I tore myself apart. Memories of the Order flashed in my head. The Priest's screams as I attacked him in The Principal's office. Images of blood and destruction followed and left me to wince and look away from the monster in the reflection.

I stepped out when the elevator came to a stop and made my way to the apartment door. I entered the code again, pushed the handle down, and walked in. The familiar scent of expensive cologne and cigars hit me in the murky amber gloom of the apartment. My steps slowed on their own the moment I saw the crime scene tape stretched across the end of the hallway, then I caught sight of the destruction in the living room.

I didn't want to see what waited on the other side of that yellow tape, and yet I was helpless to stop myself, gravitating toward the shoved-aside sofa and smashed coffee table. Tiny glass shards crunched under my boots, and larger pieces were scattered across the floor of the room. The place was a mess.

*Jesus...*

I stopped at the end of the hallway, unable to will my feet to move a step more. There was blood on the sleek tile floor. The large pool was now dried to a russet brown. A dining room chair sat overturned in the middle of the floor. I knew in an instant this was where he'd died. His screams tore through my head again, playing over and over as I found remnants of zip ties on the floor.

My stomach clenched as revulsion made me brace my hand

against the wall. *They killed him...they fucking killed him.* All because of what we'd done. And the sick thing was, I'd do it all over again in a goddamn heartbeat, even knowing what would happen. Because there was no way I'd leave her.

Not in this lifetime.

I forced myself away, stumbled to the study, and hit the light. The room brightened instantly, and I headed for the desk. There were no files on the surface. I pulled out the chair and sat.

I knew Evans, probably better than I should. We'd shared far too many damn late nights studying after stumbling into our first ethics and the law class together. And if I knew him at all, then I knew he'd have information on those who'd done this. Information I needed. I opened the drawers, pulled out the files, and found one with my name right on top.

I opened the file and splayed the contents across the desk. Black-and-white images sat on top, and underneath them was information about the men surrounding the Hale Order. Evans might have been awkward and quiet in real life, but his investigative skills outshone everything else. He'd been known in class and at the firm as 'the geeky genius'. The person who dug up all the dirt on our opponents, giving us the edge when we'd needed it.

And it looked like he'd done that one last time.

Only this time, for me

St. James, Killion, Hale, and many others were listed in detail. Names, dates of birth, addresses, and more. My pulse jumped as I scanned the information. I rose, shoved the pages back into the file, and closed the door behind me as I left the study. But before I left, I looked at the living room again. I had one more stop before I descended on London St. James. One more nail in my coffin.

I headed out of the apartment building, climbed back into

the car, and made my way to the Evanses' estate further west of the city, then pulled up outside the towering wrought-iron gates. The house could barely be seen from the street, mostly hidden behind towering weeping willows and the sweeping driveway that led to the house. Guilt made me come here. Now that I was here, hell if I knew what to say...

I leaned out, pressed the intercom, and flinched when it was quickly answered by an icy, curt, feminine tone. "This is a private estate."

"Mrs. Evans, it's Caleb Banks."

"Caleb?"

I swallowed the taste of acid in the back of my throat. "Yes, ma'am, it's me."

"Let me grab the gate," she said, and a second later, the barrier opened in front of me.

I made my way to the opulent limestone house that loomed ahead and pulled up in the middle of the circular driveway. The front door opened, as I pulled up and killed the engine. *You piece of shit*...the words rose as I climbed out and made my way around the rear of the car, meeting Francine Evans at the base of the front steps.

She stood tall and stoic, her chin jutted high, accentuating her hawk-like features. But the defiant act was just that—an act. Her bloodshot eyes shone with fresh tears. Ones she swiped away as I closed the distance between us and wrapped my arms around her in a gentle hug.

She patted my arm with a trembling hand, not allowing herself to give into the emotion.

"I'm so sorry." My voice was husky. "I just can't believe this happened. One of the guys sent me a link this morning. They're calling it a home invasion?"

I pulled away, watching her reaction. She looked away, taking a step backwards, desperate to gain some distance. Her throat muscles worked as she swallowed and spoke. "That's what they're saying."

My pulse raced. "Do you think it could've been something else?"

She gave a shrug. "I don't know. I don't know anything anymore." She was starting to close down right in front of me, wrapping her arms around her waist. "It was nice of you to come, Caleb. But you shouldn't have worried yourself."

"It was no worry." Memories of my own mother hovered far too close. I wanted to ease this woman's pain...but what could I say? *It was my fault...all my fucking fault. But how was I to know?*

"Thank you for coming," she said, dismissing me. "Give my regards to your mother."

*Your mother...*I winced and slowly nodded. Her grief was making her forget the fact she'd stood next to our family at the foot of my mother's casket mere months ago. "Sure," I murmured. "I can do that. Please, don't hesitate to call me if I can do anything."

"You're very kind." She took a step toward the house. "But we'll be fine."

Only she wasn't going to be fine. I lifted my gaze to the house, knowing that inside, Gerald Evans was at that moment in his last months of life with stage four cancer, and now their only child was gone. Francine Evans was alone, alone and hidden behind the walls of this estate where one day, she too would die...still alone.

I gave in, nodded, and made my way back to the car. I climbed in and started the engine, headed back to the gate, and shifted my gaze to the file on the passenger seat beside me.

London St. James' address was written on the first page, scribbled in Evans' handwriting, almost like an afterthought. Was he guiding me?

I punched the address into my phone just before I pulled out of the Evanses' driveway. St. James lived not far away...a few streets actually, although the streets looked more like the ones we lived on, and not the sprawling acreage like the one I'd just left behind. I pushed west, finally taking a left on Sunset and then a right on Rayne, slowing as I scanned the house numbers. But I didn't need to...

Two guys stood at the back of a midnight Chrysler in front of a three-car garage. Identical twins by the looks of it, the same age as Tobias, and I knew in my gut this was the place. The trunk was open and two gym bags sat on the ground at their feet. I pulled up, parked in front of their driveway, and killed the engine.

Ryth was all I thought about. Ryth and her pain shining in her eyes. Pain I never wanted to see again. I was out of the car before I knew it and reached around to pull the gun from under my shirt as I climbed the steep rise of their driveway. "St. James, right?"

Identical gazes turned. "Who the fuck is asking?" one snarled, his gaze narrowing as I lifted the gun and pointed it point-blank at his brother's head. *Then* the asshole's gaze widened.

I jerked the gun toward the house. "Inside."

They didn't move. Not at first, fear freezing them to the spot. But I wasn't messing around. We were too far gone for that. I closed the distance and pressed the muzzle against the asshole's head. "I will pull this fucking trigger and splatter your brains all over your car."

"Okay, man." The other twin stepped backwards. "Whatever you say. Just take it easy."

I herded them toward the house and glanced at the empty third parking space. The other car was a hotted-up Bronco, and there was no way in hell I saw London St. James driving

274

anything like that. They shoved a key into the front door and stepped inside, leaving me to follow and close the door behind me. The foyer was adorned with charcoal pieces of art that looked expensive. But I wasn't here to rob the place. Instead, I listened for movement. "Who else is home?"

"No one," the other twin snapped. "So take whatever the fuck you want and get the hell out of here."

They thought this was a home invasion? *Did they not hear me call their damn name?*

"We have money," the idiot standing in front of me said. "There's gotta be ten thousand in the safe. It's all yours. We won't even call the cops."

"Of course you won't." I stepped closer, staring into his eyes. I'm not after your fucking money. Where is your father?"

His brow furrowed and slowly, realization ignited in his eyes. He looked like his father in that second. The same calculating stare, the same predatory gleam. My grip tightened around the gun. It was St. James I wanted, St. James I'd make scream. Anything to get the information I needed to save Ryth.

But I hadn't come to kill him. No, that I was saving for Killion.

"Our father?" the asshole repeated as he glanced at the gun.

"Yes," I snapped. "Your goddamn father."

The other twin took a step closer and growled, "What the fuck do you want with him?"

"Let's just say we have business," I answered coldly, and pressed the gun harder into his brother's head.

He held my stare, no doubt committing my face to memory as he answered. "Then I guess you're shit out of luck, aren't you? He's not here."

My breath stilled. *He's not here..."*Where is he?"

His lips curled in anger. "The same fucking place he's always at...he's gone to see *her*."

*Vivienne.*

Panic thundered as those stark hallways and locked security doors filled my mind. "The Order."

"Yeah," the son in front of me answered. "The fucking Order."

# THIRTY-EIGHT

## *caleb*

THE ORDER...

"Who the fuck *are* you?" The asshole in front of me narrowed his gaze.

I flinched, my head shaking on its own. "Doesn't matter."

"I think it does." His brother took a step closer. "I think it matters very much."

The gun in my hand wavered, suddenly feeling too heavy. My pulse raced as I lowered it. I wasn't here to shoot them...I just wanted... "He won't let her go." I held the twin's stare as he took another step closer. "You're after her, that's it, isn't it? We won't let her go, not now." His voice was nothing more than a savage growl. "We *own* her, you get that? You can't have her, because *we* own her."

Own her...

The words resounded inside me. I didn't just see London St. James in the eyes of his sons now, I saw myself. Own her... That's what I wanted, right? It was the same hunger, the same insatiable longing that rode me. Every second spent with Killion wasn't about me saving her. It was about me controlling her, taking her, *fucking her*. My body trembled with the compulsion. Ryth burned inside me like a drug, one I'd tasted in the walk-in pantry in my family home with my mouth while I'd fucked her with my fingers. One I wanted to taste again.

It was more than love...

Darker than desire.

This was a sick compulsion.

An obsession I couldn't avoid.

*Because I didn't want to.*

"You get that?" I flinched at the voice, jerking my gaze back to the twin in front of me as he reached out, grabbed my shirt, and warned, "Vivienne belongs to us."

I tore myself out of his grasp. "Get the fuck off me."

"Who the fuck are you?" he repeated.

I didn't stand around and answer, just stumbled backwards before I turned and hurried for the door. I was outside in an instant, sucking in hard breaths as my fingers twitched and my legs shook. I barely made it to the car before my knees buckled. I clawed the door handle, yanked it open, and slumped behind the wheel.

My hands were trembling as I shoved the key into the ignition and started the car.

*Beep...*

I thrust my hand into my pocket and yanked my phone free, seeing a notification blinking. I pressed the button, illuminating the screen. There was a message from Killion...

My fingers shook as I punched in the code and opened the message. It was a video, but the screen was dark, too dark for me to see what it was. So I hit play...

"Hold her down!" The roar boomed through the speaker. I jerked, my gaze fixed on the screen...darkness crowding in as I heard Ryth unleash a moan, then in an instant the video brightened. Ryth bucked, screaming, as they strapped her down on a stainless steel table. The buzz of a tattoo gun followed. I watched helplessly as they yanked her pants down and set to work, marking her skin.

A hiss tore free from her throat, deep, harsh, and hateful. I clenched my grip around the cell until it shuddered in my grasp. She howled, thrashing under their holds. *"NICK!"* she shrieked for my brother. *"TOBIAS!"*

My heart clenched tight. I knew it was coming, but still I wasn't prepared.

*"CALEB!"*

She howled for me. *She howled for me*...I closed my eyes as agony ripped through my chest. "No...*no...no*."

*Beep.*

I yanked open my eyes and fixed my gaze on the screen as I exited the video and killed the sound of that tattoo gun as it hummed. A voice message waited from Killion. I didn't want to listen, but I was incapable of ignoring his call...not when there was more than my life on the line—there was Ryth's, too.

I clenched my fist, then pressed the button, listening to Killion's coarse tone echo through the speaker. "I've decided to change my mind, Caleb. I want the ruined bitch after all." His tone grew deeper, fighting through the thud of familiar music in the background. "I've been promised her," he said, and I could almost see the smirk on his face. "The contract is signed, and we're coming for her. It's only a matter of time, Caleb, and the little Castlemaine cunt is mine...I'm going to enjoy shouting your name when she gags on my cock."

I closed my eyes as I rocked back against the seat. Inside my head, I was screaming, tearing myself apart with desperation. *I'll kill him... I'll fucking kill him.* My hand shook as the recording ended, but instead of deleting the message, I pressed the button again, replaying his threat once more. But it wasn't his voice I narrowed in on, it was the music in the background. The same familiar beat I'd heard before. The Hale Club.

A twitch came in the corner of my mouth. The hell club...

He was there, goading and threatening me. I lifted my gaze to the St. James house and couldn't stop the desperation unraveling inside me. The gun pressed against my back and it was all I could think about, driving the muzzle into Killion's face and pulling the goddamn trigger.

I wanted it more than I'd ever wanted anything before.

I shoved the car into gear and punched the accelerator, stabbing Nick's new number into my phone as I drove.

He answered on the third ring. "Where the fuck are you, C?"

"I'm going to the Hale Club, Nick. Killion's there...Killion..." *I want the ruined bitch after all.* The bastard's voice resounded in my head. I couldn't shake it, couldn't get out from under the crushing weight of this rage. "Killion is there, and I'm going to kill him."

"What the fuck are you talking about, Caleb?" he barked. "You go there, and you'll be killed. Can't you get that?"

I did. Maybe deep down, I'd always known it'd come to this. Me against him...

"Come back. Come back and we'll talk about this," Nick pleaded, but I could hear the anger in his tone.

"No, I don't think so, not this time." My words dulled, sinking all the way to that murderous thrum that resounded in my chest. "Tell Ryth...tell her...I love her."

"Caleb..."

I lowered the phone.

*"Caleb—"*

And pressed the button, ending my brother's scream.

I was okay now, quiet, still. My gaze was fixed on the road ahead as I made my way through the residential streets and back toward the city. I knew what I needed to do now. I knew how I was going to reach absolution...for her anyway...

One kill at a time.

## THIRTY-NINE

*ryth*

"CALEB!" Nick practically screamed, and I jumped. *"Goddamn it!"* he roared, and lowered the phone, pressed the button again, and lifted it back to his ear. *"Answer me! Answer me, you stupid sonofabitch!"*

"What's going on?" I stared at Nick as he listened to the phone ring...and ring...*and ring*. Goosebumps raced along my arms as I stepped across the kitchen. "Nick?"

He just dropped his hand, ended the call, then stared at me for a second. No, he stared right through me, as though he didn't see me at all. "Fucking idiot!" he snarled as his gaze came into focus and fixed on me.

"What is it?" I slid my hand along his arm. "Tell me."

"He's going after Killion," he answered. "The stupid idiot is going after Killion and he's going to get himself killed."

"What the fuck?" Tobias snarled, walking into the kitchen as he tugged down his shirt. His face was still flushed after coming back from a run. "What do you mean, he's going after Killion?"

Nick just looked my way. "He said to tell you that he loves you."

"No." Tobias jerked his gaze to Nick. "*No fucking way!* Get him on the goddamn phone, Nick. Tell him to get his ass back here. Tell him—"

"He's not answering."

I stared at Nick while my mind raced and my heart howled. "What the fuck is he thinking?"

"What do you mean *'what the fuck is he thinking'?*" Tobias snapped. "You think he's *thinking* about anything other than you?"

"Me?" The word hit me. "No. You can't put this on me. I didn't ask—"

"Can't put this on you?" Tobias cut me off. His lips curled in a sneer as he closed the distance between us. "Are you blind, princess? *You're* his goddamn weak spot, his Achilles fucking heel. Can't you see he's trying to make amends for what he did to get you out of that place? He's taking it out on anyone who touched you, anyone who *threatened you.* He's gonna kill this Killion...even if he kills himself in the process." His tone softened as he stared into my eyes. "This isn't just a mission to save you, Ryth. It's a mission to make sure *no one* touches you again. You belong to us. You've *always* belonged to us...from the goddamn moment you stepped a foot inside our door. Whether we wanted it or not."

That night slammed back into me. Reeking of smoke and carrying nothing more than a garbage bag for my clothes, I'd crept into their home, and into their hearts. In turn, they'd crept into mine. No, not crept...collided.

Our fates had crashed into each other that night in a shock wave that changed us all. Cataclysmic. Destructive down to the core. They'd shattered me and rebuilt me all at the same time.

Now they were trying to save me...

Each with their own darkness.

With nothing more than a gun in their hands and that burning hunger.

Caleb was going to die...

*For me.*

"*No.*" Agony plunged deep. "We can't let him. Do you hear me? We can't—"

"Already on it, princess." Nick jerked his gaze to Tobias. "We need a ride. Something fast...*and move it, T.*"

Tobias sucked in a breath, tore his gaze from me...and lunged for the door. The *slam* resounded throughout the safehouse. Nick was already moving. "We need guns, princess... and lots of them."

Guns...

I hurried for the back bedroom, grabbed the duffel bag at the end of the bed, and shoved the guns scattered across the comforter back inside. *Caleb was going to die...he was going to die...*

*Unless we stopped him.*

# FORTY
## *caleb*

I PULLED the car into the parking lot of the elite Hale Club, and climbed out. The sky was darkening as dusk moved closer to night, leaving the parking lot lights to burn a little brighter next to me. There was no sign of Killion's car, or his driver for that matter, but that didn't mean that he wasn't here.

I looked at my phone on the passenger seat next to me, still hearing the bastard's smirk infecting every fucking word he'd left me. My pulse thundered. My mind was a vengeful storm, unleashing its rage inside me.

My hands trembled as I climbed out and reached for the gun pressed against the small of my back. Determination fueled me, driving me to yank back the slide and check the round. I had a full clip, that was all...

*Could I do it?*

*Could I pull the trigger and kill a man in cold blood?*

Ryth's face filled me, and the answer quickly followed. Yeah, for her I could. I shoved the door closed and strode toward the club with the gun in my hand, held down beside my thigh. Fear surged, and I swallowed it down, knowing that this was probably the end for me.

I saw it now as I made my way to the private entrance at the rear of the club. The cops would be called. Maybe I'd be taken out by the bouncers before they came anywhere near the place. If I were Tobias, I might've had a chance...but I wasn't my little brother.

I was just me...

"Hold the door open for me, Mom," I murmured, stepped up to the entrance, and pressed the buzzer as I slipped the gun behind me.

For a second, I thought the door wasn't going to open and security would swarm me before I even got a chance to step inside. But then the door opened, and the security guard was there, meeting my stare. "Mr. Banks."

I lifted the gun, aimed it at the guard's face, and stepped in. "Move."

His eyes widened with surprise before his jaw tightened. I pushed in and pulled the door closed behind me. "Killion, is he here?"

The guard didn't answer, not until I shoved the gun toward him. "Yes, yes, he's here."

*He's here...he's here...he's—*

I scanned the hallway, driving him backwards and into the back room of the club. There were no dancers in there yet, no terrified women dressed in black, red, and white, dragged from the Hale Order to fuck and control. No, just corrupt men with one intent—to corrupt and debase everything they touched.

No, the back room of the Hale Club was quiet and dark. I lengthened my stride, shoving the guard toward the front, where the music was louder.

"Stay where I can see you." I scanned the club, searching the darkness for Killion, then focused on the guard as I motioned with the gun toward the empty tables.

I hadn't come here to shoot the guard, but if he stood

between me and vengeance, then I'd have no other alternative but to pull the trigger. "Where's Killion?"

He pointed to the darkened lounges on the far side of the bar. I followed the motion, searching the gloom. My heart raced as my mouth went dry. I pushed the guard harder as I made my way around the end of the bar, drawing the gaze of the bartender as he wiped glasses.

His hands stopped and his gaze narrowed. Fear bloomed before he glanced to where the shadowy outline of a man sat amongst the tables...

*Killion.*

My heart was in the driver's seat now, forcing me forward. The gun wavered in my hand as I left the guard behind and strode toward the dark shadow sitting all alone. The closer I got, the more clearly I saw him. Killion was sitting with his legs crossed, casually sipping his goddamn cognac like he didn't have a care in the world... Maybe you didn't, when you had no conscience.

The gun didn't waver this time as I lifted my hand and aimed at the bastard's head. A flicker of confusion raced through me. For a split second, I thought this was all too easy, that this was too smooth. But then I shoved the thought away and focused on him.

"You had Evans killed," I snarled as I stepped closer. "And threatened his family."

Killion slowly placed the glass on the table in front of him and lifted his gaze to me. The heavy thud of the music resounded. But I knew he'd heard me as those beady eyes glittered.

I sucked in a deep breath, my hand steady now as I moved closer and pressed the gun to his head. "You think you can take her from me? You think you can...*steal her from me?*"

*This one...is ruined.* The echo of his words resounded in my head. All I could see was his hands on Ryth as he drove her against the wall in that room in the Order. *That mark on your face looks like the mark of a hand...like you've been beaten.* In my head, he pinched her nipple. *You like to be beaten?*

My finger curled a little tighter around the trigger. "I won't let you."

*She's perfect...I want her...*

He didn't flinch, didn't even look at the gun.

Movement came in the corner of my eye. And a cold shiver found me once more.

"I knew you'd come," Killion smiled. "In fact, I was banking on it."

*Pftt...*

The sudden sound came from behind me. Something bit the side of my neck, making me stumble sideways. I slapped my hand against the pain, knocking something free. It clattered to the floor, steel glinting from the projectile. But it wasn't a bullet...*not a bullet.* The darkened room started to sway as I staggered. I spun and found the white-haired guard from the Order striding forward, lowering the tranq gun in his hand.

Only then did Killion uncross his legs and rise. "You see, we couldn't get to her. No one we knew would talk to us, instead they spoke another name...*the Rossis.* You kept her well hidden. So well, I was rather impressed." He stepped closer, and the darkness seemed to swirl around me. My heart was thundering, driving terror through my veins.

"No," I whispered.

He slowly nodded. "Yes, I'm afraid. We needed another way to lure her back to us...and what better way than to push your buttons?" I stiffened as he moved close, lifted his hand, and cupped my cheek as those sinister eyes flared. "And you know how much I love to do that." He smirked. "This way, we get a two-for-one deal..."

My brothers...

"Nick...*Tobiiiiassss.*" My voice slurred as the room tilted sideways. I knew I was falling, but I was unable to stop it. I wanted to stop it...*I tried to stop it.*

Instead, I hit the floor with a *thud and* my head slammed down so hard I saw stars for a second.

Black boots shone as Killion came closer. I fought, lashed out my foot, and forced a howl of rage through my teeth as I tried to fight whatever poison hummed in my veins, but the room grew colder, until the darkness wrapped itself around me.

"Your brothers..." Killion taunted as he knelt beside me. "Well, we have no need for them now, do we?"

The gloom crowded in, stealing his face from me. "*Nnnoooo...*"

My voice wasn't my own, not anymore.

Just a moan.

Just a plea...

And as that last trace of consciousness slipped free, one thought screamed through my mind...*what the fuck have I done?*

## FORTY-ONE

*ryth*

THE SCREAM of tires came from outside the house. I wrenched my gaze to Nick, who grabbed the heavy duffel bag from the bed and hauled the strap over his shoulder. "Let's go, princess."

I was right behind him as we lunged along the hallway and raced to the front door, then outside. An old, beat-up muscle car sat parked on the street, rumbling and sputtering. Tobias shoved out of the driver's seat and raced around the front.

"A Charger?" Nick muttered as he tossed his brother the bag of weapons.

"You wanted fast, right?" Tobias moved to the passenger door, yanked it open with a squeal of its hinges, and pulled the seat forward.

I didn't wait, just climbed inside and clawed for the seatbelt.

"Let's see what this baby can do, then" Nick growled as he climbed in behind the wheel.

The engine spluttered again, almost dying before Nick punched the accelerator and the throbbing growl roared. The car shuddered, then surged as Tobias shoved the seat in place, dropped the bag of guns at his feet, and lunged inside. "Go...*GO!*"

I was slammed backwards against the seat, and struggled to clasp the seatbelt as we tore along the street, leaving the Rossi safehouse behind. We flew past a gleaming blur of black. I caught Nick's stare as we shot past the familiar four-wheel drive with Lazarus' bodyguard behind the wheel. I twisted in the seat, watching out the back window. But Freddy didn't follow, just left us to haul ass out of the protection of the mafia.

We were on our own now.

Three of us, desperate for one.

Caleb...

My heart shuddered my chest. I gripped hold of the seat-belt across my body and braced my hand against the door as we took a corner sideways and accelerated hard.

*You're his goddamn weak spot. His Achilles fucking heel.*

Tobias' words resounded in my head. They were all I could think about, all I could hear. My chest ached at the thought of Caleb. Hate, love, desperation, and lust roiled inside me. He was going to kill Killion...to save me.

The car surged and turned hard. I clenched my jaw, swaying against the window.

*Can't you see he's trying to make amends for what he did to get you out of that place?* We charged toward the heart of the city, taking the back streets. Nick shifted gears faster than I'd seen before. I held on. *He's taking it out on anyone who touched you, anyone who threatened you. He's gonna kill that Killion...even if he kills himself in the process.*

A car came out of nowhere, making Nick bark a curse, shift gears, and spin the wheel, throwing me against the side. Agony slammed into my shoulder and radiated through my chest. I bit down on a cry and pushed back into the seat.

"Hang on, princess," Nick growled, glancing at me over his shoulder.

Tobias turned and grabbed my arm. "You okay?" Concern flared in his eyes.

"I'm okay," I assured them, turning all my rage and focus to the road. "Just get us there, Nick."

"Working on it," he answered and pushed the car even harder.

We turned the corner onto a back street, hitting the entrance hard and scraping the bottom of the Charger. Tobias bent over and reached into the bag, and I knew we were close. My stomach rolled as I searched the night ahead, seeing the entrance to a parking lot and I realized this was it. It was too clean, too neat...too *quiet*.

Security lights showed dimly around the gloomy parking lot. I searched the darkness and spotted the sedan we'd been using...*Caleb...he's here.*

"T," Nick growled.

The passenger window squealed as Tobias wound it down and pushed a gun out, scanning the parking spaces as we turned in hard.

"There's the car," Nick barked.

We skidded sideways, lurching to a stop in front of the sedan. Tobias was out in an instant, scanning the inside of it before he raced toward the back of the club. Nick shoved the driver's door open as he turned to order over his shoulder. "Stay in the car, Ryth!"

I didn't have time to answer. He was gone in an instant, leaving me terrified and pissed off. "What the fuck?" I clawed the seatbelt release and shoved myself between the seats and reached for the duffel bag.

Their roars drifted in through Tobias' open window as they forced their way inside the club. A chill tore through me when I watched them disappear inside. I stared at the open duffel bag on the floorboard of the passenger seat.

I didn't like guns, not after what had happened to me in that warehouse and that fucking place. But I liked the idea of losing the ones I loved even less. So I shoved my hand inside the bag, clenched my grip around steel, and drew out a weapon, one that glinted faintly in the distant overhead lights.

"Come on, Nick," I whispered, and gripped the gun with both hands, trying to still the shakes.

Shadows raced toward me. I lifted my hand and took aim as Tobias snarled, "For Christ's sake, Ryth, don't goddamn shoot me."

Nick followed right after him, yanked the driver's door wider, and slid behind the wheel, shoving his gun under his thigh before he threw the car into gear. I searched the darkness, but no one else was coming. "Caleb?"

"He's not there," Nick answered.

"They took him," Tobias added.

They took him...*they took him*...I shook my head, grabbing onto the seat as I was thrown forward, then slammed back. My thoughts were a blur, a panicked, desperate blur. They were going to kill him...I knew that in my soul. They'd have to...*because he knew too much.*

He'd seen them in that place, in that room...in that *sick torment.* He knew their names, knew their faces. He knew what kind of depravity they'd done to us in there. I gripped the gun and wrapped my other arm around my waist. But I couldn't get warm. I couldn't ever get warm.

*He's gonna kill that Killion...even if he kills himself in the process.*

The bright city lights blurred all around us as we turned hard onto a major street and raced forward.

"They can't be too far ahead," Tobias growled.

I started to lift my focus to the cars in the distance. Only then did I see the blood on Tobias' fist. "You're hurt."

He looked my way, those dark eyes sunken and dangerous. "What?"

"Your hand," I nodded. "You're hurt."

He followed my gaze to the crimson drops on his hand that shimmered under the streetlights. "It's not mine." He swiped the back of his hand on his jeans, smearing the mess, then met my gaze. "It's not mine."

*It's not his...*

I looked at him once more, now seeing the kind of man he was—a dangerous man—one who'd do whatever it took to protect those he loved. They were all like that.

"There," Nick snarled, drawing my gaze. "There they are. That's the fucking car, right?"

All I saw were red brake lights, but they saw something else. Something that told them exactly what they needed to know.

"That's it," Tobias lifted the gun to the window's edge as we tore past the last stretch of streetlights heading out of the city.

Dread filled my stomach, heavy like a rock. I knew where they were going, had known the moment we'd left the parking lot of the club. "They're going to the Order."

Nick jerked his gaze my way. I saw fear there, fear almost hidden behind the brutal determination. He didn't think we were going to get Caleb back...or was he afraid we would...*at what cost?*

"Get him back," I whispered as Nick fixed his attention back on the road. I didn't care what it took, didn't care about the repercussions, didn't care about anything. I clenched my grip around the gun, my focus so fucking clear now, clearer than it'd ever been. "Whatever it takes, Nick. Whatever it takes."

Nick turned a shade of gray and winced. He looked at Tobias, and something uncomfortable echoed back.

"What?" I asked.

"Déjà vu," Nick answered. "Déjà fucking vu." He glanced at me as he shifted gears again. "They're the same words we said to Caleb before he did what he did to get you out."

My stomach rolled and chills broke out. I wanted to wrap my arms around myself. But I didn't. I just focused on the road, knowing how deep in the pit Caleb had gone to get me free. Love radiated through me. Love and desperation. *Whatever it takes...whatever it takes.*

Nick's knuckles turned white around the wheel, and the Charger's engine roared. We'd left other cars behind now. It was just us...and the hulking black SUV up ahead. One we gained on mile after mile that flew past us in a blur. The Charger throbbed and roared, the sound deafening through the open passenger's window.

"Hold us steady," Tobias commanded as he aimed the gun out the window. *Boom! Boom! BOOM!*

I flinched with each round, watching the brake lights of the car in front die. The SUV swerved, tires shrieking, as it veered toward the side of the road, then straightened.

"Hold on," Nick warned as he drove the Charger forward. "Do that again."

Tobias took aim and squeezed off two more shots that hit the back window, shattering it in an instant, and at the same time, Nick aimed our car like a weapon and punched the accelerator, then hit the rear fender of the SUV as it swerved once more.

I jerked forward with the impact, wincing at the scream of metal on metal.

"They can't hold it," Nick said as he drove us hard into the SUV again, pushing the back end of it off the road. Dust billowed, rising in dusky plumes behind us. "Move..." Nick barked. *"MOVE!"*

My pulse jacked higher as I lifted my gaze to the glint of the steel gates in the distance. We weren't going to make it. I looked at the SUV as it fought to hug the road, kicking up stones that peppered the front of the Charger like bullets. *We weren't going to make it.*

Through the shattered back window, Caleb moved into focus. No, not moved...*was pushed.* They were using him as a shield.

"Motherfuckers," I snarled.

Tobias leaned out of the window, then jerked back when a *crack* came from the passenger side of the SUV. *"Get back, Ryth!"* He angled his body in front of mine, protecting me, and reached the gun out once more, emptying the clip.

But it wasn't at the windows, or the body of the vehicle...it was at the tires. *Boom!* One blew in an instant, making the SUV fishtail hard. Nick drove us forward as the glint of steel came closer in the distance and the gates of the Order opened.

*"Nick, no!"* I screamed.

Only it wasn't me I screamed for. If they made it inside, Caleb would be lost. Lost for good...

In the shattered back window, Caleb turned his head and looked at me...there was blood on his face, and his unflinching eyes looked strange. I knew that dazed expression better than I should. It was the same look I'd seen in my own reflection after they'd brought me to the Order. They'd drugged him. I clenched my grip tighter around the gun. They'd *goddamn* drugged him.

"You will not take my fucking brother." Nick forced the words through clenched teeth. "Over my dead fucking body."

Nick drove the car forward again, this time hitting even harder than before. The SUV fishtailed and spun wildly in the middle of the road, then came to a shuddering stop. We shot past it in a blur, all three of us wrenching our gazes behind us.

"Hold on!" Nick roared a second before I was thrown sideways.

I didn't have time to brace for the impact. I didn't have time to do anything at all but hope and pray we didn't roll the car. The acrid stench from the engine filled the car, the scent choking as the Charger skidded sideways, the tires squealing for purchase on the asphalt, and rocked to a stop. But before my body settled, Nick shoved the car into gear and slammed down the accelerator, throwing us forward, headlong toward the blinding headlights of the SUV.

We were going to hit...*we were going to hit.*

I closed my eyes and braced for the impact.

But it didn't happen. We skidded to a stop without hitting. I opened my eyes, to see the doors of the black SUV flung open...and two men stumbled out. Tobias was already shoving his door open and lunging out. Headlights blinded me as the four-wheel drive from the Order hurtled our way.

*Crack!*

*Crack!*

*CRACK!*

Gunshots slammed into the car as Nick threw his door open and reached for me. *"Ryth, MOVE!"*

We left the weapons behind as the mercenaries from the Order flew closer. But they didn't slam into us. They didn't seem to hit us at all.

Instead, they fired at Tobias as he killed one of the men running toward us.

*"Over here!"* a man roared.

And it took me a second before I recognized the voice. It

was him...*him,* the man who'd shoved me against the wall and groped my breast. A chill tore through me as Tobias lunged, taking shelter against our side of the car.

Gunshots fired over our heads stopped us from getting to Caleb. On the other side of the SUV, another SUV raced out from the Order. I gripped the gun and shoved against the car, rising to my feet.

"Ryth!" Nick roared, yanking me back down. *"Stay the fuck down!"*

His hands were all over me, shielding me, comforting me.

But there was no room for comfort.

*"Nick!"* Caleb screamed.

I didn't wait a second longer—*I couldn't.* I shoved against the car, tearing out of Nick's hold, and lunged forward as Caleb screamed once more, *"GET RYTH!"*

Only it was too late. Doors were flung open as more men rushed forward from the second SUV. Men who watched me as they dragged Caleb into the other four-wheel drive. I ran...ran harder than I'd ever run before. I lifted the gun, my hand shaking under the weight. *"Leave him alone!"*

I squeezed off a shot. But it went wide, hitting nothing.

I ran...

And ran...

And when the second four-wheel drive shot forward, heading for the open gates of the Order, I ran after it. My focus was on those red brake lights burning in front of me as I punched my boots into the ground.

They can't have him...

*They can't have him...*

*BECAUSE HE'S MINE!*

## FORTY-TWO

*tobias*

"RYTH!" I screamed and lunged forward. Agony roared through my thigh as my leg buckled. I looked down, to see my black jeans darkening. I didn't need to reach down to know it was blood...I felt it, warm and wet. I slapped my hand against my thigh and screamed through clenched teeth, then drove myself forward again.

She was fast...too fucking fast.

I limped and ran, driving my boots against the asphalt. Each step was agony.

"Get her back, T!" Nick roared.

I risked a glance over my shoulder as a guttural snarl that wasn't my brother came behind me. One asshole from the SUV stumbled toward him, gun raised, before he squeezed off a shot. I waited for a second, watching Nick dive to the ground.

He'd be okay...even with his hand over the wound on his side, he'd be okay. I had to keep moving. I turned my attention to Ryth as she raced for the gates of the Order. "Ryth, for Christ's sake, *STOP!*"

She was slipping away, second by second...*she was slipping away*.

I unleashed a savage sound and pulled my hand from my thigh. Agony collided with rage. I used it all to drive myself forward. My body responded as adrenaline took over. My muscles clenched, settling into the momentum they knew. My strides lengthened and my breathing deepened. I focused on Ryth as she raced through the open gates, heading for the trees.

It was so dark there...too dark. "Ryth, stop!" I roared and pushed myself harder.

She was slowing...and I was gaining. That pushed me even harder. She ducked under a low branch, sinking into the shadows for a second. I lost sight of her, so I kept on moving, hitting the same branch a few seconds later. But I couldn't see her...

"Ryth?" I risked calling her name.

Movement came from the corner of my eye. For a second, relief hit me as I turned my head. "Jesus, you scared the—"

*Thump.* The fist came out of nowhere, blindsiding me. I stumbled backwards as the white-haired guard from the Order charged forward and, with a roar, tackled me to the ground. Fear slammed into me harder than his fists. I shoved sideways, rolling as his blow slammed into the ground inches beside my head.

*Ryth...*

I tried to scan the trees and shoved up from the ground, then stumbled sideways and dragged my gun upwards.

*Boom!*

I flinched as pain tore across my shoulder. The bastard took aim again. I couldn't do anything except lunge for the trees. Agony blazed through my thigh, clenching my stomach. Warmth seeped, slipping down my thigh to tickle my knee. I could feel it. feel it in my movements, feel it in my thoughts.

*Boom!*

I flinched and dove behind a tree as a bullet slammed into the trunk. One frantic glance behind me, and I leaped backwards, racing to the next one, trying to put as much distance between us as I could...and I looked for Ryth. She was all I thought about, all I ran to because without her, *I was nothing*.

"Where are you, you fucking punk?"

The yell came from behind me. I kept running, searching the trees for the faint flicker of lights from the Order. I'd have heard her scream...I would've if they'd taken her, right? *I would've...*

Desperation drove me forward. I rounded a tree trunk and stepped out.

"There you are."

I spun around, lifting my gun. I squeezed off a round and was rewarded with a grunt as the bastard staggered. My hand went to the base of the grip, steadying my aim. "Come on, you ugly motherfucker."

A low chuckle spilled out of the dark. "Ugly, huh? I guess looks don't matter to the cunt you call a stepsister, do they, Banks?"

I stiffened...watching as he stepped into sight. "She didn't mind my looks then, when I cupped her pussy and made her feel good."

Cold. Hard. Rage tore through me. "You what?"

Even in the gloom, I caught the smirk. "She didn't tell you?"

In my head, all I saw was her sad, broken smile, the one she'd fought so hard to shake. She had...she'd come back to us.

"She screamed a little," he added as he stepped closer. "I'm sure she's gonna scream again by the time I'm done with her."

"You fucking piece of shit!" I growled, and stepped out into the open myself. "You lay one fucking hand on her and I'll cut it off and shove it so far up your ass you'll choke on it."

He smirked. That sickening sight grew bolder the closer he came. "How 'bout I assfuck her instead?"

I sucked in a hard breath and lifted the gun, aiming it at the bastard's face.

"She'll scream," he took another step. "But I like it when she does that. I like it a whole fucking lot."

His words slammed into me, driving me forward, until the darkness shifted beside me...and a guard came from nowhere. The blow came from the side, hitting my head with a *thud!* I was thrown sideways and hit the ground hard. The guard was on me in an instant.

Fists drove into my face, over and over...and in the blinding blows, the image of the asshole from my father's office came back to me. His screams. His blood. My vengeance. I felt it now. *She'll scream...but I like it when she does that.*

Vengeance.

Rage.

*Love.*

Love made me savage. Love made me dangerous.

My head snapped to the side. The pain and thoughts of Ryth brought him into focus. When his fist came again...I *moved. My* head snapped to the side and his fist met my forehead with a *crunch.* His scream followed, and it was like music to my ears.

I drove my fist into his ribs, then shoved, slipped around him, and gripped my gun, lifting it to squeeze the trigger point-blank against his chest. *Bang!*

Our bodies muffled the sound as he went still. I shoved, trying to force him off me.

*Boom!*

The asshole on top of me jerked as the bullet hit. I kicked out and shoved the body from me as I lifted my gun to the white-haired fucker who took aim once more.

*Boom!*

*Boom!*

Gunshots cracked through the night. I rolled to a stand and drove myself toward the trees as he came for me. My head was booming, my thoughts too goddamn slow. I sucked in the icy night air and moved sideways. It wasn't about finding Ryth right now.

I had to leave that for Nick...praying he fucking found her, and turned my focus on the bastard in front of me.

"Gotta be hurting," the fucker called. "I know I got you at least once."

I glanced at the sting in my arm. But it was nothing compared to the one in my thigh. I ground my teeth, scanned the darkness, and moved again. All I needed was one clean shot...

I lunged for the next tree.

*Boom!*

Bark flew from the trunk in front of me and peppered my face. I winced and ducked, then fired back, and was rewarded with a snarl of frustration. It was now or never...*no, or lose Ryth.*

I tightened on the biting pattern of the grip and forced my body to give me just a little more. The night closed in around me as I raced forward once more, lunging toward a bank of trees just ahead.

*Boom! Boom!*

His shots went wide as I ran. My boots skidded on damp fallen leaves. I windmilled my arms, trying to keep my balance, and heard the thunder of steps behind me. *Move...MOVE!*

I ran like it wasn't my life that depended on it...*I ran like it was Ryth's.* Agony carved deeper, slicing like a hot knife all the way to the bone in my thigh, making my leg tremble. I knew the moment I wasn't going to make it. My leg went numb, and I lost control. The thunder of boots behind me grew louder.

"Fucking punk," the bastard roared, and tackled me to the ground.

I attacked with brutality, unleashing the rage inside me. And that empty part of me took over, the one that lived in hate, that seethed with desperation. I lashed out, cracking the bastard in the jaw, and he stumbled backwards.

That's all I needed. That second where I stole a breath and gathered my senses was all it took. I drove forward and into him, grabbed him around the throat, and shoved him backwards until his head slammed against a tree. My other fist was already cocked, and it plowed through the air and into his face over and over again.

His head rocked sideways and his eyes turned glazed.

*She'll scream...*

*But I like it when she does that.*

*Thud!*

My fist found his jaw, once...twice, until I heard a sickening *crack*. He stayed there, hard against the tree, held there by my fist alone. I looked down, searched the ground for my gun, and found the glint of steel near my feet.

"No." The word was a gurgle.

But there was no stopping this. I shoved him aside and bent. The gun was in my hand in an instant. "You touched what belonged to me." I lifted the muzzle. "You caused her pain." My finger wrapped around the trigger. "There is no universe where I'd allow that to happen again. She is mine. She is *ours*. And we are...*hers*."

*Boom!*

The gun kicked in my hand. But he was already moving, charging through the gloom toward me. I squeezed the trigger again as he slammed into me, driving me backwards...

I flew through the air, falling backwards into the darkness. Icy air rushed all around me. I hit something with a brutal thud that stole the breath from my lungs. Still, I kept on falling, down an embankment until I slammed against the ground... and stopped.

The white-haired bastard was on top of me again, his weight crushing me into the dirt. But my hand was empty, and cold against the ground. My thoughts spun. I reached out, searching...

The piece of shit on top of me gave a grunt and shoved against me trying to get away. How the fuck was he still alive? Panic kicked in my chest. I reached out further, searching for steel amongst the cold, wet leaves. But the bastard gave a groan and slumped back down, his weight a blow once more. I shoved, punched, and drove my boot against the ground as I titled my hips.

He rolled and fell off me, then was still. My breaths were so hard and heavy. I sucked in the cold air, and stilled for a second. My pulse boomed in my ears, the sound deafening until the tiny crack of a snapping twig drew my attention to the gloom.

Out of the shadows, movement came, but I didn't have my gun, and my movements were slow and weak. The shadow sharpened, and as my eyes adjusted in the faded light, I caught sight of a familiar face. For a second, I thought it was Nick. My brother had found me, and relief washed through me. But he didn't move like Nick, and he didn't sound like Nick...

"Tobias."

I scowled. "Dad?"

He moved closer, until I saw him clearly enough to see the shine in his eyes...and in his hand. He lifted the gun, taking aim. But it wasn't at the white-haired bastard at my side. It was at me.

My breaths stilled. Fear trembled through me...*real fear.*

Our relationship had been strained since mom died. There was always that seething undercurrent of anger between us.

But not this...

Never *this*.

I lifted my hand, my fingers trembling as I whispered, "No."

# FORTY-THREE

## *nick*

BANG!

I flinched at the sound and wrenched my gaze toward the bank of trees in the near distance. The gunshot was close...*real fucking close.* I pressed my hand against my side and tried to find a location for the sound. I'd lost sight of Tobias and Ryth as I fought the asshole from the SUV. But the moment he'd slumped in my arms, I took off, running toward the open gates of the Order.

Desperate to find them. "T?" I called my brother's name, wincing at the sound of my voice in a quiet night air. It didn't reach far, but it was loud enough.

Loud enough to draw the attention of anyone near me. I moved forward, searching the trees, and kept going, making my way in the direction of the Order. Wet leaves smacked my face, making me panic for an instant. I punched aside the branch stumbled forward, and found myself on the edge of the driveway that snaked through the trees, heading towards the building.

Headlights came out of nowhere, white and blinding. I jumped backwards, desperate for the safety of those trees once

307

A.K. ROSE & ATLAS ROSE

more. The growl of a sedan cut through the darkness before it tore past me in a blur. I stumbled out of the safety of those trees, seeing a pale image in the back window.

A woman pressed her hands against the glass, the whites of her wide eyes shining brightly, her mouth open in a silent scream. An ache bloomed in the back of my throat at the sight. I glanced at the license plate, finding the words St. James illuminated by the lights. I knew exactly who it was.

The woman who'd helped Ryth escape...Vivienne...

And the man driving had to be London St. James.

The car skidded sideways as it raced for the gates of the Order. I tried to catch my breath, looking at the beat-up Charger.

Part of me wanted to chase after them, to hunt London St. James down, because I knew that somehow he was at the heart of this, that if I could force him to tell us why all this was happening, I'd be able to stop it. Then I glanced toward the building looming ahead. Caleb was there, and Ryth and Tobias were somewhere out here.

They were my priority...

I had to find them. I had to save them. I kept pushing... toward the building.

*ryth*

*WHATEVER IT TAKES...*THE words rolled through my head as I kept running. All I saw was the red brake lights of the four-wheel drive in front of me. All I felt was love. Love for the man who'd risked it all to save me. Love in the wake of hopelessness.

Movement swarmed in all around me. Mercenaries with guns watched me as I ran. I didn't care about them, I *couldn't* care about them. "Caleb!" I screamed, and pumped my arms. *"CALEB!"*

I lifted the gun as the four-wheel drive skidded hard and stopped in the middle of the driveway. My heart kicked in my chest as fear and desperation collided. I gripped the gun, just like Tobias had shown me, and aimed at the man who shoved open the driver's door and climbed out.

"Let him go!" I screamed. "Let him go *NOW!*"

The guard raised his hands and stepped forward, yanking open the back door. "He's not going anywhere, Ryth." That cold, forceful voice was devoid of all emotion. "But you can get in."

*"No!"* Caleb screamed. *"No, Ryth. NO!"*

My steps slowed, but my pulse kept thundering. I gripped the gun, aimed it at the guard's chest, and stopped at the back of the vehicle. Caleb howled and bucked as he fought the man at his side. There was a grunt, then the thud of fists hitting flesh.

"Ryth!" Caleb moaned. *"Ryth, no!"*

Shadows moved all around me. I didn't need to look to see I was surrounded and outnumbered. Still I gripped the gun as I wrenched my gaze from Caleb's darkened outline in the back seat to the man standing beside the open door.

"Your choice," the guard declared as he stepped forward to close the door.

*"Wait!"* I cried. "Wait..."

My breaths were brutal, tearing from my chest. I forced myself to move, taking a slow step forward. The door hadn't quite made it, stopped an inch before sealing my fate. The gun wavered in my hand, then lowered as I got closer.

There was a pleased glint in the guard's eyes and a curl at the corners of his mouth as I stopped in front of him. He opened the door, then reached out and took the gun from my hand. "You won't be needing that."

All I cared about was Caleb as I climbed through the open door and onto the seat beside him. His hands were cuffed behind his back. Still, he leaned into me as I threw my arms around him. "Caleb," I cried, burying my head against his neck.

"You fucking stupid idiot," he groaned as the door closed with a *thud.*

I smothered his words with my mouth as the echo of the driver's door came and we were moving once more. As I kissed him, all I heard were those words...

*Whatever it takes.*

Caleb had risked it all to save me; his life, his sanity. Now it was my turn to do the same. I clenched my arms tighter around him, crushing my mouth against his. But still it wasn't enough. It would *never* be enough. Tires squealed as the four-wheel drive pulled up in front of the building.

I didn't want to look at the cold concrete structure looming through the windshield, didn't want to feel the icy blast of air as the doors opened and especially didn't want to feel their hands on me as they pulled me out. But I felt and saw it all. My arms were torn from around his neck. Rage flashed in his gaze as he glared at the man behind me. *"Don't you fucking hurt her! HEY! Don't you...Ryth...RYTH!"*

I bucked, kicked, and clawed, fighting with all I had to get back to him.

*"No, you don't!"* the guard growled, his breath hot in my ear as he pinned my arms against my sides and hauled me backwards.

I slammed my head back and impacted with something hard. With a grunt, we fell and slammed against the ground. But my arms were free. I shoved against the cold pebbled driveway and lurched upwards. "Caleb!"

But the guard In the driver's seat had a gun aimed at Caleb's head. "Fucking try it," he goaded. "And I'll splatter his brains all over the fucking seat next to you."

Fear stopped me cold. I stared at the gun, then at my step-brother...the man I was in love with.

The guard fumbled with the door handle, then yanked it open before he slid out backwards.

"You're fucking feisty, aren't you?" the asshole behind me growled, and grabbed the back of my neck with a cruel grip. "Try that again and see what happens."

His fingers bore into the base of my neck, sending spears of agony into my shoulders as he yanked me backwards. "You fucking escaped before. You won't again, got it?"

Fear gripped me with an icy hold as he whipped me around and drove me toward the side door of the Order. It was already open...and The Principal waited.

"Ryth," he snapped, anger seething in his eyes. "You stupid...*stupid* little whore."

"Fuck you!" Caleb roared behind me. "You *fucking bastard!*"

The Principal looked past me and those dark eyes grew colder as they fixed on Caleb. "Mr. Banks. he said carefully. "My brother is looking forward to seeing you again."

Caleb bucked and fought. I searched the darkness for the others, desperate to see Tobias charge out of the shadows with a gun in his hand and vengeance on his face. But there was no one. No Tobias and no Nick. An icy feeling of dread washed through me.

Only I didn't have time to panic more than I was already before the piece of shit with his vise grip around my neck shoved me forward. "Move," he barked as he pushed me past The Principal and back inside the place I hated the most.

These were the stark white walls of my nightmares. The sharp, clinical scent of my panic attacks. I'd barely survived this the last time, now here I was again...

The sound of boots filled the hallway as I stumbled through the doors. There were guards waiting for me, watching as I was pushed along the hallway and back toward the infirmary where I'd escaped. The ratchet sound of cuffs came from behind me. I didn't need to look to know it was Caleb they'd released. They had us inside now, like rats in a cage.

The Priest waited, his arms crossed over his chest and his face a mess of bruises, along with a swollen, busted lip. He stared at me with a blood-red eye as I neared. "Nice to see you back, Ms. Castlemaine."

"Fuck you!" I screamed. *"Fuck you all!"*

From the end of the hallway, movement drew my gaze. It was my mother. Her hair was wild, and it looked like she'd been running...*to save me?* Hope flared as she strode forward, her cheeks blazing red.

"Mom—" I started.

She wrenched her hand back and unleashed, striking me across the face with a *slap!* My head snapped to the side as fire lashed my cheek.

"You fucking *cunt!*" Caleb screamed behind me. "I'll kill you! *Do you hear me...I'll fucking kill you!*"

*"Get him into the interrogation room,"* The Principal roared. *"NOW!"*

I ignored the fire and swallowed the pain, wrenching my gaze to the men behind me as Caleb kicked and fought, his focus for me only. "Don't hurt him!" I lunged, trying to tear myself from the guard's hold around my neck. *"Don't hurt him!"*

"Ryth!" Caleb reached for me as they closed in... *"Ryth!"*

*"CALEB!"*

A guard swung, and his fist connected with Caleb's cheek, rocking him backwards. His knees buckled, and he fell, as the other guards quickly closed in around him. One grabbed him on either side and hauled him along the hallway, away from me.

"No!" I screamed. *"NO!"*

"You shouldn't have run," The Principal's bitter words hit me as the hallway blurred through my tears. "You only have yourself to blame for this."

"Fuck you" I croaked as tears slipped from my eyes and I turned to the woman who'd given birth to me. *"Fuck both of you!"*

She didn't flinch. She didn't look like she cared at all. Had she ever? The grip around my neck tightened as I was driven forward past my mother and toward a room that waited further along the hallway. The door was cracked open and the light was on. It was all I could do not to break down and wish for the end.

Because in death, I wouldn't have them...

In death, they couldn't save me once more.

I managed to fling my gaze behind me and caught sight of Caleb as the guards marched him along the hallway, then through the set of double doors before they finally disappeared. Grief swallowed me, the kind of emptiness where I wasn't sure I existed outside of pain.

My body moved on its own, the feet shuffled, the breaths burst in and out. But I was sliding deeper into that emptiness that I'd only tasted once before...but it was here now. It waited for me in that room. Footsteps sounded behind me, then forward to the door and into the room, but I didn't even bother to look up.

The table in front of me blurred. All I saw were shadows until I blinked, then the only color sharpened in the room and my heart clenched at the sight. Red. *Red*...the door closed with a thud behind me. Footsteps sounded all around.

"Get undressed," The Principal ordered.

That punishing hold ripped from me as he shoved me forward. I threw my hands out as I almost hit the corner of the table. But the bright crimson was all I could see. Dread filled me at the sight. "No...*no.*"

"No?" The Principal repeated. I closed my eyes as he came closer. *"No?"*

A pathetic sound ripped from me. But he didn't touch me, just stood behind me. "We've been here before, Ryth, only this time you've proved to me just how much of a problem you really are. So I'm going to tell you again...*get dressed.*"

Torment plunged through me as I opened my eyes to see

the neatly folded lace negligee. "No," I whimpered. There was *no way* I'd willingly put that on. Footsteps moved closer. I held my breath as those cruel hands found me once more.

"No!" I screamed, bucking and swinging as the guard tore my shirt.

The sound of ripping fabric filled my ears as they lifted me from the floor and slammed me onto the table. My head cracked backwards, hitting the hard surface until white stars danced in the back of my eyes. That second was all they needed. They tore my boots free and someone fumbled with the button on my jeans. I kicked and thrashed, screaming until my throat burned.

"You will obey me, Ryth," The Principal kept speaking.

They pulled my jeans off, and my panties were next. Cold air reached between my thighs. Tears blurred my vision, but still I fought. Caleb's face was a brand in my mind. But it was all useless. They finally stepped back, leaving me in nothing but my bra. I sucked in a hard breath as they moved away.

I whimpered and cried, kicking out at the movement as The Principal stepped closer to the table. He picked up the red negligee and held it out. "You need to get dressed, Ryth."

More tears slipped free. "No."

I stared at the color, knowing instantly what it meant.

"No more white." He stared down at me as I lay almost naked on the table. His stony stare drifted along my body. "No black. This time it's red. Red because I want you gone, even if it is at a sacrifice."

I shook my head. "No..." *Please...*the word rose, but it never made it to my lips.

"Red because you've been sold."

The words stopped me cold.

That soulless stare pierced mine. I slowly shook my head, dislodging the tears in my eyes. "No."

The door opened behind him...and a man stepped into the room. My stomach clenched. "No...*please...no.*"

Killion looked down at me. His sickening gaze lingered between my thighs. I clenched my thighs and closed my legs tight. "No."

"They're not going to save you," he insisted. "No one is going to save you, Ryth. This is your life now. You exist solely at the whims of the Order...as you always have."

I jerked my gaze from Killion to The Principal and moved, snatched the red lace from his hand to cover my body as I rolled off the table, stumbled backwards, and hit the wall. "No." I shook my head.

Killion smirked. The guards held the remnants of my clothes in their hands. They held my life. My jeans. My boots. The panties and the clothes Nick had bought me. "No."

"No one is coming," The Principal repeated, as though somehow the words would hit home. "Not your brothers, or the man you call father."

*The man I call father?*

I tried to control my breaths, tried to stop the shudders. But they continued to rip through me. "My father."

He smirked, and I'd never seen such a sickening sight. "He isn't now...or ever was, your father, Ryth." He glanced at the red lace in my hands. "Like I said, you belong to the Order. Always have, always will. We're not abducting you." He met my stare. "We're reclaiming what was already ours."

He turned and strode toward the door, leaving Killion behind.

*What was ours...what was ours?* "What do you mean?" I cried as a guard opened the door for him.

His footsteps resounded as he walked out and left.

*"What do you mean?"* I screamed. *"Come back here! COME BACK!"*

But he didn't, just left me behind with Killion and two of his men. Men who were dishevelled and bloody. Killion lifted his hand to the swelling corner of his mouth. "You've cost me a car, and at least a few of my men."

I sucked in a breath and tore my gaze from the closed door to the monster in the room as he stepped closer, cruelty and rage glittering in his eyes. "It was an expensive car."

My pulse thundered.

My stomach clenched.

I pressed my spine against the wall, shivering.

He lifted his hand and brushed a strand of hair from my face. "I'm going to enjoy making you earn every goddamn dollar to repay me." He smiled. "Very...*very much.*"

# FORTY-FIVE

## *caleb*

"GET THE FUCK OFF ME!" I drove backwards, charging for the double doors as they closed behind me.

My arms ached and throbbed from when my hands were cuffed behind me. But they were free now, and I'd fight. Through the glass panel in the door, I'd watched as Ryth was driven out of my view. The image of that had torn free something savage inside me. I spun, lashed out, and drove my fist into a guard's face. His head snapped back and blood spurted from his nose. I didn't stop, just charged forward, reaching for the ID card at his waist.

Until they tackled me from behind. They swept my feet out from under me and slammed me down to the floor. Something inside my mouth cracked, and pain followed.

"Get him inside."

I lifted my gaze to the Priest as he stood over me and grinned. His face was badly bruised, one eye blood-filled and weeping. I'd hurt him bad...I guess this was payback.

"Fuck you," I spat as they hauled me to my feet. I didn't help them, letting them grunt with my weight. "Give her back to me, or the next time, I won't leave you alive."

The Priest stepped closer, pinning me with that bloody stare. "What makes you think there'll be a next time?"

Fear moved through me, cold and heavy in my gut. But I didn't let the bastard see the truth. I just held that focus, making sure he felt every fucking word. "You kill me, and they'll still come for her. You won't be able to fight them all... one of them will find you. They'll find you and they'll kill you. My bet is it'll be Tobias. It won't matter then, not any threat or any promise you can make."

The Priest just smiled. It was a knowing smile...

A chilling smile.

My own gaze faltered as he turned to the guard at my side. "Get him in the room."

They wrenched me backwards. But I couldn't get that gleam from my mind...that smirk which carved all the way to my soul, and my little brother's face rose swiftly. *Tobias*...

My steps were slow as they shoved me into the room. *No*...

I stopped inside the doorway and turned, meeting that bastard's gaze once more. "No. No..."

"No?"

"I don't believe you." I held his stare, searching the bloody eyeball for the truth. T wasn't dead...he couldn't be. *He couldn't be.*

"Get him on his knees," the Priest commanded, not once breaking our stare.

The guard shoved me backwards and I stumbled, throwing out my hand. The face of my baby brother burned in the darkness. I refused to give in to grief. Nick was still out there. Still fighting, still trying to save her. He'd need to now—more than ever before.

The guard came for me again, kicking the back of my knees and shoving down my shoulders. I folded, hitting the floor hard.

"You got the drop on me before," the Priest said as he reached for the guard's gun and drew it from his waist. "But you won't get that chance again."

My pulse was strangely steady, nothing more than an occasional skip as the door opened behind him and The Principal stepped inside. I saw the resemblance now, saw the same empty stare as he stood next to his brother. The same hardness...the same coldness.

They were just like Tobias.

"Mr. Banks," The Principal murmured. "I'm sure you realize this is the end of our relationship. I'm afraid we cannot allow any more issues...where Ryth is concerned."

That skipping in my chest kicked at the sound of her name.

"Don't worry," the bastard continued. "Killion will take excellent care of her indeed."

"No," I whispered as an icy blade of fear plunged all the way to my soul. "No."

The Principal took a step closer. "I'm afraid the contract's already been signed...and right about now, Killion is taking possession. You've caused a lot of problems for the Order, Mr. Banks...you and your brothers."

"Fuck you," I hissed.

He just smiled, looking down at me, and for a second, that smile faltered. There was sadness as he breathed, "You were never meant to fall for her."

I sucked in a harsh breath as those words hit home.

*You were never meant to fall for her.*

He gave a slow nod, and the Priest lifted the gun, the muzzle pressed point-blank at my temple...

Until the sharp ringtone of a phone cut through the air. I stared at The Principal as he looked down at the screen and scowled. He lifted a finger to the Priest, swiped the screen, then answered. "Yes?"

I caught the faint sound of a voice on the other end. He straightened and paled. "I see." He forced the words through clenched teeth. "I won't be intimidat—" he started, and stopped before snarling, "Fine."

He lowered his hand and pressed a button. "You're on speaker."

"Caleb?"

A stranger's voice came through. I didn't know who it was, but I answered anyway. "Yes."

"Have they hurt you, son?"

The calm, careful voice on the other end was etched with compassion. I tried to pull back from that chasm where I'd been prepared for the end and answered. "No."

"And my daughter, have they hurt her?"

My pulse kicked...*raced*. "Jack?" I murmured. "Jack Castlemaine?"

"Yes. Have they...hurt my daughter?"

My pulse raced harder with the words. The Principal tensed his shoulders as I met his stare and answered. "Not that I know of."

"Good." That was all he said, but then his tone grew colder. "You're going to be okay. Both of you will be okay," he said, comforting me, before all trace of warmth left his voice. "He is not to be harmed, do you hear me, Riven? You harm a fucking hair on my daughter's head, or any of the Banks boys, and there will be hell to pay. I'll unleash a war, the kind you'll never survive. You think you have problems now, I'll have the FBI, the cops, and the DA on your doorstep by morning. They'll tear you apart, well before Mr. King can get to you."

The Principal stiffened at the name.

*Mr. King...*

"So you can either follow my demands or die screaming alongside your brothers and that piece of shit, Hale."

"That's a serious threat, Castlemaine," The Principal muttered. But I could see he was scared. Really fucking scared. Whatever Jack Castlemaine had on the Order, it was enough to give him power over them...that was all I needed to know.

"Would you like to test me?"

The careful words carried all the weight of the world. There was a twitch in the corner of his eye before he spoke once more. "Your terms?"

"Let them go."

The Principal's lips curled with fury. "You know that's never going to happen."

"Then let Caleb go to her. My daughter is not to be sold or trained *in any way*. Do I make myself clear?"

There was that twitch again, one that told me Castlemaine had hit a nerve. I clawed for hope, desperate for anything as long as it kept Ryth safe.

"You will allow Caleb to stay with her. They are both not to be harmed. Believe me, if they are so much as threatened, I will call the hundreds of contacts I've gathered and I'll send them enough information to bury Hale and expose every vile piece of shit that ever bought or sold a woman through the Order. I'll expose you utterly."

The Principal's grip tightened around the phone.

"I'll be calling this number at this exact time every day. I expect to speak to them, *both of them*. The moment the call isn't answered, I'll hit send. The moment I even suspect the voice on your end isn't my daughter or Caleb, I'll hit send. I will hit send the moment you come for me. And then we'll see just how much heat your employer can withstand." Castlemaine was quiet for a second before he spoke again. "Give my daughter a hug for me, Caleb. Tell her I never left her...tell her no matter what, that she is the most important thing in my life. I love her more than I ever told her. Stay safe, son...and protect her."

Then in a heartbeat...the call went quiet...and the screen on the phone went dark.

*Jack Castlemaine...*

*He was alive.*

*More than that, he could save us...he could save* her.

"Riven," the Priest murmured.

The man Jack had called Riven jerked his gaze toward his brother. "You fucking heard him. Do you really want to test him?"

"We don't know exactly what information he has." His brother stared at me with bloodlust in his eyes.

"Precisely," Riven answered, then glanced at the guard. "Take him to her. Make sure they're locked in, and for Christ's sake, don't let anything happen to them."

The guard gave a nod, and the bastard limped a little as he came for me. I stared at the Priest as they hauled me to my feet once more. My legs shook and my mind screamed. I had been prepared for the end...prepared to meet my maker and finally atone for what I'd done.

Now I had hope...

The guard dragged me toward the door. I stopped and turned. "My brothers."

The Principal clenched his jaw. He turned his head and met my gaze. "You will be taken to her. Consider that a win."

The guard shoved me forward, out the door, and back into the hallway I never thought I'd see again. There was no fighting this time. Instead, I lengthened my stride, almost running to the doors. *"Ryth!"* I screamed her name. *"RYTH!"*

The seconds were like hours as I pushed through the doors. I scanned the hallway, frantically searching for a sign, and heard a whimper...one that came from inside a door up ahead. I lunged forward, my will moving faster than my body.

Through the glass panel on the door, I saw Killion as he

hovered over her. She was backed against the wall...naked. "The fuck!" I screamed and slammed through the door.

I was across the room before I knew it, swinging my fist at his closest guard before I went for him. The glint of a gun shone in the corner of my eye before the guard behind me roared, *"NO!"* He flew into the room, sucking in huge breaths as he lifted his hand. "He's not to be harmed...by order of The Principal."

I grabbed Killion and yanked him away from her. He was still clothed, still hadn't...I swung again and connected with the bastard's jaw. He stumbled back, stunned. I couldn't stop myself. Rage and desperation collided, and under it was a kind of grief that knew me all too well.

I dove forward and lashed out again. My fist connected with Killion's nose. Blood sprayed, causing him to unleash a howl of agony and clutch his face. I wanted to kill him...I *needed* to kill him.

"No," The Principal's guard stepped out from behind me and got between us. "No, you've done enough."

My knuckles throbbed, the ache so fucking familiar.

"You're here." The guard glanced at Ryth. "And so is she. That's all the allowance you get, understand?"

"Caleb," Ryth called my name. I sucked in a breath and looked at her, then turned back to Killion. "You will never touch her again. Do you understand me?"

Killion just clutched his nose as blood dribbled between his fingers. His threatening stare was pinned on me before he fixed on the Order's guard. "He's supposed to be dead!"

The guard shook his head. "By order of The Principal."

*"Fuck The Principal!"* Killion bellowed as he lifted his finger and stabbed the air toward Ryth. "I paid good money for that *cunt!*"

I took a step and moved in front of Ryth. Only then did I see the clothing she held against her. *Red...red...*I took a step and snatched the negligee from her hands, then turned and threw it in his face. "Then I guess you're shit out of luck, aren't you?"

I'd never really felt violent before, not the true emotion that changed a person, that turned someone proud of the law into a murderer.

Until this moment.

I was going to kill Killion. I knew that in my soul.

Maybe not right now, but it was going to happen.

As soon as I got us out of this place...and mourned the death of my brother.

*You were never meant to fall for her.*

The Principal's words stayed with me as I yanked the buttons on my shirt and tore it from my body, shielding her as best I could. "Look at me, Ryth," I pleaded. Her shoulders were curled forward and she held onto her stomach as though she was in pain.

But I knew it was shock...I also knew this was just the beginning, and the worst was yet to come. I took another step and wrapped my arms around her. "Hold on to me, princess," I whispered, and pulled her tight against me. "Hold on..."

*Tobias.*

My brother's face drifted in the darkness of my mind. I didn't know how I was going to tell her.

I didn't know if I even could.

She wrapped her arms around me, her body shaking so hard her teeth chattered.

*Whatever it takes.* Nick's words surfaced. I felt them now, clearer than ever before. "I will, brother," I whispered into her hair. "I will."

VIVIENNE

"RYTH!" I screamed, slamming my hands against the window. *"Ryth!"*

"Shut the *fuck up!*" The bark tore through the car, making me flinch.

Still, my gaze was fixed on a shadow under the trees. One that streaked across the driveway before it stopped. But it wasn't Ryth...it was a woman...one who looked like her, though it wasn't. She turned her gaze and saw me, then she was gone.

The car swept around a bend. I slammed my hands against the glass once more, catching the wide stare of a male as he appeared out of nowhere. "Please, *help me!*"

He took a step toward me and, for a second, I thought he was going to come after me...that somehow, he *could* help me. But then we were gone, skidding hard before we tore through the open gates of the Order...and past two vehicles parked sideways in the middle of the road.

"Fuck!" Came a burst from the front.

I turned then, pressed my spine against the seat, and faced the man who'd taken me...*London St. James.*

One glance at the door, and he hit the locks. "Try it," he threatened from the driver's seat as I met his gaze in the rear-view mirror. "And see how far it gets you."

My pulse was thudding as chills raced along my arms. I knew what he'd do if I tried to run...but I also knew what he'd do if I didn't. I slammed my palm against the seat, holding on as the car swayed erratically, the snarl of the engine throbbing through the leather seat under me.

"You push me."

I tore my gaze from the darkness ahead to the rear-view mirror again.

"You fucking push me."

I stayed like that as we raced for the bright lights of the city, one hand against my seat, the other against the passenger headrest in front. "I'm sorry," I whispered.

He snapped his gaze to the mirror. "Don't fucking lie to me." He punched the accelerator, spearing us up the on-ramp of the freeway. "You can do many things, Vivienne. But one of them is *never fucking lie.*"

I tried to think, tried to find a way out of here. One that didn't get me killed...or worse, *fucked.* The fighter rose quickly. "You can't...you can't touch me. The contract—"

*"Fuck the contract,"* he snarled. His gaze shifted in the mirror, lowering to my body.

I crossed my arms over the white negligee, hiding myself as best I could. He can't do this...*he can't do this.* He'd be in violation. Then they'd put me in the Order for good. Use me. Train me...*still it would be better than this.*

We sped up, leaving the freeway before I knew it, slipping through the streets on the way to his house. I'd been there twice...and each time...*each time he almost broke the agreement with the Principal. Each time he almost...*

I closed my eyes, my pulse frantic. By now the Principal would know that I was missing. By now he'd have men on the way. One look in the cameras and he'd know who took me. So it was only a matter of time before they'd come and take me back.

The tires squealed as we turned, and turned once more, speeding past expensive houses before he finally slowed. I wrenched my gaze to the steep driveway as we hit the entrance and braked hard, coming to a stop outside his house.

The locks disengaged with a *clunk*.

"I will take you down on the front fucking lawn if you run... and I'll take you there, as well...by force if I have to."

My pussy clenched with those savage words. One look in his eyes and I knew he was telling the truth. He would. He'd rape me, right in front of the neighbors, and they wouldn't do a goddamn thing because he was London St. James. A man they were scared of...*a man I was terrified of.*

My fingers shook as he climbed out and slammed the door shut. Through the dark tinted windows, he rose like a monster and rounded the back of the sedan before he yanked open the door and commanded with a snarl, "Inside...*now."*

I shook my head, unable to move. "No."

He lunged faster than I could track, reached in to grab me around the throat, and dragged me out. "You *will* do what I say."

I kicked, clawed, and grabbed hold of the door handle before he snatched my hand and wrenched it free. We left the door open as he dragged me toward the house. "Open the *goddamn door!"* he shouted.

*No...NO!*

I fought, even as the lock sounded and the door opened in front of me. Then I sailed through the air, tripped and fell, and hit the floor hard. Gasping breaths sounded. The *snap* of a lock cracked like a gunshot in the air. I shoved against the cold tiles, lifting my gaze as footsteps sounded and the shine of black shoes filled my gaze.

"I warned you, Vivienne." Heavy breaths punctuated his words. "I warned you."

White lace spilled over the slate gray tile as I shifted, closed my legs, and lifted my gaze to the two other men in the foyer. Men who looked identical. They were all identical. Father and sons. The same ravenous stares. The same cruel lips.

"I told you there'd be consequences," London said, and took a step closer.

He reached down and grabbed me around the throat once more. His grip found the same pattern and the same ache as he dragged me to my feet. "Move," he commanded.

He drove me backwards and this time, to stop from falling, I had no choice but to obey. I stumbled backwards, leaving the foyer and the twins behind until his grip around my throat stopped me. He leaned over, punched in a code on the outside of a door, then shoved it open. "Down," he urged, his eyes sparkling with a terrifying glint. "Watch your step."

His hold eased, guiding me more than punishing as I took a step, then slipped, flailing until he lashed out and grabbed my arm. "I *said* watch your goddamn step."

My heart was hammering. Fear crowded my thoughts. He was going to put me in a dungeon, some kind of cell, and leave me in the darkness. A sob escaped at the thought and for a second, fear gripped me so tight I couldn't move.

With a bestial snarl, he bent, grabbed me around the waist and lifted. I slammed onto his shoulder, my hair falling across my face.

"No!" I kicked and bucked, slamming my fists against his back.

But he didn't stop, just kept walking even as I punched and writhed.

*Slap!* "Enough!" he yelled and stopped.

I sucked in the air and twisted, desperate to see where he was putting me. But I could barely see. The hallway was gloomy, leaving barely enough light to see the door beside us before London yanked it open and strode inside. He dropped me, catching me at the last second before I hit the floor.

My pulse slammed against my chest as my feet hit the floor. I stumbled backwards as a soft light came on, illuminating the floor, then the thud of the door, followed by the click of a lock. All I wanted was away from him. I stared at the monster and kept moving until I hit something hard in the middle of the room.

"The contract specifically says no part of my body can enter you." His voice was husky and raw as he took a step forward. "I'm prepared to obey the rules..."

Those bottomless eyes shone in the darkness. "Stay away from m-me." I hated that my voice stuttered. "Just stay the fuck away."

"I warned you what would happen if you got involved with the Castlemaine bitch." He kept moving, ignoring my pleas. "I warned you what would happen if you tried to run."

He grabbed me, only this time it was around the back of my neck, and pulled me forward. I lashed out, my palm landing on his cheek with a hard *slap!* A sting licked my palm, searing. London stopped cold, his eyes widening in shock before darkening.

I'd never seen evil, not until they took me to the Order.

Now I knew it well...in all its forms.

And one of those stood in front of me now.

He lifted his hand, his fingers touching his cheek. Even in

the murky light, I caught the flesh reddening. "You fucking touch me, and I'll kill you."

"Touch you," he said carefully, his tone dangerous.

Still, he reached for me again, grabbed my neck, and pulled me close. "Let me show you something. A very special something I had made especially for you."

He dragged me by the neck around to the base of what looked like a bed...one that had straps and shackles on the sides, to some kind of machine at the foot...

"No part of my body can enter you...that's written in the contract. But it doesn't say anything about what I can control."

He yanked a black covering free...revealing something that made my blood run cold.

"I tried to warn you, Vivienne. I tried to do my best...but you didn't obey." His hold around my neck eased, sliding to my jaw. His fingers were bruising as he forced my gaze to his. "Now tell me you understand."

I couldn't tear my gaze away, unable to comprehend what I was seeing.

Heat burned inside me, making me tremble and quake, and he noticed, lowering his gaze. His other hand fingered the shoulder strap of my negligee and dragged it lower until the hard peak of my breast bounced free.

"Say it...say what I want to hear," he said, his breaths deepening. His thumb brushed my nipple, making me flinch and tremble. He rolled that sensitive flesh, pinching until I moaned as he commanded once more. "Say it or we will start right now."

"Y-yes..." I whimpered.

"Yes...*what?*" He met my gaze.

I stared into those soulless eyes, finding the depths of depravity as I said the words he wanted to hear. "Yes, daddy."

He smiled. "Good girl."

*Want more? I've written an extra scene with Ryth & Caleb just for you ♥ click here to start reading*

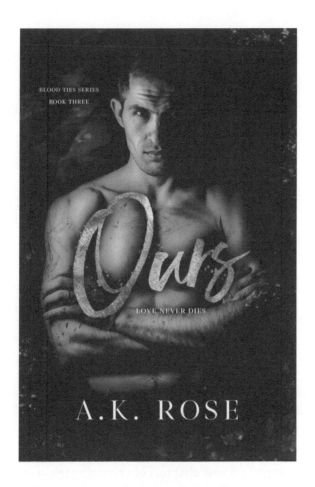

BLOOD TIES SERIES

BOOK THREE

*Ours*

LOVE, NEVER DIES

A.K. ROSE

***Preorder your copy here!***

No one is safe from us.

Not even so called blood...

No one touches what's ours—not while we're alive.

Want NSFW (Not Safe for Work) Pre-release Digital Versions of my books? Join my exclusive club on Patreon and be the first to read *all the steam...*

- What you get by joining:
- Pre-release copies (limited to the next release before it goes live on Amazon)
- Discrete ebook covers
- NSFW Art
- Exclusive content
- Teasers and new chapters of upcoming releases
- Monthly short stories based on your favorite characters and more...

Click here to join

Made in United States
Troutdale, OR
12/30/2024

27421458R00206